THE *Beauty* BOX

THE *Beauty* BOX

BONNIE DUNLOP

thistledown press

National Library of Canada Cataloguing in Publication

Dunlop, Bonnie, 1950-
The beauty box / Bonnie Dunlop.

ISBN 1-894345-70-3
I. Title.

PS8607.U55B42 2004   C813'.6   C2004-900866-8

Cover painting by Brad Pasutti
Cover and book design by J. Forrie
Typeset by Thistledown Press

Thistledown Press Ltd.
633 Main Street
Saskatoon, Saskatchewan, S7H 0J8
www.thistledown.sk.ca

Thistledown Press gratefully acknowledges the financial assistance of the Canada Council for the Arts, the Saskatchewan Arts Board, and the Government of Canada through the Book Publishing Industry Development Program for its publishing program.

ACKNOWLEDGEMENTS

Heartfelt thanks to my editor, John Lent, for his insight and skill and for making this final edit a joy.

Special thanks are due to the following mentors for their support and encouragement: Rod McIntyre, Dianne Warren, Shelley Anne Leedahl and Ron Marken.

I am grateful to the Sagehill Writing Experience, the writer-in-residence program at the Cypress Hills Community College and the Regina Public Library, the Saskatchewan Writer's Guild Mentorship Program and for the support of the Saskatchewan Arts Board.

"The Merc and Me" first appeared in *Up All Night*, an anthology published by Thistledown Press. "Kenny" has been published in *Grain* magazine. "The Blue at the Base of Her Throat" (then titled "Wings in the Morning") has been broadcast on CBC for *Gallery* and a version of "Aurora Borealis in the Churchill Sky" is slated for broadcast on CBC at a later date.

In memory of Carson Albert Lines, voracious reader
For Stevie, and Luke

CONTENTS

The Outright Murder of Baby Birds

Dr. Eric Anderson's invitation came in the morning mail on benign, cream-coloured stationery. It looked harmless enough. He'd graduated from Benson High in 1968 at the head of his class. Beneath his yearbook photo it said: *Captain — Benson Bombers, Math Club, French Club. Most Likely to Succeed.* He checks the calendar on the wall behind Heather's shoulder. 1988. Twenty years? Unbelievable.

His mother, no doubt, had passed along his current address. His mother. Now, there was a case, and he'd be the first to admit it, psychiatry his passion. When her bird phobia had finally tipped into madness, his mother had insisted on wearing a full Scott air-pack, even in the shower. The heavy tanks and the full body harness had worn deep grooves in her bony shoulders. The hose from her face mask to the tank and the mask itself made her look like a creature from the deep.

Eventually, she even refused to leave the safety of her home. It was an embarrassment to his father, long-time mayor of the town. There were openings and important parties to attend. Official business, official people. Firm handshakes and wine in fluted glasses. When his father's administrative assistant had offered to be his official escort, it had made perfect sense. "No fault of Susie's," his father had said, "things just went from there." No damn wonder Eric avoids going back.

"Reunion committees," he mutters, loud enough for Heather to hear. "They could track down a ghost."

"What's that?" she asks. Click, click, click. Eric hears steel against granite, sees the flash of the sharp-honed blade. Heather flips the translucent slices of steak into a marinating sauce with the tip of her knife. She wields it like a surgeon, with precision and grace.

Eric tosses the invitation onto the island, barely out of range from Heather's flashing knife. She washes her hands, dries them on her jeans and picks up the envelope. She slides the invitation out, lifts it high, like it was holy, before she seats herself on a wrought iron stool and begins to read. Eric doesn't wait for her reaction.

"There's no decision there," he says. "Send a note. Tell them we'll give it a pass."

"Our first reunion in twenty years? I wouldn't miss it for the world." She sticks the invitation front and centre on the fridge, anchoring it with two magnets that discretely advertise her plastic surgeon's name, phone number and office hours. Cheap bastard, Eric thinks. For each operation, she only gets one?

Eric lets the screen door slam and heads for the garage and the soothing company of his tools. A reunion. Shit. Bones left long buried might be dug up all over again. Delicious Donna Desmond. Long dead-dreams.

When it was over between them, Eric dated any girl who chased him hard enough. As Heather eventually had. His roommate had introduced her to him when they'd shared a table in Koffee and Krumbs, a busy little pastry shop across from the university in Saskatoon. She'd reminded him they'd both taken business from Miss Bellamy back at Benson High. All Eric had remembered about Miss Bellamy's class was their teacher's amazing cleavage. Boobs Bellamy, the nickname coined by his buddy Paul.

When Heather had come knocking a few days before Christmas — with gingersnaps and coconut macaroons — he was happy enough to see her again. The homemade cookies didn't hurt. "Thanks," he'd said, taking the tin from her hands. He hadn't asked her to come in. Considering what he knows about Heather now, Eric muses, he's probably lucky to be alive. No doubt she was in the kitchen right now, slamming utensils into the sink, banging the pots and pans, sulking like a spoiled-rotten child just because he wasn't up for a troubling trip down memory lane.

Sometimes, he wonders if he'll ever be forgiven for ignoring Heather during high school. He'd married her, hadn't he? After Donna, pure unadulterated adoration was the one drug he craved. Besides, Heather's always been a damn fine cook. He's never told Heather that ignoring wasn't exactly the word. At Benson High, he hadn't been aware she was alive.

Donna Desmond balances the invitation on her palm. She recognises Sally's backhand slant immediately. Cute little Sally with her halo of carrot-red hair. *Please come —I'm dying to see you again. Stay at my place, we can gab Friday, after the wine and cheese. We've got a rock and roll band for Saturday night. Let me tell you, they're not very easy to book anymore. Makes me long for Bullfrog Frank and the Crooked Creek Boys. Remember them? Being on*

THE BEAUTY BOX

the committee has been pure hell, but it's all coming together now.

She'd signed the note *Stressed-out Sally*. Underneath, she'd drawn a lop-sided happy face, with frazzled hair.

So, Donna thinks, Sally and friends have finally taken the idea, made it fly. A reunion. The people she'd put into a little box in the back of her mind stirred and stretched. She feels a cramp as they begin to move. Eric. Will he be there? She licks her forefinger, smoothes it up and down the crease in the vellum paper. Is he still so handsome it almost stops your heart? She runs her palm over her board-flat belly. Tries to relive the long-ago flutter of her baby's first kick.

She slips her feet into her satin slides and dream-walks downstairs to the storage room where her photo albums are lined up on a shelf above the wine rack. She pulls out the red one. It's worn, ready to fall apart at the spine. It flips open of its own accord. There's Eric, leaning against the gymnasium wall, and Paul, with his shy little grin, right beside him, as he usually was. Behind them, a mere shadow against the red of the brick, Heather, the woman Eric had eventually married. Donna wonders what's she's like. How she was the one who'd ended up with Eric.

Eric and Donna and Paul. Joined at the hip. Donna holds the photo closer, studies Eric and Paul. Maybe, in the photo, Donna thinks, I should have seen a sign. The only one missing is me.

An hour passes like wind through the willows on a hot summer day, gusting and gone. She replaces the album and climbs the stairs, sees the invitation lying on the table in the hall. She drops it into a wicker basket by the door. She needs time to think.

14

Paul Jackson slips off his blazer and slings it over his arm. His muscles bunch against the crispness of his sleeve as he loosens his tie. Spring this year is unseasonably warm. He opens his mailbox, grabs the bundle of bills and flyers and steps inside to the cool of the hall. He's about to drop the papers on the antique sideboard when he sees the postmark from his old hometown. He rips the envelope open, unfolds the creamy paper and begins to read.

He'd left Benson High in a hurry, without even the chance to tell his friends goodbye. He drops the invitation in front of his wife, who's sitting at the kitchen table, her tea cooling in a flowery china cup. "Look at this," he says. "Came today. Twenty years already. That just blows me away."

His wife picks up the invitation between two fingers, scans it and drops it back on the table.

"Let's go," he says. "Do you think your parents could watch the kids?"

"Why would I go?" she says. "I wouldn't know a soul. I'm surprised they even thought of inviting us."

Me, he thinks. They invited *me*.

He realizes that he'll most likely be attending by himself. Again. He doesn't understand his wife's compulsion to spend every minute with the kids. Even when his mother-in-law phones and offers to babysit, he can't talk her into going out for a nice, quiet dinner or even just taking a drive in the countryside, talking, like they always used to. Kids are great, he thinks, but they can't be your whole life.

He walks to her chair, touches the tendrils that curl on the nape of her neck. "Call your mom," he says. "I bet she'll jump at the chance."

She turns away. Years ago, he was tongue-tied around women, lisping a little, searching for something to say. Now his words flow smoothly, like water over round river rocks. He's never at a loss, except with his wife.

"I'm going for a run," he says, peeling off his tie.

"Down memory lane?" his wife asks.

"Something like that."

A tree-lined park, showing hints of palest green, abuts his property. Paul stops to check the lilacs, swelling in bud. He knows just how they feel. Pressure has been pushing against his breastbone ever since he opened his mail. The promise of his run hasn't provided relief, like it usually does. Paul looks up at a patch of azure sky, framed by the unfurling leaves. "Memory lane," he murmurs and picks up his pace. At the fork in the path, he jogs to the left.

As long as he can recall, Eric's always turned the ladies' heads. Even now, with his hair turning grey, he gets double takes. Heather fumes at the attention other women pay him. He's seen her stomp across a restaurant, tell some poor staring woman that Eric is taken. The pitch of her voice carries too well. Eric thinks she hungers for the chance to make a scene. He imagines the gossip over the years. How does he put up with her hissy fits? Why's she so damn jealous?

In their wedding pictures, which Heather insists on displaying in the formal living room, it's clear he and Heather hadn't really fit. Eric picks up the picture, studies the photo, yellowed with age. His tuxedo strains across his

chest, shoulders crowd the left edge of the picture. Hair long
and blonde. He's calling to the camera, well aware of how
he looks. Heather's light brown hair is piled in careful curls
on the top of her head. His hand rests at her waist, nipped
in for their wedding day with some kind of girdle, double
panelled, extra strength. He remembers searching for the
feel of her soft, willing flesh. She's looking at him with
pinwheel fireworks bursting in her eyes. He turns the
picture sideways, as if it were a hologram that he's trying
to decode.

Sometimes, Eric thinks, life just doesn't make sense.
First, there was Heather's accident, a direct result of a
winter storm. Even then, before the elective surgeries, she'd
been on a quest for physical perfection. She dieted herself
model-thin through sheer determination, worked out every
day.

Heather had called him from the General Hospital.
When he'd heard the panic in her voice, he'd cursed his
laziness, lying in bed while his wife drove herself over sheets
of ice to her early morning workout. He'd heard the
warnings on the radio as she'd prepared to leave, thought
about getting up, but instead, had pulled the down
comforter closer and hit the snooze button one more time.

"My nose," she kept saying, "I think they're going to
amputate my nose."

Heather's nose had never been her strong point: slightly
curved, beaklike and large. His father secretly called her
the little owl. The surgeon was an artist. He had her pert
little nose settling into her face as if she'd been born with
it. But that was years ago, Eric muses. He can hardly
remember what she looked like before.

He opens a beer, the tab making a satisfying pop in the silence of his garage. He hefts a hammer, the silk of the handle oiled and polished. Something about being alone with his beloved tools puts Eric in a reflective mood. He thinks of the changes in Heather. She'd certainly jumped on the plastic surgery bandwagon after her nose job turned out so well. Next came the boobs. Those he'd had to pay for and he's not entirely sure it was a deal. The goddamn things are noticeable now, to say the least. Embarrassing. At his company's last Christmas bash, while everyone was mingling, Heather showed up a half an hour late in a black sheath dress, the fabric slithering to a deep V above her breasts. Conversation stopped. The bartender forgot to mix her drink, and had stood there like he'd been struck to stone.

Eric doesn't get it. She doesn't seem to care that guys no longer make eye contact. Sure, she gets all kinds of attention, but no one shows a lick of interest in anything she has to say. Men always focus on her magnificent tits.

If only they knew, Eric thinks, taking another pull on his beer. He replaces the hammer. The symmetry of the pegboard, laden with tools, causes an iridescent bubble of happiness to rise in his chest, like a good long toke used to do. He sometimes wishes he could get the same feeling of pure joy when he looks at his wife. Sure, her boobs look good, but you might as well put your hand on the Rock of Gibraltar. Not much fun in that.

Gawking guys. It'll be the same at the reunion. Hell, Heather gawks herself. He'd watched her in the bathroom mirror as she'd stripped to shower. Sweat from her workout glistened on her breasts. She pressed her hands up her sides, past the bulge of her bosom, across her collarbone.

She licked her index finger, circled her nipples. They rose to her touch, like berries, purple and ready to burst. Heather bowed her head, as if her breasts were sacred objects she'd been longing to kiss.

"Heather?" he'd called, and she'd dropped her hands.

1970, Eric thinks, New Year's Eve. The night I drew the *Get Out of Jail Free* card, but I was too drunk to realize the stakes were so high. He and Ben had shared a small house with not much room to spare. He was living close to the bone, but the old man had come through with some cash after the divorce. Jeez, Eric thought, I know he's been ordered to make payments to Mom. I wonder why he's paying me? Can't he just say he's sorry and leave it at that? He'd counted the zeros three times as he'd held the cheque in his hand, knew he should deposit it *tout de suite*. What the hell, he'd thought, as he walked into Music Man, it doesn't cost a cent to look.

The stereo he'd bought was a thing of beauty, the latest technology the salesman said. When he'd offered to throw in a wireless speaker that worked great in the bathroom, Eric was hooked. Talk about luxury, he thought, music to shit by. He'd even read the instructions before he hooked it up; he didn't want to blow his speakers first time out. It had taken him all morning to set it up, but when he'd finally turned on the tunes, he could feel the bass vibrating deep in his chest. He'd danced alone in the living room, wrapping his long arms around his own waist and laughing out loud for the sheer joy of it.

A New Year's Eve bash in a place of their own. Heather was playing hostess, finding extra ashtrays and filling bowls with pretzels and nuts while he and Ben had run down to the Belmont to pick up some Pil. The party was no big deal, until a blonde with a strange familiarity had walked across his living room. She was balancing red wine in a plastic cup, and a napkin laden with nuts, as she carefully lowered her slender body into his sling-back chair. When she crossed her legs, Eric's eyes lingered. Legs that didn't quit. Donna Desmond. Of course, Eric thought. I should have seen the resemblance right away. Who'll be kissing Donna when the clock strikes twelve tonight? And where?

Much later, when he went upstairs to take a piss, he noticed red wine had spilled down the front of his shirt. He'd walked to his closet, looking for something clean to wear. When he'd seen a blonde in his bed, he thought it might be a dream. He sat down, shook her shoulder, and knew she was real. She turned at his touch, arching her back and somehow, his hand ended up on her breast. He fondled the fullness of the firm, round breast, and then, of course, Heather walked in.

"You bastard," she said. "You and any long-legged blonde that happens to be around. All my fucking life I'm going to have to live with that."

Heather had stormed down the stairs. The music died suddenly and Eric heard two loud thumps and a tinkling crash. He took the stairs two at a time, bare-chested, his quest for a clean shirt forgotten.

Heather had thrown two heavy glass dishes full of peanuts at the wall, denting the plaster, shallow with her first shot but with her second she scored a perfect ten. Chunks of plaster powdered the carpet, littered with peanuts and diamond shards of glass.

She was crouched beside his speakers, her eyes darting and wild. In her hand, she clutched a bouquet of colour-coded wires. In three strides, he was beside her, muscles bunched as he tried to hold her back. Heather threw him off like a bothersome gnat and he stood watching in helpless horror as she systematically destroyed his stereo, smashing the turntable, kicking the shit out of the speakers and pulling every wire he'd so carefully strung.

"Oh, sweet Jesus," Eric had said, downing a glass of whiskey, neat, that someone had left. Finally, he bowed his head, Heather's frenzy hurtful to his eyes. When he heard front door slam, Eric wished he'd found the courage to end it, start the New Year on a different path. When he finally lifted his head, he refilled his glass and wondered where his friends had gone.

A car door slams and Heather starts her Honda. Eric sinks to the cold cement floor of his garage, lost in the long-ago moment when his hand had finally found its home on Donna Desmond's breast.

A sparrow thumps against a window. Eric stands. Maybe he should put up orange reflective tape for the dimwit birds. Either that, or quit polishing his mullioned windows, taking such meticulous care of his retreat, the only place in the entire house that's really his. He takes a soft chamois from the cupboard, folds it over twice and begins to buff the chrome around the headlights of his haze-green Beemer, hand moving in slow concentric circles.

Birds, Eric thinks, will they ever really let me be? Whenever birds nested in the eaves of Eric's childhood home, his father would drag out a ladder and knock the nests down with an old Ping putter. Not a very dignified pastime for the mayor of the town. If his father procrastinated, as he often did, the eggs would be hatched before he knocked the nests to the patio below. Eric's father would call from atop the ladder, demand that Eric remedy the carnage on the deck.

Eric can still feel the pulse of the translucent gut-sacks heavy in his palm, see the line of pale yellow edging the gape of baby bird beaks, grape-skin eyes squeezed closed. He remembers the goose-bump texture of baby bird skin, buds of feathers not yet ready to sprout.

The cyclical and inevitable return of birds intent on nesting was a springtime plague on Eric's life.

"They're back," his mother would say, cowering near the patio doors, pointing to a few blobs of mud and a twig or two that had fallen to the bricks below the resurrected nest. From the protection of the family room, she would scream if a swallow so much as swooped. "Eric, shoo them away!"

She'd pace, unable to rest, until he'd hosed down the entire patio, removing every trace of the birds. As his mother's phobia increased, so, it seemed, did his father's business, taking him out of town more and more. Eric had been left to contend with the destruction of the nests and the outright murder of baby birds.

Benson High: October, 1964: Paul threw the pass to Eric, threaded it through at least three hulking guys intent on solid defence. Eric pivoted, snagged the ball with one hand and sprinted thirty yards. Touchdown. Five seconds left. Cheerleaders flashed their pom-poms, breaking into the beginning bars of the school song. The clock ran down. The entire team rushed Eric, who led their frenzied dance. Paul saw Donna waving from the stands. Number 13: Lucky Eric

Anderson, MVP. Shit, Paul thought, edging from the pack. I throw a miracle pass and Eric gets the glory. If he wasn't such a nice guy, I'd have to hate the prick.

Benson High: January 1965: The birds. Always the birds. God how Eric longed for a normal, boring life — a brother, a sister, hell, even a pet. When he read the ad in the *Clarion* — *To Give Away: Budgie . . . with cage* — he'd made the call. He fully intended that his whacked-out mother would never find out.

How would she? She refused to clean his room. "Stinks too bad in there," she said. "Can't you leave your bag outside?" He explained how he had to bring his hockey gear in, dry it off before he could play in it again. "I don't care if you are an all star winger, the stench is too much," she said. "Make sure you keep the door closed and the window open. I'm becoming more sensitive to all kinds pollution, especially in the air." She never set foot inside his room again.

He was playing a game of pool, the click of the balls soothing his soul, when the pool hall owner came over. "Eric," he said. "Just took a message. You're supposed to hightail it home."

At home, the doors were open wide; his mother nowhere in sight. Fire and ambulance vehicles were parked in the drive, lights flashing, and two cop cars were pulling up in front. Eric bounded up the steps. "Mom," he called, "What's going on?"

Silence in the house.

He found her in the front hall closet, curled into a foetal ball. He helped her to stand, stroked her golden hair. He felt her fragility like a head of over-ripe wheat ready to crumble.

"A bird in the house," she kept saying, "means a death in the family. Do you have any idea how many germs ride on the wing of a single bird? Oh, my god, the little thing was fluttering so and I was breathing in the very same air. It kept whooshing past my head; it almost got tangled in my hair."

They couldn't calm her.

"It's an omen," she kept repeating, "an omen from God."

Eric sat beside her. "A bird in the house doesn't mean a thing," he said, patting her hand. "It's just Bob, from my bedroom . . . he's a budgie, tame as can be." When she realised there had been a bird living in her house, she bent from the waist and puked on his shoes.

Benson High: January, 1965: Paul Jackson Jr. had no idea that Wednesday would be his final day at Benson High. He was in his homeroom, wrestling with History Of English Literature, wondering what kind of drugs the author of "Ode to a Tree" had been on and trying to see up Donna Desmond's skirt. By some lucky alignment of the stars, his pen had rolled from his desk at the perfect moment and as he'd bent to retrieve it, she'd sashayed by.

The worst and best part of the year had been the miniskirt. Their school had adopted the thirteen-inch rule: *Skirt length: Thirteen inches minimum allowed from waistline to hem. Violators will be sent home for appropriate apparel.*

Donna was in flagrant violation once again. Good for you, Paul thought, a little civil disobedience is a good thing. Especially for me.

The worst, for the guys with active imaginations like Paul, was leaving your desk at the end of a class. It's hard to stand straight when you've got a boner as big as Texas pushing against your pants. He put his mind to the stupid poem, hoping for the best.

Later that day, his mother had dropped the bomb. "Pardon me?" Paul had said.

At first, he'd failed to understand.

"It might be hard to leave just now," she'd said, "but it's the opportunity of a lifetime. The Little Flower parish has offered to pay your tuition and room and board, even your books. You're such a promising young man, Father Kilbourne says."

She'd patted his hand. "Your father and I are grateful. Now you'll have the best."

To Paul, the bus ticket she'd pushed into his hand might as well have been a ticket to the end of the world. A boy's school, he'd thought, of all the rotten luck. How could it possibly happen to me?

His father had carried his bag, and surprisingly, kissed him good-bye. He'd never been kissed by his father before. Somehow, it had made his leaving more final than it already felt. Jeez, he'd thought, as the bus pulled away, by the time I graduate from Saint Andrew's, the miniskirt craze could be over and I'll probably never see Donna Desmond again. He'd briefly considered bailing from the bus and ending it all, but he didn't think the monsignor would approve. Christ. There are more churches per capita in my hometown than any city in North America and I get sent *away* to a religious school. Gimme a break.

Donna slows, turns the Mustang into the experimental farm on the west side of town. Oh my, she thinks. I'd forgotten how beautiful it is. The tall double rows of pines offer protection from the prairie winds; profuse peonies grow along the lane; volunteer pansies — clumps of yellow and purple — hide beneath the peony plants, peeking at the sun. This was her home.

Wedding parties came from town to get their pictures taken in the perennial gardens. Three Tudor houses sat on the grounds like jewels in a crown. Donna and her father, David, a microbiologist, had lived in the largest one.

Somewhere in a distant field, she hears a cow's plaintive bellow as it calls for its calf. She remembers her father's obsession with Valda: a cow with a hole in her stomach. Well, maybe not a hole exactly, she decides, more like a porthole, so you could look in and watch the green sludge swishing around. The scientists clocked how long her meal stayed in that particular stomach, opening the porthole and taking samples of the goop inside, testing for nutrients from the different types of hay. The first stomach handles the rough stuff, breaking down the feed, the second refines it further and the third, strangely enough, does more of the same. In the fourth chamber, nutrients are leeched into the bloodstream and the roughage is given one more good squeeze before the whole mess gets moved to the lower gut. By then, it's shit.

"Four stomachs," her father often marvelled. "Imagine that!"

Occasionally, Donna attended official banquets with her father, but only under duress. "I'd like you to meet my beautiful daughter," he'd say. Donna could have died. She often got stuck with a dinner guest intent on explaining every detail of his meticulous experiments. She didn't want to be rude, but she didn't think she should have to pretend that she cared. Thank god for Eric and Paul, she thinks, if it hadn't been for them, I might have gone strange.

She eases her black Mustang into a parking space in the visitors' lot. A gardener is emptying his clippings into the compost bin.

"Can I help you?" he asks, pulling his little cart closer to her car.

"I grew up out here," Donna says. "Do you mind if I wander around?"

"It's not allowed," he says, pointing to a *Tours by Appointment Only* sign in the shadow of the pines.

"Too bad. For years, I've dreamed about this place." She bites her lip as an uncomfortable silence stretches between them like a thick rubber band. "Oh well, I guess they're right. You can never go back." She picks up her reunion itinerary from the passenger seat, where it's fallen, and tucks it back into the visor of her car.

"Aw, go ahead if you want," the gardener says, glancing over his shoulder. "There's no one around."

Not much has changed — the house where she withdrew from the world until the baby was born still looks the same — except for the trim colour, now periwinkle blue instead of her father's favourite 4-H green. The gardens are more extensive, the curving flowerbeds extending further west and closer to the trees. The trees have grown in twenty years, their branches touching as they bend above the lane.

It's almost like a cathedral, she thinks. She stares at the back of the house, the shades drawn, windows blank. She makes herself breathe slowly and deeply and fights the urge to flee.

She picks out her bedroom window, second floor, third from the corner. She can see the room, the sloping ceiling, shining oak planks on the diagonal across the floor. The sun was strong in the mornings, and she ordered a special blind so she could sleep. She'd been a prisoner. As if staying out of sight, dropping her friends before she started to show would fool a single soul. Her father had forbidden her from seeing Eric, even from talking to him on the phone.

I wonder if his voice is still fluid and soft, she thinks, like the mercury we poured from test tubes in Chemistry 2E.

Her father had insisted she make her peace with the Lord. "God is good," he'd said. "He forgave Mary Magdalene, didn't he?" Every Sunday, when the pastor came, he'd insisted Donna join them for tea. She didn't understand how it could be okay for the pastor to see her swollen belly when it was off limits to every other person on God's green earth.

She didn't get flowers when the baby was born, but Eric brought her flowers on graduation day. She was allowed to attend graduation — a miracle wrought by her father — and precipitated, she guessed, by the large scholarship offered by the experimental farm.

Donna drives around, killing time. She idles along the gravel road on the extreme west edge of the community, where the houses are old and widely spaced, finally giving way to open clover. The fair's coming to town. The grass at the grounds is flattened by trucks hauling in cattle and horses for the 4-H shows and rodeo stock. Mid-way trucks, loaded with illusions, travelling across the country and right into town.

Eric's father, as mayor, had led the Homestead Day parade in his 1964 Cadillac convertible: bright metallic green. The parade marshalled at City Hall, at the top of Central Avenue. It meandered along for at least a mile before it crossed the bridge and ended up at the fairgrounds on the south side of town. Donna remembers how Eric's father had waved — and waved, and waved — throwing Double Bubble and Mo-Jo candies to children scavenging for candies at the edge of the crowd.

She parks and walks to the edge of the chain-link fence. The hawkers are stringing lights, filling the shelves inside their booths with teddy bears. Toss the rings, shoot the gun, get your girl a prize. Pink bears, black bears, red and white and blue.

Donna dreams, sometimes, of Ferris wheels, of wheeling through the inky sky. She rises on the Ferris wheel like a sparrow riding an updraft, feels the freedom of a fluttering bird, the vastness of the sky holding her up as she drifts and dreams. The Ferris wheel rotates, graceful giant cartwheels spinning in the night. Yellow lights flash.

Eric's edgy. He decides to take a drive. He leaves Heather back at the motel, still fussing with her hair. Sure, he thinks, they could have stayed with his mother, but why put themselves through the misery? He passes his childhood home, sees every window still covered with blackout paper. He'd tried to remove it from the patio doors Easter weekend, when he'd last came home.

"The birds," his mother had said. "The glass calls to them like hookers on a corner. They can't stay away. They whack against the windows, fall to the deck. What if a budgie breaks in?"

Eric drives past the experimental farm. *He's in Donna's house, standing behind her, cupping her breasts. Shades are drawn, light is dim, but he can see their reflection in the full-length mirror mounted on the back of her closet door. Pregnancy has made her breasts heavy, like melons in his hands. He traces the swollen blue veins beneath her skin with the edge of his thumbs.*

Donna cradles a loose bundle of daisies and ferns: a talisman for her parents' graves. She bought the flowers at Smith's Florists, where Eric had ordered her graduation corsage: a single coral rose. The cemetery is immaculate, the grass so green Donna wonders how Memory Gardens can afford their water bill. The rest of the town is already parched, the hot wind sucking moisture from the soil, and from faces as well, if the taut feel of her own skin is any indication. She walks to the northwest corner of the cemetery. There are a lot of new graves.

Her father wanted a large obelisk: black marble. It had given her a grim kind of pleasure when she'd ordered the flat granite plaque — its soft grey matched to the aged patina of her mother's — and had them install it flush to the ground. She wanders the northwest corner three times over, flowers clutched tightly in her hands. When she notices the damage she's doing to the daisies, she loosens her grip.

Finally, she finds her father's grave. She bends, pulls a clump of prairie grass that's taken root at the base. Dirt falls from the dangling roots. Nodules cling. She places the grass in the sun, centred on her father's stone, so the roots will wither and die.

She turns to her mother, dusts the fine film of dust from the inscription with the palm of her hand. *Margaret Desmond. Beloved wife and mother, 1910 – 1955.* So young. No wonder her mother's face is a sepia-colour blur.

She leaves her parents, and, suddenly dizzy, perches for a moment on the edge of another grave. Ellen Hollister, *dearly beloved wife*. Who was she? Ellen, did you do what you wanted? Did you have a good life? Donna gives Ellen three daisies and two stalks of fern. Then she drops daisies and ferns on graves throughout the entire section. She feels peaceful, as if, for once in her life, she's done something good.

Cradled again by the heat of her hot leather seat, she pulls a journal from her handbag, writes quickly, before she starts her car. *Note to self — leave instructions — Tombstone inscription: Donna Desmond — Where's she dancing now?*

The day of the reunion dawns hot, with high hazy cloud. The everlasting prairie wind has ceased. A miracle, Donna thinks. She opens the closet door in Sally's spare room, rifles through the clothing she'd hung earlier so the wrinkles would fall. She tries on three different outfits, modelling for Sally, who's already dressed and sitting in the kitchen, checking last minute changes in the evening's agenda. Sally talks her out of wearing the loose, yellow sundress.

"Jeez, Donna," she jokes, "are you not aware of the old saying, 'If you've got it, flaunt it?' If you're going to go looking like a librarian, you might as well stay home." She eventually decides on a simple denim miniskirt, which somehow, the way things go, is all the rage again.

Heather's little black dress is shot with streaks of silver that sparkle when she moves. A bit much, Eric thinks. Heather hands him her locket. "Will you fasten this?" The point of the heart falls in the cleft between her breasts, like an indicator sign, highlighting cleavage that gleams with 'Silver Shimmer Pink', a liquid body shimmer that cost him forty bucks. Oh well, he thinks, I hope it makes her feel beautiful, if anything really can. She's been primping for hours and she isn't ready.

"Let's go," Eric finally says. "I want to be on time for once."

Donna is leaning on the bar, waiting for her wine. She tugs at the hem of her miniskirt when she notices the amount of leg she's bared. She'd forgotten how often her long legs got her into trouble. Benson High: the thirteen-inch rule.

"Hi beautiful," Paul says as he grabs her from behind, twirls her around and holds her to his heart.

"Paul? I can't believe it's you." She wipes her eyes with the back of her hand before she kisses him, full on the lips. "What have you been up to for the last twenty years?" she asks, still standing in the circle of his arms.

"University," he says, "travel, getting married. The usual stuff."

She realizes where she's standing and takes one step back.

"You know," Paul says, "I finally got over being sent away, but I've always wished I'd had the chance to tell you and Eric good-bye."

Donna reaches up, brushes his cheek with the tip of her fingers. "Me too," she says.

"I should have written," Paul says. "But I didn't know what to say. It was like I'd stepped out of one world and into another with no bridge in between. By the time I finally came home, I was afraid to call in case you'd already forgotten."

"I'll never forget," Donna says. "Your desk, empty, between Eric's and mine. Boobs Bellamy telling us you'd gone away. God, everything changed for us when we didn't have you."

Donna touches his shoulder. "Just making sure you're real."

Paul rubs his chest with the heel of his hand, feels a sudden, swift ache for all he'd missed. "I probably shouldn't tell you this," he says, "but you followed me for years."

Donna bows her head and listens. His voice, like a soft pastel pencil, draws pictures in her mind. Paul — a white-sand beach in Mexico, a perfect star-filled night — smoking a little pot and wishing she were there.

"Oh, Paul," she says, when he's finished. "That's beautiful. It almost makes me cry." She steps closer again and gives him one more hug.

"Dreams do come true," he says. "Donna Desmond in my arms and they're playing a waltz. Want to dance?"

They waltz halfway across the gym, the glow of white garden lights looped along the walls gentle on their faces. Donna feels the purr of Paul's soft humming as he keeps time to the familiar music. When he is suddenly silent, Donna looks up, sees him craning over the crowd. "It's Eric," he says. "He's finally decided to show. Over there.

God, wouldn't you know it, he still looks the same." Paul waves. "It's been too damn long."

Eric, less than twenty feet away? How could she have missed him? There was a time when she could sense if he was anywhere near, even in a room packed full of people. Donna tries to spot him, but the dance floor is crowded and she can't see a thing

Longest damn dance of his entire life, Eric is sure. He's been tracking Donna Desmond from the corner of his eye. She's been dancing with Paul. When the music finally stops, he takes Heather's elbow, guides her straight to Paul and Donna, who are scanning the crowd from the edge of the floor.

"Donna," he says, her name catching on the lump rising in his throat.

She moves from Paul, straight into his arms. He hugs her long and hard. Their bodies remember.

"Hi," he whispers in her ear, inhaling the sweet clover scent of her long, blonde hair. She lifts a delicate hand, feathers her fingers across his craggy cheek.

"Hi yourself," she says. "Eric Allan Anderson, how in the world have you been?"

"Earth to Eric," Heather says impatiently. "Could you get me a drink?"

He releases Donna, returns to the land of the living. "You remember Heather?"

"Of course," Donna says. "Heather, it's been a long time." She gives Heather a quick hug. Heather retreats, adjusts the neckline of her little black dress. The locket falls from her cleavage and skitters into the crowd on the floor. Paul chases the gold, picks it up and puts it in her hand.

"I'll be right back," Heather says, the broken heart open on her palm as she walks from the gym.

When the first chords of "Oh Donna" play, Eric takes Donna's hand. "Our song," he says. "Remember?"

"Mmm," she murmurs.

"Tell me. Do they still clear the floor when you start to dance?"

Donna doesn't answer — steps into his arms — and they move in perfect unison across the polished floor.

Paul leans against the warm brick of the old school gym, feels the roughness grab, pinning him to the wall like he used to pin dragonflies to cardboard in Science 2E.

The moon is high. The dance is over, but no one wants to go home. The party eventually reassembles down at the gentle bank by the swimming hole where Donna spent weeks of her life as a bikini-clad girl soaking up the sun. They are — all of them — caught in the delicate silver web of yesterday, old memories like drops of dew glistening in the morning sun.

"Let's go to the fair," Donna says. "Once more. For old times' sake." Hypnotized by the lantern moon reflecting on the glass of the creek, languid in their mutual memories, no one responds except Eric and Paul.

"Come on," Donna coaxes.

Paul offers his hand, pulls Heather from her seat on the grass. She turns to him, moves in close.

"Remember the pavilion?" Heather says, as if moving has broken her trance. "And how we used to dance on Saturday nights? Bull Frog Frank and the Boggy Creek Boys?" She keeps holding onto his hand.

Paul nods at his friend's wife, takes one step back. Maybe I danced with her a time or two, he thinks, when I couldn't stand there one second longer, watching Donna and Eric out on the floor.

Donna and Eric are halfway across the park, their shadows in the moonlight wavering one moment, solid the next.

"We better boogie," Paul says. "It doesn't look like those two are about to wait." Paul takes Heather's elbow and guides her across the rolling grass. The bodice of her dress is like fireflies flashing and Paul wonders why she didn't change into shorts and tee shirts like the rest of them had. When her heel catches a ridge, Paul steadies her for a moment before he hustles her along. The desultory murmuring from the creek bank recedes. Paul hears the soft cry of a mourning dove somewhere in the canopy of leaves.

Paul sees Eric and Donna step from the shadows of the magnificent old elm trees and into the golden glow of the crosswalk light. Donna looks back, waves them closer. "Look at that Ferris wheel," she says, "Do you think the one that came to town when we were kids was anywhere near as big?" The lights of the Ferris wheel twinkle and flash.

Arms linked, they walk the short distance across an open lot to a wire mesh gate that guards the secrets of the fair.

"I've always loved the Ferris wheel," Donna says. "Everybody game?"

Heather finds a spot where she can rest against the fence. "You guys go ahead," she says. "I'm feeling kind of queasy."

"C'mon," Paul says, "take a chance. What the hell, it might be worth the ride."

Heather shakes her head, smoothes her glittery dress across her breasts and adjusts the side slit of her skirt so her upper leg is partially revealed.

It's late. Sheet lightning licks the edges of the blue-black sky. Soft yellow squares of light pour from open windows, pool on the sidewalks, like hopscotch in the night. Half-grown farm boys are streaming to their cars. Plush pink puppies, won for their girlfriends at the ring-toss booth, are tucked beneath their arms.

The multi-coloured lights on the Ferris wheel flash. Donna digs in the pocket of her miniskirt. "I'll buy," she says. "I've got a twenty somewhere in here."

Thirteen inches, Paul thinks, I'm sure she's over the line.

"Here," he offers. "Allow me." He pulls out his wallet and somehow, drops it in the sawdust at Donna's feet. As he bends to retrieve it — he's suddenly fifteen again and cannot help himself — he does his best to look up Donna Desmond's skirt.

Paul buys the tickets, joins Donna and Eric in the short line-up. The carnie barely glances at their tickets, clangs the safety bar. "Up and away," he says, eyes sliding from theirs as he flips the switch. Paul fingers the cold yellow metal, checks on the latch, catches the sweet smell of cotton candy drifting in the air. Brilliant blue lightning forks across the clouds.

They wheel into the sky. Below them, silver shocks from Heather's dress fade, dimmer and dimmer, until they disappear into the dense fog of shadows that blanket the ground. Donna reaches for Eric's hand, and Paul's, and holds on tight.

"The old home town," Paul says. "Bird's eye view."

Eric flinches, squeezes the bones of Donna's dainty hand. Twice, hard. The way he used to. *I love you.* He hopes she remembers their code.

A raindrop falls.

Donna surreptitiously drops Paul's hand and runs her fingers through her sun-streaked hair. She touches the spot at the base of her skull. Walnut sized and growing, but she doesn't feel a thing.

Wickham's Corner

Karen and Sheila, suspended in the hammock, are barely breathing. The heat is sticky, Karen's arm slick against Sheila's where their bodies touch. Karen's eyes, slitted against the sun, shadow the community hall across the road, and further down, the faded blue paint on the back of the store. She knows if she turns her head just a bit, she'll be able to see the elevator and the three scraggly houses opposite the town sentinel. She knows this town so well she could walk the streets blindfolded without so much as tripping on an unfamiliar bump in the road.

It's a lucky day because she gets to spend more time with Sheila before the harvest starts. After that, Karen might as well be marooned on a desert island for all she gets to see of the outside world. Her mother had called before noon, extending her reprieve. "I won't be able to come to town before supper," she'd explained, "I have to help Dad move machinery, at least until the boys get home. They're picking up parts and I'm not sure how long they'll be." Karen had counted her blessings.

Sandals slap and Glenda walks by, orange Popsicle dripping down the inside of her wrist. She glances toward Sheila's yard. Karen nudges Sheila with her toe and they close their eyes. Glenda's only twelve and she sticks to Karen and Sheila like a burr to a woollen sock.

"If she comes over here, pretend you're asleep," Sheila says quietly, her lips barely moving. High above them, cottonwood leaves stir.

A shrill voice pierces the silence. "Sheila, where's Pete? I thought he was out here with you." Sheila's mother is lugging a heavy basket of whites to the clothesline. The sheets will no doubt dry immediately, Karen thinks, their wrinkles intact.

For a moment, Karen wishes she'd offered to help Anne with the wash. She loves to feed the clothing through the wringer, watch the water cascade from one side and the flattened fabric rolling out the other.

"Don't know," Sheila says. "He left with Butch." She unwraps a Double Bubble and pops it in her mouth.

Anne folds a sheet, edges together, giving it a good snap before she pins it firmly to the line. "You better go find him."

Sheila shrugs. "He'll show up sooner or later."

"Later might be too late," her mother replies. "Auntie Edna called last night. She'd seen Butch's motorcycle out on the highway. Said he must have been doing sixty at the least."

"So?" Sheila blows a huge bubble.

"So, Petey was riding on the back." Her mother hangs another sheet, snapping the corners harder this time. "If he's out riding on the highway with Butch and doesn't bother telling me, God only knows what else he might be doing. And I don't appreciate hearing about it second-hand, especially from your Auntie Edna. Thank goodness she didn't go straight to your father."

"What did Pete have to say for himself?" Sheila asks, pushing her black curls back from her brow. Her hair is frizzy from the heat.

"He promised me it's the only time he's done something crazy like that, but I've got a feeling he may be telling a little white lie. Easy enough to learn, hanging around with Butch."

Sheila spills out of the hammock and Karen follows, thinking when it comes to lies, Petey's got more than a trick or two of his own. They've already caught him watching them through a peephole in the back of the outhouse. It was Karen who noticed the wide-open eye. She'd turned her back and motioned to Sheila, then sauntered outside as if she was done. Pete had his face plastered to the back of the can and he just about shit when she'd grabbed him by the collar. They were going to tell, but he promised never to do it again. The girls plugged the hole with a twisted-up bit of Sheila's old shirt. They thought they were safe. A week later, they noticed a smaller hole, lower and on the side. Petey, of course, knew nothing about it. Crossed his heart and hoped to die.

Karen doesn't envy Sheila her task of forever having to look out for Pete. She thinks it's unfair, but she doesn't say anything. And Butch is always bad news. Most of the parents in the countryside have banned their sons from hanging around with Butch. That leaves Pete. He's only ten, but he's drawn to Butch like a moth to a flame. Maybe next month, when Butch turns sixteen and can actually go out on the highway with his bike, he'll widen his search, find new pals. Right now, he's stuck hanging around town. Karen's dad says that if Butch's parents had bought him a pitchfork and a pair of coveralls, it would have done him a lot more good than that goddamn bike.

"Okay," Sheila says, stretching and yawning. "We're on Petey patrol." Karen notices the burn across Sheila's shoulders and the freckles multiplying on her face. Her friend has skin like Snow White. It looks great with her black hair, but the sun is always murder on her. This year, Karen feels sorry for Sheila. She's suffered more than her share.

They check the store first, the most logical place to find Butch and Petey. The store is deserted, except for Mrs. Tilley, who looks up for a moment from sorting the mail. Her glasses have slid down her sweat-slicked face to the tip of her nose and she peers over the top of the frames. The letters she's holding are a fan in her hand and she flips them back and forth in a futile effort to generate a breeze.

Karen closes her eyes, inhales the sweet scents of the store. She could walk over to the jawbreaker box with her eyes closed, count out ten and put them in a bag. She can see the Black Cat clock on the wall above the canned goods, ticking and tocking, its eyes moving from side to side, in time with its tail.

"No, they haven't been in," Mrs. Tilley tells them. "But if they stop by, I'll tell Pete to head for home."

Outside, Tommy and Danny Walker squat on the sidewalk, intent on their task. Karen sees the magnifying glass and thinks they're probably trying to burn a bug.

She almost tells them it's not going to work, but changes her mind. They'll figure it out soon enough.

The girls turn toward the elevator and the three remaining houses. The first they pass without checking. Nick, the eccentric bachelor who barricades himself behind thick wooden shutters, welcomes no one, especially children. Pete would never dare go there, not even when he's pumped up with the bravado he seems to borrow from Butch. Pete's told the girls that old Nick keeps a loaded gun right by the door and he's just waiting for an opportunity to use it. Karen thinks Petey made up the whole story to scare himself. He's told it so often even he believes it.

In the next yard, there's a tricycle and a small denim jacket thrown on the ground, but there's no one around.

That leaves the elevator agent's house, a pale yellow clapboard with off-white trim. In the veranda, books and papers are piled high, almost covering the wicker rocking chair. Empty wine-bottles are lined up beside the settee. A crystal wineglass is on its side on a cushion. At one end, someone has draped a red chenille throw. To Karen, it looks like a movie set.

"No sign of him here," Sheila says. "Let's go home. Maybe he's already there." There's an eight-foot slab fence around the back yard, the boards dried and twisted, weathered silver-grey. Behind it, someone laughs.

"We better check the back," Karen says.

They find Butch's motorcycle parked by the back gate.

"Darn that brat." Sheila frowns. "Pete's not supposed to hang around the Welgans. It's not like they even have kids. Mom won't be happy."

"Why not?" Karen thinks of Mrs Welgan, how pretty she is, especially when she smiles. She's always down at the post office, either mailing in her latest assignment or checking to see if her marks have arrived.

"Mom thinks she's strange," Sheila says, lowering her voice as they get closer. "When they asked her to join the Busy Bees, she wasn't even interested. Said she's too busy, if you can imagine that."

Karen shrugs, wondering why it's so important that everyone join the community club.

"Anyway," Sheila continues, her voice a raspy whisper, "I don't see why she's still worrying about getting a degree at her age. Cripes, she must be thirty! What's she gonna do with a university degree in this town?"

Sheila unlatches the gate. Mrs. Welgan is lying facedown on her chaise lounge. The strap of her two-piece is undone and Petey is rubbing lotion on her already golden back. He's running his hands slowly up her back and down her sides to the bulge of her flattened breasts, his eyes drifting, dreamy.

Butch is draped across the back step, watching. Seeing Karen and Sheila, he lifts a sweat-beaded coke and motions to them. "Wanna join us?"

Sheila's face is red. "Petey," she says sharply, and Pete stops his slow circles, his hand resting on Mrs. Welgan's side, close to her breast.

"We're havin' a picnic," Butch says. "Want a pop?"

Sheila stomps to the lounger, grabs Pete by the arm and hauls him back a few steps. Pete digs in his heels, tries to jerk his arm away, but Sheila's got an iron grip. Mrs. Welgan holds her bikini top to her breasts as she sits upright, careful not to knock over her glass as she swings her long legs to the grass. She smiles, and Karen notices the whiteness of her teeth, the gold of her skin, and that even in the middle of an ordinary day, she's wearing glossy lipstick and green eyeshadow.

"Sorry you have to leave," she says. "Come on over any time."

Once the gate closes behind them, Sheila gives Pete a shove from behind and he stumbles. "What do you think you were doing?" she asks. "Mom'll kill you if she finds out. You know you're not supposed to be hanging around over here."

"Finds out what?" Pete asks. "I was just helping her with the lotion. She asked me to." He's watching Karen and Sheila with a strange, flat-eyed stare, as if waiting for some response. Karen looks away, her stomach doing strange twists.

"Never mind," Sheila says. "Just keep your mouth shut for once."

The heat rises in waves from the road, punching through the soles of Karen's sandals. By the time they pass the community hall, she's in a heat-induced haze herself. There's dance music, soft and far away, an orchestra, playing a waltz.

At times, her mother, caught by a tune on the radio, has interrupted her work and grabbed Karen, her arms guiding her lightly as they dance their way across the kitchen floor. Her mother, intent on teaching her an old-time waltz. Karen often tries to pull away. Her mother doesn't give up though and tells her someday she'll be grateful she's learned how to dance. There's nothing more beautiful, she says, than a man and a woman claiming the dance floor, moving smoothly to the rhythm of a waltz.

Sheila stumbles. The music has stopped.

"You finally found him," Sheila's mother says, greeting their return with ice-cold lemonade and peanut butter cookies, Petey's favourites. "Let's have a picnic." She sets the tray on the table, which she's pulled into the shade.

Sheila shoots Pete a warning glance.

"I made us a lunch," Sheila's mother says.

Karen waits for an interrogation, the "Where were you young man and what were you up to?" The way Sheila's mother was snapping the sheets, Karen fully expects the shit to hit the fan. When *she* does anything suspect, her parents dog her for weeks until they get the entire tale. Here, no questions are asked and Sheila offers no information. Everyone is suddenly mute. They munch their cookies. Petey chews slowly, deliberately, crumbs sticking to the moist fullness of his lower lip.

Karen squirms, feels the silence stretch. She checks her watch, anxious now for the hands to move, for the gravel splatter sound of her mother's car pulling up outside. She can't bear it. "I gotta phone mom," she says, to no one in particular. Inside the house, she picks up the receiver, cranks out one long ring and two shorts, and waits. Please be washing dishes, she thinks, and not be in the garden, hoeing the corn. Karen hears the faint click of other receivers picking up. Probably Aunt Edna, and Mrs. Tilley, too, if she doesn't have any customers bothering her. She often wonders why people like to rubber, especially on *their* party line. All they're likely to hear is someone talking about the weather or next week's meeting.

She rings again. "Hi," she says when her mother finally picks up after the fourth ring. "It's me. I'd like to come home."

"Don't tell me you've had enough already," her mother says. Karen hears soft country music spilling from her mother's bright kitchen into the phone. "Yesterday you were absolutely going to die if you didn't get to town. Maybe you're not such a city slicker after all." Her mother is laughing, and Karen wonders why she doesn't pick up on the edge in her voice. Mom, Karen thinks, will you please *listen* to me?

"Just come, okay?"

After her mother hangs up, Karen stands for a long time, holding the receiver. Finally, she drops it into its cradle and pushes herself away from the wall. Her feet count each step from the phone to the yard. The minutes stretch, like McIntosh toffee left sitting in the sun. Karen begins to hum, slicing the silence. She waits.

Harvest has begun. The smell of hot grain drifts into the kitchen where Karen and her mother scramble to prepare lunch. Karen knows they'd better not keep her dad waiting. He loses his perspective during harvest, and everyone hops to his tune. Karen's seen him jump up from the table and stomp across the kitchen, slamming the door hard enough to rattle the china when her mother mentions a leaking tap, as if anything outside the harvest itself is an insult to him.

Last September, Karen forgot and asked him if she could attend a school dance.

"Jesus H. Christ, Karen! I don't want to hear another thing about it! I got enough on my mind as it is." Karen had been ironing a dress. When her father raised his voice, she forgot what she was doing. Now the smell of scorched cotton is a harvest smell; it brings back the lesson she'd learned.

The whole world disappears at harvest and it doesn't return until her father's grain is safely in the bins.

"Ready?" her mother asks, slicing the sandwiches neatly on the diagonal and reaching for the cookie jar. When the truck roared through the yard five minutes earlier, it was their signal to fly into action. Karen hears the auger growl, gauges how much time she has. Not much. She quickens her pace.

She clinks a serving spoon into a sealer, pours the coffee from the old tin perc. The spoon will keep the glass from exploding when the boiling coffee hits the bottom. The smell of strong coffee makes Karen want to taste it, although she knows from experience that coffee doesn't taste as good as it smells. Her father likes it boiled so long "a spoon will stand up in it." Washing the inside of the coffee pot is a criminal offence. After the coffee's poured, Karen carefully wraps the jar in newspapers, held tight with a sealer ring, and slips it inside a stray woollen sock.

"Coffee's ready," she says.

Her mother has been packaging freshly baked cookies. The cheese and onion sandwiches on homemade bread — white and fine, her father doesn't like rye bread or brown, "peasant" food — are already wrapped.

"You better get out there." Her mother hands her the sandwiches and the coffee, holding the jar by the knot in the top of the woollen sock. She kisses Karen's forehead. Karen, at thirteen, thinks she's too old for such foolishness.

She waits on the front step. When she hears the truck leave the bin, she'll sprint to the middle of the yard, ready to pass off the precious lunch to her father as he idles down for her hand-off. It's a relay race, the prize her father's smile.

He's different today. He's stopping the truck and opening the door. "Want to come?" he asks. "The durham's going over thirty at the Wickham place. No more room in the bins. I'll top this load up and then we'll have to take her to town."

"Sure," Karen says, a sudden lilt in her voice, eyes shining.

As they head to the field, Karen thinks about the harvest, how the Wickhams, whoever they might have been, have always been a part of her life.

Her father bought their land before she was born, but still talks about that half section of his land as Wickham's corner. She wonders how many years they'll have to be dead or gone before the name will finally change, not only on the municipal maps, but in the minds of the farmers themselves.

It's three miles across the flat to the corner and another three before they cross the railroad tracks and into town. It usually takes an hour to make the round trip, including waiting time at the elevator.

"Look at those clouds." Her father points out the mare's tales whisking across the sky. "Don't mind seeing those at harvest time." Karen has learned all about cloud formations. The thin cirrus are not significant, their pretty streamers of white and sliver floating high above. The nimbostratus, hanging low in the sky and dimly lit from within, are cloud formations that make her father fret. They mean a weather system moving in, and will almost always deliver on their threat of rain. Karen's eyes search the skyline and she spots the elevator, a distant smudge.

Karen smiles, thinking of seeing Sheila again, having some time to talk to a normal person, someone not affected by harvest madness. It's been two long weeks. She wonders what's up in town. Sheila's life seems more interesting than hers.

During harvest, it's just her father and her brothers and their sacred work. Sometimes, Karen gets caught in the soft cloak of the tasks she shares with her mother — taking cookies from the pans and setting them on racks to cool, buttering fresh bread, peeling and mashing the hard-boiled eggs — her mother chattering away, just slightly above the twang of country music that's always in the background, but she'd rather be in town.

When harvest is over, Karen and her mother take a whole day off. Karen's father goes to town, buys Kentucky Fried Chicken and salads in plastic containers, and store-bought buns. Karen and her mother spend the entire day taking care of only themselves, reading the latest magazines with mud-masked faces, drinking mugs of sweet tea while the mud cools and sets. They give each other manicures and play soft music. They burn scented candles in the middle of the day.

Her father is driving more slowly than usual. Karen pours a cup of coffee for him, first shaking the sealer to make sure the sugar from the bottom has dissolved. He takes his chipped mug from her hand, sucks the hot coffee from its lip, sips and sips again. "Ah-h-h," he says, "The nectar of the gods." The sealer is warm in Karen's hands. He crunches his cheese and onion sandwiches and, catching her watching, gives her a wink. The wink is their 'good girl' signal. Karen feels happy just being around him.

He starts on the cookies, dipping them in his coffee, managing to bring them to his mouth in one smooth movement, no dripping or losing half the cookie in his cup. He dances like that too, a graceful economy of movement.

Karen seldom gets to spend time alone with her father and she watches him shift — up, down, over — all the while singing. He never sings a whole song, just a line or two from one, then on to another.

> *"Never speak harsh words to your true loving husband*
> *He may leave you and never return.*
> *And today's the day the teddy bears have their picnic."*

As her father sings and steers the loaded truck over the rutted roads, Karen watches the cords in his arms, the white skin on the inside of his elbow where he's finally made a concession to the heat and rolled up his sleeves. She's never seen her father in shorts or without his ever-present long-sleeved shirts. She wonders how he can stand it in the golden heat of the harvest sun.

His face is craggy, his eyes bluebell blue, with purple ringing his iris. There are streaks of grey in his thick black hair. Karen has noticed that women take a second look when they pass him on the street. She wonders if her mother has noticed it, too.

Her father hands her his empty cup and Karen puts it beside the sealer in the brown paper bag. She notices a hint of sweet onion lingering in the air.

She wonders if her father makes time to kiss her mother during harvest, at night, when they're all finally tucked into their beds. Can her mother still smell the onions, on her hands and on his breath?

The line-up at the elevator is six trucks long. "Damn, this is going to take a while," her father says. He takes a red polka-dotted bandanna from his pocket, mops at the sweat forming on his brow. "I hope that stupid kid has enough brains to check the hopper and wait for me if I'm not back in time. That's the last thing I need, my grain pouring out the back of the combine and me stuck in this godforsaken line."

Karen knows her father doesn't put much stock in his sons. She realizes he always expects the worst from them, and quite often gets it. She's not sure of the dynamics, having read about the *yin* and the *yang*, but she wonders if her life will be different. The book talked of expectations, how putting good vibes out to the universe would attract good fortune and how expecting trouble would attract it to you for sure. Karen is expecting only good things, so according to the book, that's exactly what she'll be getting.

"You may as well go visit for a bit," he says. "It's gonna be a while. Unless you want to stay and ride up in the truck."

"No, that's okay," she answers quickly. The last time she'd come, her dad had insisted she stay in the truck as it was raised into the air on the hoist inside the elevator. She never told him of her sick certainty that the shaft would jam at the top and she would never get down.

"Be back in half an hour," he says, and she wonders if she'll be able to tell when a half an hour has gone by. She holds her palm horizontal, its edge touching the bottom edge of the burning sun and tries to remember. How many fingers make a half an hour? Two? Maybe three? She's always had trouble telling time by the sun, but her father's a master. Her brothers, too. At least they're good at something, Karen thinks.

She heads for the store. Mrs. Tilley is sorting through flyers, moving slowly from the counter to the mailboxes lining the wall. Her pendulous breasts sway gently, as if dancing to a melody only they can hear. She doesn't notice Karen. Seeing nothing in their box, Karen leaves, making sure that the screen door snaps shut, scattering the flies. Mrs. Tilley has suspended sticky, amber fly strips from the high tin ceiling. By the middle of summer, the strips are studded with tiny black bodies.

The wooden sidewalks make a hollow clunk beneath her feet as Karen heads for Sheila's. As she crosses the street from the dancehall to Sheila's house, she envies her friend. Karen wonders if Sheila and Pete sneak over to the Saturday dances and watch the dancers, or the people outside, smoking, taking swigs from dark bottles. I'll have to ask her, Karen thinks. If they were careful, they could probably get close enough to hear some good jokes or a whispered conversation. If *she* lived across from the dance hall, she'd be out there every chance she got. It would be wonderful, hearing the music, watching the dancers holding each other, gliding across the freshly waxed floor.

She knocks on the door, and, hearing nothing, opens it and steps inside. "Yoohoo, anybody home?"

Sheila rubs her eyes and squints in the dimness of the kitchen, puts her fingers to her lips. "Shh, Mom's asleep."

When there's trouble at Sheila's house, her mother hibernates. Karen hasn't figured it out. What good does sleeping do?

"Can you come out?" Karen asks, her voice soft and low. The place is unusually quiet. The shades are pulled and the doors to the adjoining rooms are closed. It reminds Karen of her grandfather's house before his funeral, everyone afraid to laugh or talk out loud, her family already whispering over his grave. A vase on the table is overflowing with sweet peas, their scent overpowering in the closed-up kitchen.

Sheila, still holding a finger to her lips, scratches out a note for her mother. She tiptoes across the floor, pushes Karen into the porch and quietly closes the door.

"Where's Pete?" Karen asks, as they head across the road, past the dancehall and down to the store. For once, he's not tagging along.

"He's grounded," Sheila replies and offers no further explanation. They've reached the old rope swings, behind the store. The timbers used to be painted yellow. Now they're weathered, mostly grey, but the structure is solid, still straight and strong. They seat themselves and start their lazy swinging, barely moving, angling their heads backwards to get an upside-down picture of the vast prairie sky.

The seesaw motion and the moving clouds make Karen dizzy. She puts down a toe, anchoring herself. "What did he do this time?"

"I'm not supposed to tell," Sheila says, bending further back and taking in a larger panorama of the sky. "Mom made me promise."

Karen's stunned. Sheila is her best friend; they talk about everything. The silence is filled with the background hum of combines. "I'll never tell a soul," she says. "You should know that by now."

"Okay," Sheila says. "I'll tell you. But you can't say a word. Cross your heart and hope to die?" she asks.

Karen solemnly crosses herself, spits in the dust and hopes to die.

"He filled up Glenda's hole with peanut butter and jam."

"That's the stupidest thing I've ever heard you say," Karen says, grabbing the rope of Sheila's swing, turning her so Karen is looking into her eyes. "And it's not even funny. You better quit going around saying things like that or someone might believe you."

Sheila's eyes are dark. Her freckles stand out, like a heavy sprinkle of cinnamon on a pale pastry. There's no sign of a smile on her sun-dried lips. "It's true. They've been playing doctor all summer and finally got caught. Glenda's mom was doing the wash and noticed the jam in Glenda's panties. I guess she thought Glenda was a little early getting the curse. Anyway, her mom went in to give her the talk. When Glenda told her what was *really* in her pants, Mrs. Anderson totally lost it. That's why my mom's got a headache and Pete's grounded. I guess he used a little too much jam."

"Jeez," Karen says. "What's the matter with Glenda? You'd think she'd have more brains. Even if Petey doesn't."

"I don't know," Sheila looks at Karen, a question in her eyes. "Pete told me it was his idea the first time, but ever since then, it's Glenda who brings the stuff. I've been thinking," she says. "Pete loves the taste of peanut butter and jam. Do you think he . . . um, you know?"

"Sheila, that is too disgusting," Karen says, jumping from the swing. It's there again, that feeling in her stomach. She can almost touch the pain with her palm. "Come on, I haven't got all day. Let's go do something."

Karen heads for the station. Maybe there's a train. They could haul the mailbag up to Mrs. Tilley. She's always happy when someone helps her out. When Sheila realizes where they're headed, she hesitates.

"Not sure if I can go in," she says.

"Why not?" Karen asks.

"My dad," Sheila tells her. "Last time he got a load on he came down here and made a really big scene. I guess Pete and Butch had been hanging around the station. They got into the office and read some girlie magazines, tried to steal a few. They got kicked out and told not to come back."

"Oh," Karen picks up a small smooth stone, tosses it at a red-winged blackbird sitting on the power line. The stone misses by a mile, as Karen knew it would, but the bird flies away.

"Dad was so mad I thought he might kill Petey. He said if he ever heard anything like it again, he'd kick Pete's ass from here to breakfast. And he probably would have, if it hadn't been for Mom."

Karen starts up the stairs to the platform surrounding the station. "C'mon," she says to Sheila. "You worry too much."

Inside the cool and shadowed waiting room, Karen and Sheila check the train schedule. It's a half an hour before it returns from its run up the Leader line. Karen wishes that she and Sheila had more nerve. She'd seen Butch and Pete put pennies on the track moments before the train comes through. The weight of the wheels turns the pennies to molten sheets of copper, smooth and curved and thin enough they can almost see right through them. Karen has heard you can derail a train doing that, but still, she wishes for the nerve to try it.

"This place is a morgue," Sheila says, running her hand across the smooth oak railing around the ticket wicket. "Let's check the store."

They walk along the lane, shoulders sometimes touching, until they reach Mrs. Tilley's store. Tommy and Danny are standing outside, their bikes flopped on the sidewalk and Sheila and Karen have to step around. Sheila cuffs one of the little boys, and tears spring to his eyes. "Move those damn bikes. A person could break a leg."

Karen looks at Sheila, eyebrows raised.

"It's the heat," Sheila whispers, as they climb the steps to the store. "Or maybe it's my goddamn rag."

For a moment, Karen is blinded by the contrast between the boiling sun outside and the dimness in the store, but she walks straight to the penny candy like a seeing-eye dog. She fingers the candy until Mrs. Tilley notices and glares at her over the top of her silver rims. "Take one, leave the rest," she says, wiping the countertop, her eyes on Karen.

Karen spends her dime, settling on thirty jawbreakers: three for a penny. She loves their licorice sweetness, how the flavour lasts forever on her tongue. She even loves the way they turn her teeth black.

She sits on the front steps, recounting the jawbreakers, hoping she didn't rip Mrs. Tilley off, but also hoping that if anyone got short-changed, it wasn't her.

"Why does that woman make me feel so guilty?" Karen asks, when Sheila finally saunters out. "I've been trying for years and I haven't got the nerve to steal a single thing. Chicken, I guess."

"I'm not," Sheila says, pulling an all-day sucker from the cuff of her shorts and peeling off the cellophane.

"Looks like the boys high-tailed it home," Karen says.

"Good thing," Sheila says. "They hang around way too much and sometimes, the little bastards get on my nerves. Maybe if someone checked on them once in a while, they wouldn't be wandering all over town getting into trouble."

Karen thinks of Sheila's mom, who always has Sheila checking on Pete and the trouble he's gotten himself into, despite her efforts.

Suddenly, Karen remembers her dad, by now probably waiting for her back at the elevator by now. "Shit," she says. "I better run. Dad'll be furious if I've kept him waiting." She turns to her friend, grabs her arm. "Don't worry about Petey. Things will turn out fine. Even if he is a pervert, it's got nothing to do with you."

"You think?" Sheila says, looking at Karen through eyes veiled by thick, black lashes.

Karen nods. "I'll call you tonight." She notices a bank of leaden clouds building in the west as she hurries to the elevator. It seems a long time since she last saw her dad. The soft dust swirls as she runs down the road. She's sweating. The dust sticks to her body in a fine, slick film. She rounds the bend. Her father's truck is parked outside; he's been weighed and emptied. Waiting. Karen wonders why he hasn't come looking, or at least honked the horn, his usual 'time's-up' signal.

She runs up the ramp to the elevator. The creaking ropes give her a sudden chill. "Dad?" No answer, just the sound of the swallows fluttering against a window, and the wind, moaning through an opening somewhere high above.

She runs across the scale, the guts of the elevator rumbling as she grabs the heavy brass handle on the office door. She's been here a million times, but the place seems strange, everything changed, like a lens has dropped and the view is slightly skewed. She shakes her head, tries to refocus.

She wants her dad, wants out of this place right now, wants to be back on their farm, in the kitchen with her mother, doing useful things in her mother's slow, meticulous way, the rhythm of their work as soothing as a song. She longs to hear her mother's melodious voice, crooning country songs at the kitchen sink, her hands soapy and scented as she washes the china teacups.

Mrs. Welgan is sitting on the corner of her husband's desk, tanned legs crossed, one sandal flipping negligently against the darkened wood. She's wearing pink shorts — very short for a woman her age, Karen thinks — and cherry lipstick. Her pink top is cropped, with an edge of crocheted lace in a deeper shade of pink. Beneath the lace, Karen sees a line of golden skin. Mrs. Welgan's head is tilted to one side and a waterfall of hair, shot through with sunlit streaks, shades her eyes from Karen's view. She's intent on Karen's father, who hasn't yet noticed her, doesn't move.

"Dad?" Karen hears herself whisper.

"Oh, hi Karen." Mrs. Welgan turns. "Your dad and I were just talking. For some fool reason, I've signed up for another year of classes. I came over to break the news to Allan, but I found your dad instead."

Karen looks at Mrs. Welgan. Her dad? Talking about anything other than how many bushels his crop might go? About anything not connected to his precious farm? During harvest?

"Dad?" she says again.

Her father peels his gaze from Mrs. Welgan. He stands up, straightens the collar of his shirt and runs his fingers through his unruly hair. His movements are slow, disoriented, an ordinary man drugged by the heat of the harlot sun.

Marking the Goddamn Spot

Tongues were wagging all across town before Merle Williamson reached the railroad track in his battered International three-quarter ton, with Truck Puppy and Twyla sniffing the breeze from the bed of his truck. Truck Puppy is purebred Blue Heeler, a wizard with cattle. Twyla's just a mixed-breed bitch some jackass had dropped off on the road to his ranch. She'd been a walking skeleton when he'd rescued her from the ditch — sides gaunt, ribs like razors — brown eyes clouded and caked.

The first Tuesday of every month Merle buys supplies. Lorne watches from behind the counter as Merle pulls up in front of the Lucky Dollar in a swirl of yellow dust. His order is always the same: fourteen cans of Libby's deep browned beans, a big bag of Uncle Ben's instant white rice, ten cans of Aylmer's crushed tomatoes and five ten-pound bags of Kibbles and Bits.

Twyla still gobbles up food as if every meal might be her last.

"I've got some real nice lettuce," Lorne offers as Merle plunks his groceries down and the turntable starts to move. "On sale, too."

"Don't know much about making salads," Merle says. But he goes to the cooler, takes out two bags of romaine hearts and some green onions that have seen better days. "Never too late for an old dog to learn new tricks," he says, placing the greens on the counter beside his usual fare.

While Lorne rings up his groceries, Merle whistles softly, ambling up and down the aisles. Lorne hears a thump as something gets knocked off a shelf.

"Jesus H. Christ on a Shetland pony!" Merle curses from the bowels of the store.

"Lookin' for something?" Lorne finally asks.

Merle clears his throat, comes out from behind a black, wrought-iron rack packed full of garden seeds, the pictures on the packages not even vaguely resembling the gardens that grow in Coleman, with its alkali-laced soil.

Merle is looking at his boots. "Actually," he says, "I'm looking for Pampers."

"Pampers?" Lorne almost screams.

"Yeah, number twos, I think."

Lorne points to a shelf above the feminine hygiene products, coughs as Merle reaches for a super-size box. Merle is a sixty-three year old bachelor, the same age as Lorne. Merle has lived alone on his isolated ranch his whole life. When he's not checking the health of his herd or riding fence, Merle reads. The town librarian says she's forever ordering in new books for him. Where Merle gets his extensive reading list, she has no idea. He never reads Louis L'Amour, even though she's got lots of those on hand. He's intelligent, she says, although definitely strange.

Merle pulls three boxes of Pampers from the shelf and piles them onto the turntable and watches as Lorne pushes the button and the Pampers travel slowly toward the till. Lorne adds the total to Merle's bill.

"Expensive," Merle says.

"Yep," Lorne replies. He thumps the Pampers box. "You got some company we haven't heard about yet, or are you diapering your dogs these days?" Lorne looks up, winks at Merle. "If you are, you been out there alone too damn long."

Merle smiles and picks up his grocery bags. Lorne hurries to hold the door, craning to see past Merle. He watches as Merle piles groceries on the empty seat of his truck.

When Merle pulls around the corner, Lorne flips his 'Back in Ten Minutes' sign on the door and scurries across the street to the coffee shop.

Charlotte heard a change as the motor geared down, the whine of the wheels diminishing as the Greyhound slowed. Soft green smudges dotted the edges of the railroad track and further away, roofs reflected the slanted golden rays of the afternoon sun. The blur of the power poles began to focus, and poles passed, one by one. Charlotte blinked, looked twice when she saw a single chair by the edge of the highway.

"Coleman," the driver announced. "Your stop, ma'am."

"Here?" she asked, dazed by the expanse of nothing assaulting her Toronto blue eyes. The horizon was so far away it hurt. She'd never seen that much sky before.

"Yep," the driver said. "I expect someone will be along soon. And if you get stood up, it's an easy walk. Express bus," he explained, "don't go into town."

Charlotte looked at Danica, asleep on the seat, the July sun basting her forehead with sweet baby sweat. She eased Danica into her arms, and turned sideways in the narrow aisle to squeeze past two blue-haired ladies perched behind the driver.

One of the ladies gave Charlotte a shy smile and offered her the grubby Winnie the Pooh that had fallen from Danica's arms. "She'll be needing this when she wakes," she said.

"Beautiful little girl," the other said.

"Thanks," Charlotte said, "And I'm sorry about the noise. Your trip will be a whole lot quieter now."

Danica had been fussing for what seemed to Charlotte a few hundred miles and she'd been grateful the ladies hadn't complained. She nodded to them as she stepped from the bus.

Damn, she thought, setting her suitcase beside the red plastic chair. What have I done? The heat of the day had softened the seat and it branded her buttocks as she hauled a howling Danica onto her lap. Diesel fumes fouled the air.

"Shh, shh," Charlotte said. "It's gonna' be okay."

Dust devils danced and a green International three-quarter ton slowed, rolled to a stop ten feet from the red plastic chair. A man of about six feet, wearing Levis and a battered brown Stetson, soiled at the brim, stepped from the truck.

"I'll be jiggered," he said. "I wasn't sure you'd really come."

"Merle?" she asked, shading her eyes with her hand. Sun bounced from the spider-web cracks on the window of the truck. Merle's silver hair was blazing with light, his face in shadow. She felt a small thrill of relief when she saw the sudden white flurry of his smile.

Two dogs stared from the bed of the pick-up truck. The smaller one was silver-blue, the other, black and white, with long, smooth hair that looked like it had been recently brushed. They leaned over the edge of the truck bed, tongues lolling, watching their master.

Danica spotted them, reached with her baby-fat hands.

"Do you want to pet them?" Merle asked, and when Danica shook her head yes, he scooped her up, held her close so she could touch their silky hair.

"Truck Puppy and Twyla," he said. "They're going to be your friends."

Making ends meet living in the heart of Toronto was, for Charlotte, like waging an on-going war. Her meagre weapons — her hard, young body and the ability to carry a full tray of beer through a standing-room only crowd — had barely kept her head above water.

And living had become a lot more complex since Danica had come along. Simple things Charlotte had never given a thought to before. With Danica in tow, even a trip to the grocery store has become a chore. Window-shopping a thing of the past. And money disappears faster too, like water sucking down a drain, and she has to calculate everything twice before she spends. Children complicate things.

When Luanne, manager down at Second Hand Rose, called to give her an early-bird shot at their annual brown bag sale, Charlotte blessed the helping hands of friends. Luanne knew all about Charlotte's struggle to make ends meet and she helped out whenever she could. Her timing was perfect because Charlotte had ten whole dollars in her pocket, thanks to a drunken patron down at Tucker's Bar and Grille.

"Come on Sunday," Luanne had said, "I've got a couple of things set aside. I'll be there all afternoon tagging stock. The back door will be unlocked."

Chimes tinkled as Charlotte opened the door.

"Hi," Luanne popped up from between two racks of jeans. "Sale officially starts tomorrow, so don't tell the boss."

Charlotte gave her a victory sign and tugged on Danica's hand. "My lips are sealed," she said.

"Give that little sweetheart to me," Luanne said, coming out from behind the racks and taking Danica into her ample arms. She set Danica on the counter, tickled her chin and her delighted giggles blended with the music of the Japanese serenity ball Luanne had placed in her chubby hands.

"Room two," Luanne said. "Take a look."

Charlotte tried on four dresses before she found the perfect one, black, fitted to the curves of her body, the rounded neckline showing off her slim neck and prominent collar bones.

"Wow," Luanne said, as Charlotte turned before the mirror. "You look transformed. When you'll get a chance to wear a classy outfit like that is beyond me."

"Do you have any accessories?" Charlotte asked.

Luanne hoisted Danica from the counter and balanced her on her generous hip as she sorted through a box beside the till. She came up brandishing a small, black-beaded purse and a pair of almost-new charcoal pumps, size six. She also held a purple shawl, fringed with multi-coloured beads. "The shawl might be a bit much," she said. "But try it anyway."

When Charlotte left the store, she had an outfit she could wear anywhere.

"Come again," Luanne said, blowing kisses to Danica. "Bring my sweetheart too."

As she walked along the street, Charlotte's hand strayed to her green canvas bag. She fingered the soft edge of the shawl, its silky softness slipping through her fingers like the elusive edge of a dream. Charlotte had always loved to pretend, creating her own perfect world. Charlotte's hand slid to the side pocket of her bag, fingered the ironwood toothpick holder purchased from a street vendor. It perfectly concealed the reefer she'd been longing to light. Pot hazed the hard edges of reality, skewed the lens for Charlotte so the impossible seemed entirely true.

One night, down at Tucker's, Charlotte had heard Larry and his new buddy Carl talking about George, one of the regulars, famous for how long he could nurse a bottle of stout.

"Professional mourner," Carl had said. "The old bugger attends every funeral within walking distance of his flat."

"Maybe he's got something there," Larry had said. "He probably eats better than most pensioners. Think of the free lunches and all those grey-haired ladies hungry for a man. Hell, maybe we should tag along a time or two. Get George to show us the ropes."

Charlotte had wiped sticky spills from the length of the bar, moving away from Larry and Carl and their snickering grins. But later, she found herself replaying their gossip, over and over, like a movie in which she'd missed an important piece of the plot.

Finally, inspiration struck and she'd found a way into another world, even without the pot. Charlotte scoured the announcements in the social pages of the Toronto Star for weddings at fancy hotels, like the Palliser downtown, or political conventions; large events where acquaintances mingled freely.

At weddings, she timed her arrival halfway through the cocktail hour. Usually hosted in vast, informal spaces near the foyer, the functions were easy enough to spot and slip into uninvited.

Trays laden with food — caviar on crackers, pinwheel sandwiches, radishes cut to look like tiny, perfect roses and dainty pastries on silver trays — floated through the crowd, born aloft by tuxedo-clad waiters. Food was plentiful, free. Working nights at Tucker's Bar and Grille while Danica slept at Darlene's apartment next-door didn't allow for luxuries like caviar. It barely covered necessities, and Charlotte hungered for more.

She learned to drift from conversation to conversation, careful to stay on the fringes, never staying longer than ten minutes at a time. She nodded and smiled, scanning the room like she'd lost track of her date.

At the last reception she'd attended at the Palliser, she'd forgotten her self-imposed rule. A man of about thirty, deeply tanned, with a sharp-edged haircut — one that Charlotte knew would need a trim every third or fourth day — was sitting on a couch in the corner. He looked at her and smiled and she noticed his perfect Chicklet teeth. She walked over, sat beside him on the embossed velvet couch.

"Wow," she said, as a piper, clad in a moss green tartan marched in and began to play, the high ceilings absorbing the wail, softening and sweetening the notes, echoing them throughout the entire room until she felt feathery fingers move up and down her spine.

"Who'd have thought the pipes could ever sound so good," he said, stretching his long legs. "Better than they do on the streets of Glasgow. Acoustics, I guess."

He flagged a waiter, offered her champagne. "Thanks," she said, looking into his slate-blue eyes over the top of her fluted glass.

"Splashy do," he said. "Trust Tony. Nothing but the best for any kid of his."

She was gazing at the bride, who had just floated into the room, trailing a train of iridescent, ethereal white "Yeah," she replied. "What a beautiful bride. Her dress must have cost a fortune."

"I'm wondering," he said, his eyes suddenly smoky with suspicion. "Which side of the family are you on?"

Since she didn't know the names of either side, or even that you had to take sides at a wedding, she only looked at him and shrugged. That was it. He actually took her elbow and ushered her to the door.

"How'd you bust me?" she asked, pulling her elbow from his hand and turning for one last look at the beautifully dressed and coiffed women standing against the backdrop of a sparkling silver fountain at the end of the room.

"A hunch," he said. "Your hungry eyes. Better work on that."

Charlotte first saw Merle behind the podium of a National Charolois Breeder's Association meeting. His long grey hair brushed the collar of his soft chamois shirt. He'd snugged up his braided string cowboy tie with a tooled silver clasp. When his velvet voice reverberated across the crowded hall

— apparently, he was a dignitary of some kind — she actually stopped munching on her ground beef meatballs impaled by red plastic swords, and listened.

She'd hung around the bar, where bottles of Crown Royal, Lamb's Navy Rum, Jack Daniels and Iceland Vodka were lined up like proud, old soldiers on parade. There were no waiters pouring discreet portions and she noticed they didn't even have a shot glass. The men freehanded, eyeing up the levels in their plastic glasses, and usually added an extra splash or two. They used the mix sparingly, as if it were liquid gold.

Merle had walked up to the bar, carrying a heavily laden paper plate, filled with meatballs and square chunks of cheddar and marble cheese. As he'd reached for a glass, three meatballs rolled to the edge of his Chinet plate.

"Looks like you could use a little help," Charlotte had said, taking a glass from the stack. "What brand and how much?"

She wasn't too surprised when he'd said, "Jack Daniels, three fingers please, and easy on the Coke."

By the end of the night, she had a clear picture of his pretty little ranch, his herd of purebred Charolais cattle and she could almost hear the prairie wind sighing over the hills above his yard.

"It's nothing fancy," he'd told her, "but I love the damn place. Coming to the city for three days straight is about as long as I can stand. No silence anywhere."

Charlotte had talked about Danica, something she rarely did on her scavenging forays.

"You look awfully young to be a mother," was all that Merle had said.

"It's a big responsibility," she told Merle. "More than I ever knew. But I wouldn't trade her for the world."

He'd taken another swig of Jack, then looked across the rim. "Don't know much about kids," he said. "They're good in theory, but I've never really been around one for long."

At the end of the evening, Merle had filled another plastic glass with Jack Daniels straight. "One for the road," he'd said. As they waited for the elevator, he handed her a napkin and a pen. "Your address?" he said. "I like to write a letter now and then."

He'd held the door for her, punched number three for his own floor, and then the lobby button for Charlotte as she scrawled her name and address above the picture of a Charolais cow.

"They'll call you a cab at the desk," he'd said. "Too dark out there for a pretty thing like you to be walking alone." He'd tucked a twenty-dollar bill into the palm of her hand.

"Thanks," she'd said, stepping from the elevator and into the muted light of the lobby.

"You pour with a generous hand," Merle had said. "Damn fine trait in a woman," he added as the steel of the elevator doors cut his final words in half.

When the bellman had hurried to open the door, she felt like a princess. "Thanks," she said, blowing him a kiss as she stepped into the cab, guilt nipping at her heels when she didn't give him a tip. She knew how precious tips could be.

The heat wave holding the city hostage had been getting on everyone's nerves. It had been been hell-fire hot for seven long days. A simple walk to the corner store had become a nightmare, ten blocks long. Charlotte thought getting a Popsicle for Danica would provide some relief, but all she accomplished was cranking up the misery index a full notch or two. The Popsicle melted quickly, stickiness dripping into the creases of Danica's neck.

"Help me," she said as the Popsicle split in half and fell off the stick, puddle on the sweltering pavement at her feet.

"There's not one damn thing I can do to help," Charlotte said, trying to take hold of her daughter's sticky hand. Danica flopped down on the pavement beside the orange puddle and howled.

When they finally got back home, Charlotte pushed bath time up an hour. As she filled the tub, she tried to ignore the rust streaks leaching brown from the chipped porcelain.

"Come here, baby," she said, and plopped Danica into the tub. Charlotte wiped Danica's flushed face, filled a red plastic glass and poured tepid water down her delicate back.

"Doesn't that feel good?" she asked as she tickled her way down Danica's delicate spine.

"Don't," Danica said, pulling away. Charlotte brushed damp hair from her forehead and sighed, then counted the hours until Danica slept.

Three times Charlotte tucked her in and three times she looked up to see Danica — dragging her blanket and Winnie the Pooh — peeking from the open bedroom door.

The third time, Charlotte snapped. She almost threw Danica onto the bed. "Last chance, kiddo," she said. "You better stay in bed. Don't think you're too damn cute to spank."

Danica's blue eyes were huge, magnified by a film of tears as she wiped her nose on Pooh. But she stayed in bed and finally cried herself to sleep. When Charlotte peeked in a half hour later, she was sucking her thumb in a sweat of tangled sheets.

Fans whirred in the bedroom and the living room, the one in the living room slightly off kilter, pinging a metallic chorus with every turn. Charlotte's head hummed.

She opened her apartment door, grabbed the mail and quickly slammed the door again before the putrid hallway smells, ripened by the heat, could push themselves further into her tiny living room.

With clarity close to pain, she suddenly smelled fresh-baked buns. "Don't be late," her mother's voice called from the verandah. "One of these days, you girls will get into trouble hanging around downtown." Charlotte turned, lifted her hand to wave but the shadows had deepened. Her mother was gone.

She'd often met her friends at the veteran's park in the middle of her green hometown. At dusk, the fountain lights came on, petal pinks and pale blue-mauves, splintered by the spray of water rising from its circular base. Chiseled on a black marble plaque set in the cement base were the words *Built and maintained by the Kinsmen Club for the enjoyment of all.*

As the water rose in the fountain, a bubble of happiness would rise in Charlotte's chest. She linked arms with her friends, happy, safe. She wondered, now, why she had been in such a rush to leave.

For Charlotte, the big city beckoned. Prince Charming was waiting, she was sure. But the good ones don't stop in at Tuckers and the ones who do are already married, just looking for a quick one before they go home. The city has become dreary viewed through the smoky, plate-glass window of Tucker's Bar.

She turned the letter over, held it to the light. When she gave Merle her address, she thought he'd probably drop the napkin on the bureau in his hotel room and leave it there, or tuck it in his pocket and forget about it. She imagined him riding, pulling out the crumpled napkin, staring at the handwriting, unable to recall where he'd gotten it, or why.

She'd been surprised when the first letter arrived, Merle's melodious words as pretty as the pictures he drew. The envelopes were beautiful, works of art. This one was completely covered by a picture of fat cattle crowded around a water trough and a windmill braced against a scud of scattered clouds. Pencil drawn. Serenity oozes from the idyllic prairie scene.

Charlotte kept his letters in a green shoebox under her bed. They arrived like clockwork every second week and the box was almost full.

She held the letter to her chest, walked through her stifling kitchen onto the tiny balcony. It's too small to actually use for barbeques or eating, and it's littered with Danica's toys. There's a small wooden chair wedged in the corner, and Charlotte often sits there late at night while she smokes and winds down.

She bent to light a match, inhaled deeply, and felt a faint coolness wash over her sweat-slicked skin. The lights of the city reflected from the low-hanging bank of smog, a sickly yellow glow. Below her, the bus stop was deserted, street sounds muffled by the mantle of the night. A cat yowled and Charlotte stood.

A bag lady, bent and twisted like diamond willow, was haloed by the streetlight as she dug through the trash. Her corduroy pants were rolled up almost to the crooked hem of her orange flowered dress. She ripped into a discarded Tim Horton's box and grabbed a half-eaten chocolate dip

donut with both hands, helping herself to garbage like
Charlotte helps herself to salmon pate and caviar crackers
from silver platters at the fancy receptions she attends.

The woman cackled as she unearthed a half-full bottle
of Coke, and brandished it high. Charlotte shivered. The
bag lady stuffed the precious discards into her khaki bag,
pulled her black tam low over her clotted hair and slipped
into the alley that ran the length of Charlotte's building.

Jesus, Charlotte whispered, seeing a smoky shadow of
herself follow the bag lady into the gaping black void. I'm
only half a step away. When she looked down again, she saw
the letter from Merle.

The Coleman Community Club is having a meeting and
potluck in the town hall. The low buzz of desultory conversation ceases entirely when Merle and Charlotte walk in.
The whole community knows that Merle has hooked up with
some fancy city woman, stashed her out on his ranch. Got
a kid with her, too. But until now, they've had to get their
information second-hand from Lorne at the Lucky Dollar
Store. He insists that Merle has married the woman, but
no one knows for sure.

Esther drops the lid of a roaster and it bongs across the
floor. face flaming, she chases it down. She returns to help
Trudy arrange the salads and casseroles on a trestle table
at the back of the hall.

"Should we put the buns first or last?" Trudy asks, bags
of store-bought buns dangling from her sun-damaged
hands.

"Last," Esther replies. "The line will move faster that
way."

Trudy arranges the buns and a tub of Co-op margarine at the end of the table. Esther takes paper plates from a bag, and opens packages of plastic forks and knives.

"Thank God they sprang for paper plates and plastic," she says. "Too damn hot to wash dishes tonight. Who ever thought having a potluck in mid-July would work? Even the promise of food won't get many people out to a meeting in this dreadful heat."

"Don't know," Trudy says, tugging at the damp tails of her shirt, which has come un-tucked.

Merle is standing beside Charlotte at the back of the hall, his head bent to hers. His hand rests on the small of Charlotte's back, and he holds it there until she shakes her head and smiles.

When Merle finally turns and walks over to their table, cradling a crockery pot of beans in his large, rough hands, Esther feels a sudden flush and fans herself with a paper plate she's folded in half.

Trudy notes the gold band on his ring finger, left hand, and her eyes grow wide.

"Here," he says, depositing his crock next to a pan of cabbage rolls. "Made them myself. Sort of. Added some ketchup and a few spices to my Libby's store bought beans. Onions and bacon, too."

Trudy lifts the lid, sniffs the steaming beans. She fills a teaspoon, takes a taste. "Mmm,' she says. "Good. Do you share your recipes? Russell's not real struck on my home-made beans."

"Sure do," Merle says, "a pinch of this and a smidgen of that. Easy on the salt." He winks, but Trudy is looking over his shoulder. He turns to see Charlotte standing behind him, Danica in her arms.

"Come to old Merle," he says and carries Danica over to the group of weathered men standing near the bar.

"I'd like to introduce a charming, little lady," he says. "Danica's her name. Sunshine to me." The men murmur their hellos, but their eyes never leave Charlotte's pretty, young face. Merle sets Danica down, gets himself a drink, and she toddles to her mother's side.

The president calls the meeting to order and Merle finds a seat next to Charlotte, takes Danica in his arms. When Trudy's husband, Russell, on the other side of Merle, tells Danica she's got a real pretty name, she shyly tucks her head under Merle's stubbled chin.

A string-bean young man who's sitting close by tries a little peek-a-boo, but Danica ignores him. Charlotte catches his eye, and returns his friendly gaze.

"Name's Kyle," he says. "Your neighbour for the summer."

Charlotte hears bluebottle flies as they hit the windows, bashing their bodies on the panes. The buzz is like a narcotic and she drifts into a world of her own, until Danica starts to whine.

"Okay, Sunshine," Charlotte whispers, pulling her T-shirt out of her waistband. Danica dives from Merle's arms to Charlotte's lap. When Charlotte bares her bosom, Danica snuggles closer, contentedly sucking her mother's firm, round breast.

Russell leans across Merle, his incredulous eyes darting across Charlotte's breast like a hummingbird seeking the centre of a dew-kissed daisy. He blinks, three quick blinks, then settles his gaze on Charlotte's blue-veined breast. She can feel his lingering eyes and Charlotte stifles a grin. Trudy glares daggers. When Russell finally looks up, he flushes scarlet from the roots of his hair when he sees Trudy's face. She draws the edge of her hand across her throat and he drops his eyes.

When the meeting is finally over, supper is devoured by the restive crowd. Trudy and Esther are cleaning up, bagging the soiled paper plates and covering the leftovers with foil so folks can take theirs home.

"Imagine," Trudy whispers to Esther. "Breast-feeding right out in the open like that." She shoves the leftover buns into the freezer, forgetting to twist tie the bag and slams the lid so hard it bounces. She glances across the hall to where Kyle sits, talking with Charlotte. Her brows pull together, form a solid black line, like thunder clouds before a storm.

Esther is scraping burned beans from the bottom of Merle's crock. She glances at Charlotte and Danica. "I'm sure that kid must be two, at least."

Merle's ranch is in the river hills, at the end of a winding, washboard road. No one has been to visit Charlotte since she'd moved in with Merle six months ago. She'd thought after the potluck at the hall, when she'd met Trudy and Esther and a few others, someone might drop in for coffee, but after weeks of hopeful waiting, she'd finally given up.

When she hears the purr of an approaching vehicle, she rushes around the kitchen, straightening the mess of papers, crashing crusted dinner dishes into the sink. Truck Puppy and Twyla don't even bark, so Charlotte knows whoever's coming has been here before.

Gravel crunches and Trudy appears on the tilting porch, nose pressed to the tattered screen door. "Anybody home?" she hollers and Charlotte hurries to open the door.

"Hi," she says, the door held wide like welcoming arms. "Come right in." She leads the way through the littered porch, apologizing for the mess.

"Don't worry," Trudy says, her eyes raking the kitchen, catching its air of neglect. "Got the coffee on?"

Charlotte prefers Peachline herbal tea, but she boils the coffee, making sure it's thick, black molasses, like Merle has taught her.

"Good stuff," Trudy says, blowing on her mug, steam rising in curls to bead on the fine, dark fuzz above her lip. She looks around, notices sunflower wallpaper on the west wall and cream lace curtains framing the view of the sagebrush hills.

"Making some changes, I see," she says, stirring more sugar into her cup.

"A few," Charlotte replies.

"I thought you'd have old Merle building on by now," Trudy says, "pretty tiny house. Fine for a bachelor, but things have changed."

"Merle's not into change," Charlotte replies. "He nearly had a heart attack when I moved the couch from one side of the living room to the other. Said Truck Puppy and Twyla liked it the way it was. He moved it right back."

Trudy snorts. "Heart attack's not too likely for Merle," she says. "Man's as strong as an ox."

"So I've found," Charlotte says, reaching for the coffee pot. She refills Trudy's mug.

"Is Danica napping?" Trudy asks. Charlotte shakes her head, explains that Danica is out riding with Merle.

"She just loves being tucked up on that saddle," Charlotte says. "Half the time, she's sound asleep. Must have been riding dream horses before she was born, she took to it so quick."

She shows Trudy a picture she'd taken of Merle and Danica on his biggest roan. Danica's eyes are almost closed, her sagging body supported by Merle's denim arm.

"I'll be damned," Trudy says, studying the photo. "Look at his shit-eating grin."

Merle has been hauling rocks to the corner of the yard for three days straight. The sun is hot. Dust swirls around Charlotte's ankles as she walks across the barren yard. Scrub brush struggles on the hills and a hawk soars high in the azure sky. She has come to hate the desolate landscape, and she rarely goes outside.

"What are you doing?" she asks Merle, when she gets close enough to see that he's carefully arranging the rocks by colour, a row of red, a row of cream, and a row of grey, repeated with each layer he adds.

"Making a cairn," he replies. "Marking the goddamn spot."

He gestures toward his truck. "Got the mail on Tuesday. Registered letter. Feds are going to build a dam. They regret to inform me that one of the places flooded by the dam will be the Flying Kay Ranch. Offered me a damn fine compensation package. Ain't that sweet?"

Charlotte isn't sure what to say. Merle's jaw is set, the tendons of his neck taut in the harsh light.

"Why?" she asks.

"Going to control the water to the east of here all the way from the Rockies," Merle says. "Water conservation, for the future, they say. Trying to improve on God's own plan. Bureaucratic bastards don't have a clue."

Danica nears, lugging a yellow beach pail full of small stones she's gathered from the gravel in the yard. She offers one to Merle.

"Hep?" she asks and Merle takes the rock from her chubby hand.

"Thanks Sunshine," he says. "You're a big help to old Merle."

"Mommy hep too?"

Charlotte shakes her head, walks across the burnt orange yard and stands on the porch. She imagines the water rising, slowly erasing the dilapidated barn, lapping at the crooked porch, floating the grey clapboard house away on waves of burnished steel, the leaning porch first to take the plunge.

Charlotte stands safe on the cliffs high above, holding Danica's hand. Truck Puppy and Twyla whimper.

Black water rushes and Merle floats by, his body bloated by the blazing sun. His long, grizzled hair streams in the brackish water of the flood. His right arm catches on the cairn, and his corpse grotesquely waves. Charlotte loses her grip on Danica's hand, screams as Danica dives from the safety of the cliff. Truck Puppy and Twyla follow, and Charlotte is left behind on the edge of the cliffs, the generous government cheque clutched tightly in her hand.

That night, Charlotte is haunted by dreams. She's often imagined her husband passing away peacefully and herself inheriting the ranch. She's already sold out and moved back to the city a million times. But now she's seen, with her own wide-open eyes, Danica dive to Merle and she's suddenly afraid.

Charlotte and Merle have been married for one whole year. A miracle, Charlotte thinks. She had no idea, when she'd left the city, about the reality of living on the land. It was safe all right, just like she'd dreamed, but she hadn't dreamed days of solid boredom, hours without the sound of another adult voice.

One day, as she'd sat staring at yet another segment of *The Edge of Night*, she'd finally heard Danica's muffled sobs. Charlotte had been surprised to see that three full hours had gone by since she'd put her daughter down for a nap. A nest of paper — every page of *The Free Press*, the newest one, that Merle hadn't even read — lay shredded on the coffee table. She'd stared at the palms of her hands as if searching for a clue.

Charlotte's been dreaming again, the clink of glasses, the sounds of bragging baritone voices and rock music wafting through the smoke-filled din of Tucker's Bar and Grille music to her ears. She meets a stranger's calculating eyes, accepts extravagant compliments and kisses stolen on her ten-minute breaks. She dreams of taking a toke from Larry Tucker, dodging his wandering hands as he tries to cop a feel.

"It's been thirteen months since you sent me the cash for our bus tickets," Charlotte tells Merle as they sit at the round oak table after supper on another deadly quiet Saturday night. "And we've been married for a year. We should have a party. Make the weekend mean something for once."

"Means rounding up the yearlings to me," Merle says.

Charlotte walks behind his chair, touches his long, grey hair. "Don't be such a stick-in-the-mud," she says.

"Do what you want," Merle says. "But leave me out of it. I've got work to do."

He picks up his Stetson, wipes his mouth with the beige linen napkin she'd folded by his plate and clomps across the porch. As he strides to the edge of the yard, the horses come running, snickering softly for oats.

Charlotte mailed hand-written invitations, unearthed from the highest, back shelf in the Lucky Dollar Store. The vase of irises on a lace-covered table didn't seem right, so she'd gone with a soaring hawk in a cloudless sky. *Please come,* she'd written at the bottom of the party invitations. *We're anxious to see our neighbours and friends.*

She'd cleaned and polished for an entire week.

The morning of the party, she'd spiced a thirty pound roast of beef, double wrapped it in foil and cooked it for twelve hours on low heat. The neighbour women had all phoned, offering to bring a salad or beans or desert. Their generosity had touched Charlotte and she'd thanked them over and over, until there was silence on the other end of the line.

She'd even talked Merle into lending a hand.

"Do you think we should set up one table or two?' she asked him as they hauled broken branches close to the bonfire site in the middle of the yard.

"Makes no difference to me," he said, "let's just do it. I've still got work to do."

A half hour later, she gazed with satisfaction at the wooden benches arranged in a circle near the carefully laid kindling, and the two trestle tables, one for food and one for the bar. White plastic tablecloths, anchored by large, flat stones, flutter like half-hearted surrender flags.

Trudy and Russell were the first to arrive. Charlotte was happy to see that Kyle was with them too.

Somehow, he'd picked up on her need to purchase weed and she'd often run into him on the street in town. No one has ever questioned how often she and Kyle stopped and chatted. It's easy to make the exchange. She hoped he'd brought a bag along tonight. She'd been smoking a lot and was running dangerously low.

Trudy was carrying two rhubarb pies, their crusts beaten copper, shining like new pennies in the slanted evening sun. Charlotte walked over, took one of the pies.

"Wow," she said, sliding it onto a clear spot on the trestle table. "This looks too beautiful to eat."

"Just plain fare," Trudy said. "But it should be good. Old family recipe."

When Charlotte unwrapped the roast, she didn't even have to call Merle to come and cut the beef. It was so tender it fell apart on the platter, red juice running from the plastic tablecloth to the ground, where Truck Puppy and Twyla waited, tongues hanging, pink and wet.

The supper was superb and over too soon. Charlotte and Trudy were clearing the table when Kyle sauntered over.

"Mom," he said, touching Trudy's shoulder. "Why don't you sit a while? I'll help Charlotte carry the rest of this stuff inside."

Trudy beamed, sat down on the nearest green bench, the pride in her mother eyes bathing her son.

Kyle and Charlotte carried casseroles and empty platters across the yard, the hum of low conversation and the first chords from Kurt's acoustic guitar drifting behind them in the soft evening air. The eager singers searched for a common key, started over twice and then the sweet notes of "Sing Me Back Home" followed them up the rickety steps of the tilted porch.

When Charlotte and Kyle returned, night had dropped down from the purple hills and Charlotte had a reefer tucked inside the pocket of her vest.

People were pouring drinks and popping beers, drifting around the circle of orange campfire light, telling jokes, laughing, repeating old lies.

Merle was tending the campfire, throwing on more logs even though the flames already rose high into the blackness of the sky. When he'd fed the fire to his satisfaction, he sat by Danica on a silver driftwood log.

"Hep?" she said, offering him a stick. He took it from her chubby hand and threw it on the fire.

"Horsey?" she asked and Merle hoisted Danica up on his slim shoulders. She wrapped her arms around Merle's neck, resting her blonde head against his wiry, greying hair. He snorted, galloped across the yard and Danica's delighted laughter erupted like a crystal geyser: clear and pure.

The singing seemed louder now, and the singers were repeating some of the songs. Charlotte was leaning against the corral, hungrily gulping the clean night air. Her head was swirling, pinwheels of light arching and exploding behind her eyes. Too much Jack Daniels. Not enough mix. And she'd never been good at mixing booze with pot. Trudy walked over, a Labatts Light in her hand.

"You okay?" she asked.

"Not really," Charlotte mumbled. She nodded at Merle and Danica bathed by the yellow of the fire. "Look," she said, "peas in a pod."

"Yeah," Trudy said, "sweet to see."

Merle, dressed in soft beaded buckskins, saw Charlotte watching and waved. Then he took Danica's small hand, and waved it too.

Truck Puppy and Twyla sat by the fire, eyes on the ridge. A coyote howled and the dogs replied, their barks bouncing like lasers from the valley walls.

Charlotte lifted her hand to wave, but the movement threw her off balance and she wretched, a choked, rasping sound.

"Jesus, look at him," she moaned. "I thought he was rich. Thought he was old."

Trudy wheeled, stared at Charlotte from the shadows of the corral. "You came out here hoping to end up a rich widow?" she asked, her voice rising like the flames from Merle's well-fed fire. "Merle might be old," she said, "but he's healthier than either you or me. Indestructible."

Trudy took a pull on her beer, spit something onto the ground.

Charlotte heard a liquid splat, close to her feet. "Kiddin'," she mumbled, suddenly aware of the damage she'd done.

"Let's hope so," Trudy said, "let's goddamn hope."

Merle is consumed by the threat of the impending dam. He spends his days writing letters, calling his MLA, anyone else in government who'll listen to him rant. One night, he brings Charlotte a letter, the envelope covered with pictures of a flooded valley, bloated corpses of cattle and dogs floating across the flap. Charlotte turns white as she gazes at a scene straight from her dreams.

"Read it," Merle says. "Tell me what you think."

She studies the writing, struggles to decipher his words but all she can see is rotting carcasses floating in the flood, and at the edge of the envelope, the secret shadow of Merle's mottled face.

"Sounds okay to me," she says, dropping the letter into Merle's outstretched hand. "But will anything change?"

"Not likely," Merle says, sadness tugging creases at the corner of his eyes. "But I can't just sit back and let 'er go."

Charlotte clicks off the kitchen light and walks out to the porch. Merle follows. "Can't you see?" he says, spreading his arms wide, encompassing the yard and the hills beyond. "This will all be Danica's some day. She won't thank me if the horses have all swum away and the goddamn corrals are under twenty feet of water."

Charlotte shivers. The desolate landscape looks like the far side of the moon.

"Danica's?" she says.

Merle is on the porch, mending his bridle. Danica sits on the top step, beating a dirge on the saddle soap can with a willow twig.

"I'm ready for the Murphy's," he says and Danica hands him the can.

"Thanks Sunshine," he says. Merle soaps the leather slowly with a soft flannel rag and rubs it again and again.

Danica watches, leaning on his leg. When he's done, he takes her hand, runs it over the reins. "Good as new," he says. "Always fix problems as soon as they start. Amazing. Can't even feel those hairline cracks."

Danica's curious fingers are stroking the leather.

"Softer than finest silk," Merle says. "Beautiful too. Just like you."

Charlotte tokes up when Merle is out riding pasture. Her stash is hidden in the shoebox with her letters from Merle. She'd expected Merle to be against pot-smoking, considering his age, but she didn't expect him to be so stubborn. He remained dead set against drugs, even harmless ones, like pot. She wasn't to have it anywhere on his spread and he wasn't about to change his mind. Not even for her.

Anyway, Charlotte prefers to dope alone. She inhales dreams of the city — of smoky lights and dancing and noise — hazy nights that are just beginning when the sun sinks low.

"Let's pretend," she says to Danica. "You're a brave explorer. See the fence at the edge of the yard? That's the edge of the world. You can go anywhere, look at anything. Just don't step past the edge of the world. Go on, go ahead."

Danica loves the game. She spends hours examining smooth, shiny stones, a hawk's feather, mushrooms growing behind a crumbling log. She pockets the prettiest rocks, saves her treasures to show Merle.

When she's done exploring, she returns to the porch, to oatmeal cookies and a glass of her favourite cherry Kool-Aid that Charlotte has placed on the floor beside Danica's chair. She's learned to wait in the rocker until her mother finally comes. Truck Puppy and Twyla sit by her side.

Danica has worn herself out exploring the yard. She falls asleep in her highchair and Charlotte carries her to bed without washing her mashed potato face.

The kitchen taps gleam in the fading light, reflecting the brief flare of Charlotte's match. She inhales deeply, the roach in her hand a doorway to another world. Headlights top the rise. She finishes the butt and drops it in the sink, fumbles with the taps, mesmerized by the swishing sound.

"Water's precious around here," Merle says, reaching from behind her and turning off the taps. Charlotte can't stop giggling, wipes her streaming eyes with the back of her hand.

"I'll drink to that," she says, and tries to hold a glass under the suddenly silenced tap. She giggles again. The glass slips into the sink, shards exploding across the butcher block counter and onto the floor. Merle gets the broom and dustpan and cleans up the mess.

"Jesus, Charlotte," he says. "You promised you were going to quit smoking that shit."

"Just took a couple tokes," she says. "Anyway, Danica's asleep."

"As if that has ever made any difference to you," Merle says, shaking his head.

Charlotte is sure she hears a piper, the plaintive notes rising above the lavender hills, echoing across a field of pale blue and sunshine alfalfa in full, fragrant bloom. She scans the horizon, but sees only transparent tatters of the gauze-strip clouds.

A white half-ton tops the rise, and Charlotte flips her thumb. Danica stands beside her, clutching her Pooh bear. "Merle comin'?" she asks.

"No, Honey," Charlotte says, reaching down and scooping Danica into her arms. "Merle can't come. Not today."

She knew she'd have no trouble hitching a ride. Danica is sure-fire insurance, better than a paid-up ticket on a Greyhound bus. She'd made Truck Puppy and Twyla lie in the ditch. She smiles at the young man as he opens the door.

"Hop in," he says. "Going far?"

"Just into Coleman," Charlotte replies. At the sound of her voice, Truck Puppy and Twyla tumble from the deep grass, trailing clouds of black mosquitoes. They're both busy sniffing the tires of the truck.

"Do you mind about the dogs?" she says.

"Tell them to hop in," the man says, getting out and dropping the end gate of his truck. "Damn nice dogs."

He shifts smoothly as he drives, and Charlotte can't help noticing the muscles rippling along his arms and shoulders, his skin a smooth gold sheen.

"What brings you way out here?" she asks.

"Surveying," he says. "For the new dam."

Charlotte turns, looks him in the eye. "Be careful," she says. "There's some opposition around here. Serious, I mean."

He laughs, his teeth winter white, full lips moist and red. "I won't be here long enough to let it bother me," he says. "Anyway, I'm a lover, not a fighter. Always have been."

When he drops them off in front of the Lucky Dollar, he jerks his head, indicating the dilapidated brick hotel across the street.

"Be in the bar for a while," he says. "Buy you a beer?"

Charlotte shakes her head, looks at Danica beside her, Winnie the Pooh skimming the dust.

"Thanks," she says, "but not today."

She helps Danica climb the crumbling steps of the Lucky Dollar Store. When she opens the door, an icy blast of air conditioning raises goose bumps all along her arms.

"Come on," she says, "let's hurry. Lorne will give us hell if we heat up his store."

Inside, it's a twilight zone. The oiled plank floor gleams, gives off a pleasant, old-oak smell. The shades are lowered on the plate-glass windows and Charlotte notices a triangular tear at the bottom of one of the shades. Fingers of light probe the corner, wriggle their way inside.

"Need any help?" Lorne asks.

"We'll be just fine," Charlotte says. She takes Danica's hand and they walk down the centre aisle. In a jumbled bin at the back of the store, she finds a pair of yellow thongs and slips them onto Danica's feet. Her runners have been pinching her toes lately; she's been growing like a weed.

Charlotte takes Danica to the front, seats her on a ladder-back chair near the window. She shows her the tiny tear in the shade. "Look," she said. "You can peek outside. Keep an eye on Truck Puppy and Twyla."

Danica puts her eye to the hole. "Okay," she says. "Nice puppies sit."

Charlotte finds a lined scribbler, red, Danica's favourite colour and a six-pack of Crayola.

"Two forty-five, shoes included," Lorne says.

She digs in the back pocket of her blue jean shorts, finds a crumpled dollar, five quarters and two dimes. Lorne drops the change into the open drawer of the cash register. The clink of coins is staccato, like the shooting of a starter gun.

Charlotte walks over and squats beside Danica's chair, takes a black crayon from the box. On the front page of the coil-backed book, she prints in bold letters *Mommy loves Danica*.

"Here," she says, lifting Winnie the Pooh from Danica's arms, leaning his battered body against the leg of the chair. "Your turn. Can you draw Mommy a picture of Truck Puppy and Twyla?"

"Merle too?" Danica asks, little worry creases lining her brow, and Charlotte nods her head. She kisses Danica's soft curls and walks over to the aisle where Lorne is building an Eiffel tower of Aylmer's canned tomatoes.

"I have to run," she says, twisting a piece of hair around her forefinger, her eyes far away. "Merle's picking her up. Will you give him a call if he doesn't show? He's kind of distracted these days."

Lorne nods, not really listening because he's almost at the top of the highest tower he's ever managed to build. He adds two more cans and the tower holds strong. "Sure," he says, rolling the final can in the palm of his left hand.

Charlotte walks back to Danica's chair. "Let's pretend," she says. "The edge of your chair is the edge of the world. If you stay right here, you'll be safe as can be. And soon, a handsome prince will come along."

"On a horse?" Danica asks.

"Maybe," Charlotte says, her hand grazing Danica's cheek. She turns to the door and steps into the heat-filled haze of the dusty street.

Truck Puppy and Twyla stand, sniffing the air, their back ends flagging a frenzy of joy.

"Sit boys," Charlotte says, her eyes drawn to the highway, the traffic heading east. "You stay here."

The Blue at the Base of Her Throat

"Carrie's been crying again," my supervisor, Marlene, tells me during morning report. "And she's asking for you, as usual."

Carrie never calls for her husband, Mac, or her sister, or even Jimmy, her wonderful son. Mostly, she asks for me. For some unknown reason, I've become Carrie's favourite. The feeling is mutual, so as soon as report is over, I hurry to her room, four doors down on the left-hand side.

"She's coming again today," Carrie says, grabbing my hand. "Last time she came she was wearing my coat, as if I was already dead. Didn't even ask, just helped herself. All our lives it's been like that with Darrah and me. Darrah. It means 'in cahoots with the devil' you know."

Carrie tugs at her sheets and twists the corners into tight little knots. I pull up a chair and sit by the head of her bed. Morning sun glints on my brand-new LPN pin and I caress it as I halfway listen to another of her long-winded tales.

I'm licensed now, and I've always been practical, but I still look around when someone calls "nurse."

Carrie stops her frantic twisting. Sometimes, it calms her if you just sit by her bed for a minute or two. "I remember Mother crying the day Darrah was born and she saw the red hair." She stops for a quick gulp of air. "'Oh no,' Mother kept repeating, 'oh no, oh no, oh no. The touch of the devil's hand.'"

"'Come now, Mother,'" I remember saying. 'Look at her. She's beautiful.'" I was already seven and I'd been longing for a wee sister for years. I didn't see how it could be so bad. But Mother was right . . . Darrah's been touched by the devil. She damn well has."

I straighten the edge of Carrie's sheet. "Now, Carrie," I reply, "that's an unlikely story." I've gotten pretty good at spotting unlikely stories. Three months ago, my husband, Alvin, started buying new clothes. If I happen to be home when he comes in laden with bags from Mr. Big and Tall, he tells me a long story about why he needs two new pairs of chinos, how the blue of his new golf shirt matches his eyes. I wonder who told him that?

Alvin has never bothered about his wardrobe before. Buying his clothes has always been entirely up to me. Now he's even explained why he doesn't like plain white boxers anymore. He's trying those new hipster-style undershorts, the ones with a bit of spandex. They fit more snugly to his butt. He offers too many details. It sounds like he's already prepared an elaborate defense, and I haven't even asked the questions yet. So far, I don't have the nerve.

I fold the blue cotton blanket and place it at the foot of Carrie's bed, give her pillows a final fluff before I head for the door, checking my watch and mentally tallying the time

I have left to finish my tasks before the breakfast trays arrive.

"Elizabeth," Carrie demands, "you stay right here in this room. Don't you leave me alone with Darrah. I'm sick of her treating me like I was a bird with a broken wing. She fusses too much. If she starts up again today, I'm going to ram her with my chair. I can, you know."

"Okay, Carrie," I reply. "I'll stay, but not for long. Here, let's get you prettied up before Darrah comes. That sister of yours is always telling me to take special care of you? Bet you didn't know that."

Carrie snorts. The mere mention of Darrah telling someone what to do is obviously ridiculous to her.

"Let's massage your scalp a bit," I say, pulling a chair toward her. "Doesn't that feel good?"

Carrie sits absolutely still while I gently work my fingers through her soft, silver hair. It's amazingly thick. "Ah," she says. "I love it when you come on shift. That lazy Judy won't do a thing, you know. You have to ring at least three times before she even bothers to check. She thinks we should all be sleeping just because it's the middle of the night."

She catches my eye in the mirror, glaring at me, as if I have something to do with Judy's behavior.

"Just wait," she says, black eyes snapping. "She'll be old someday, too.

I'd like to be around to see it. Her flat in bed having to piss like a racehorse, waiting for some lazy nurse who doesn't want to leave the station. I hope she has to lie in it."

"Come now, Carrie," I say. "You don't really mean that."

"Bloody rights, I do," she replies. "Bloody well rights."

Massaging slowly, I work my way from nape to crown. She begins to relax, her head becoming surprisingly heavy. I close my eyes, concentrating on my job.

Ten years ago, when I started at Biscayne Lodge as kitchen staff, I dreamed of becoming a nurse. Sometimes, when I was delivering meal trays and found someone in distress, I'd do what I could to help — straighten their bed, help them to the bathroom — anything to relieve their discomfort. One day, when the head nurse was handing out the meds, she saw me helping a frail old fellow to the bathroom.

"Kitchen help is not allowed to assist the patients," she'd said. "Tend to your dinner trays. I'll handle this." That was the day I finally decided to go to school. Alvin was supportive — I'd talked nursing school for years — but he seemed more interested in the wages I'd be earning once I got my degree than the fact I might finally achieve my dream. It felt like I was leaving him forever the day I left for school. I was so damn blue and lonesome I almost didn't stay, but Alvin seemed happy with the bachelor life.

I sigh, wish I could crawl right into bed with Carrie, have someone take special care of me, like my husband used to. Carrie's eyelids droop. I reach across and ease a pillow from the bed, wedging it into the chair so her head is supported.

Poor thing gets herself worked up so easily, I think, although what she says about Judy is probably true. Sometimes I think the older nurses like myself — even though I'm new at this — feel their patient's pain. Some of the younger ones don't seem to care.

I tuck the blanket around Carrie and dim the lights as I leave. Maybe she'll sleep.

It's easy to lose track of time, especially at work. When I check my watch, an hour has passed. But when I'm waiting for Alvin to come home, the hands on my watch seem leaden, loathe to move. Sometimes, I wonder if it has two different rhythms.

I've been busy bringing instant relief, counted carefully into little white paper cups, to the patients on my floor. When I've finished the meds, I grab Carrie's breakfast tray from the cart in the hall and take it to her room. Just like old times. When I open her door, I find her sitting upright in her chair, eyes darting quickly like a bird about to land on the edge of a feeder. "When's Jimmy coming?" she demands. "That bastard hasn't shown up for weeks."

No one knows why she's taken to calling her son a bastard. She won't quit either, even when he gently explains that he's not a bastard, never has been, in fact. Somehow, the fifty years of her marriage have become a haze to Carrie now.

"Okay Carrie, calm yourself," I say, wincing as I bang the tin teapot against the metal of her adjustable bed table. Tepid water sloshes onto my wrist and I dry it with the edge of a cotton throw folded on Carrie's bed. "That boy of yours was here yesterday. He took you out on the terrace for tea. And he stayed, even though you told him to leave at least a dozen times. And don't be calling him a bastard anymore, either."

Carrie's son is a burly fellow, probably weighs over two hundred pounds, and stands at least six feet tall. He's about forty, but faithfully makes time for his mother. He comes to visit every Sunday, wheeling her up and down the halls when the weather's poor, and taking her to the terrace when the sun's high enough to generate some real warmth. He always checks at the desk to see if there's anything she needs, if there's anything he can do for her, other than just show up.

Sometimes, when Carrie gets unruly and we can't get her to settle, we call that lovely boy of hers. He's told us to call him at anytime. His presence is a drug to Carrie and as he sits there, patting her hand, Carrie calms down slowly, as if he's peeling away her anxiety layer by layer, until she can breath more easily and drift.

"It's okay, Momma" he croons, "I'm here, Momma, don't worry, it's okay." To see a big man like that, sitting there stroking his mother's hand over and over again, is almost more than I can bear some days. It's been a very long time since Alvin has touched me, even stroked my hand, and when I'm old like Carrie, there will be no devoted, gentle son.

"Are you sure?" Carrie asks. "Are you sure that bastard was here?"

I nod and she settles back into her chair, lifting the metal lids on her breakfast tray and sniffing each dish in turn.

"You can take this crap back where it came from," she says, dismissing her meal with a wave of her hand. "Fed better swill to my pigs, I bloody well did."

I add a little brown sugar and some creamer to her porridge. "Now, that's not so bad, is it?' I say as I offer her a bite. She takes it. Three bites later, she pushes the tray away, and me as well.

"Bugger off," she says. "You're no friend of mine, feeding me that bloody swill.

What I need is some whiskey." She's fishing in the pocket of her robe with her one good hand. "Here," she says, "I've got cash. Get me some Jack Daniels. Right bloody now."

I take the limp piece of Kleenex she pushes into my hand. "Okay, Carrie, okay, but I might be a while. Try a little more of your breakfast, why don't you?"

It's another day in paradise where you can buy Jack Daniels whiskey with one wet Kleenex. It makes perfect sense to Carrie. Sometimes, I envy her.

I tend to my other patients, but Carrie stays on my mind. Her family is appalled by her new penchant for swearing and demanding alcohol. Apparently, before her stroke, she was the soul of decorum. That's how her sister Darrah describes her. The soul of decorum. Her husband's said it, too.

Carrie's husband Mac is a robust man, even at his age. His hair is thick iron grey and the bulk of his shoulders strain against the confinement of the tweed sports jacket he always wears when he visits. He stands by Carrie's bed, murmuring as he touches her face. She usually pretends she's asleep until finally he gets tired of standing there and sits on the vinyl armchair across the room.

Oh Carrie, I think, there are so few truly good men. If only you knew. It still hurts my heart to think how quickly Alvin's nightly calls tapered off once I'd gone away. It was more expensive for me to phone home from residence and when I did try, the phone rang and rang in my empty living room.

When Carrie does acknowledge Mac's hovering presence, she's less than cordial. "Why are you standing there looking at me with that hangdog look? Go on home. Don't you have work to do?"

"He's not to be trusted," she tells me. "Made me wait on him all my life, just ask Jimmy. Ask Darrah, too, although don't put too much store in what she says. No doubt she's in cahoots with him by now. Maybe always was for all I know."

Ah, the other woman. I could tell Carrie a tale or two. If I'm right about Alvin, his girlfriend will be a blonde. She'll have a smoke-raspy voice and she'll drink Labatt's Blue. Someone petite and lively, like Alice, who moved in three doors down about a year ago. A woman who laughs at all of his jokes, even when he tells them twice. Someone not like me.

Whoever she is, she isn't too smart. She keeps calling our house and when I answer, she hangs up.

"Elizabeth," Carrie says, "do you remember that time after we'd been to a dance? Mac and me? Sound asleep in our bed, I was, and he ups and kicks me out. Landed flat on my arse on the floor. We didn't have rugs back then, just lino. Bruised my tailbone, I did, couldn't sit for a week. He never apologized either."

Carrie is glaring at me. When I don't offer condolences, she continues. "'What was that for?'" I asked Mac. I was blinking and blinking but I could still see the look in his eyes. He wasn't even sorry, not one bloody bit."

"'When you're dancing,' Mac says, 'you don't have to twirl so fast. Your dress flares out and every man in the goddamn place is ogling your legs.'"

I can't picture Carrie in a bouffant dress, twirling quickly across the floor. All I can see is Carrie wrapped in her favourite housecoat, cobalt blue.

"The son-of-a-bitch," she continues. "The dirty son-of-a-bitch. I should have left him right then, except where would I go? It's not as if I had any choices, not like you do, Elizabeth. I bet you don't put up with much from your

Alvin, now do you? You can just tell him to go to hell if you want. Not like me."

Carrie thinks I'm bold and brave. I told her how old I was when I finally went to nursing school. Sometimes, it seems Carrie's the only friend I've got. I haven't even whispered a word to anyone about our phantom caller, or the faint hint of Calvin Klein on my husband the nights he does come home.

When I'm home alone, I study the mirror, check the fit of my jeans. They're snug across my slim hips. My hair is dyed a pleasing combination of auburn and golden brown. I'm starting to get laugh lines around my eyes and I have a few creases down the sides of my face, but overall, I look pretty good. Still, something must be missing and I don't know what it could be.

"And the worst," Carrie says, "the very worst, is that I cooked him breakfast the next morning. Bacon fried crispy and two eggs, sunny side up. Served it to him on a chipped white plate. Like nothing had happened."

I shudder when she's like this, telling me awful stories. I've seen Mac standing beside her bed, coaxing her to eat, pleading with her to cooperate. "Bugger off," she'll say. "Really, I'm doing fine. Just leave me alone."

One day, she sends him away ten minutes after he arrives. She insists that he leave. When he's gone, she turns to me. "Don't let him fool you," she says. "He's not to be trusted, you know. Did I tell you about the time he brought the crabs home? Said he'd gotten them from working with cattle. Have you ever heard of cows getting crabs?"

There's really not much that surprises me since Alvin started to stray. God knows, I never dreamt he'd ever want anyone but me. "I've heard a lot of things," I say. "But I haven't heard of that." Absently, I finger the smoothness of my LPN pin.

"Oh, that awful soap. I had to wash everything twice. Hang it on the line in the dead of winter, too. It was a hell of a job, I don't mind telling you. My hands were raw from the scrubbing. Ha! I better tell Darrah about that." She's stroking her hand, as if she still feels the sting of the soap.

Down the hall, someone must have dropped a meal tray. I hear a crash and then the clink, clink of cutlery being gathered from the floor. The stench of cooked cabbage hangs in the air.

I *tsk, tsk* for Carrie but, really, I'm thinking of myself. If Mac brought the crabs home to Carrie, I am frightened to think of what Alvin may have brought home to me.

Carrie knits her knobby fingers across her sunken chest. "Darrah's moved into my house, you know. She should have gone back to Victoria weeks ago. She says she'll stay as long as I need her. Me! Only one she's helping is herself. But I don't care," she says, her good hand rubbing her arm as if to warm herself. "I just don't."

Later, when we go down to therapy, she sags onto the mats like a boneless doll. She offers no assistance as we move her arms and her legs, patterning again and again, trying to rouse her sleeping reflexes. The only part of her that seems almost recovered is her mouth, although her family says her stories are total fiction, that she's carrying on about things that never happened.

They want the old Carrie back.

I think we're seeing the *true* Carrie. I bet she's saying what's been on her mind all these years.

I roll Carrie's wheelchair down the hall to therapy — again — and she waves grandly to the nurses. Peter's the only therapist on shift and it looks like he's been busy, the chart's long list of patients stroked through with black marker. Carrie's the last today. As we crouch on the edge of the mats, manipulating her limbs with gentle determination, she glares at us.

"Haven't you done enough to this broken old body?" she demands, small droplets of spittle wetting the drooping left corner of her mouth.

"Come on Carrie, you lazy thing," I say. "You're not getting the whirlpool yet. Not till you help us a bit."

She's figured out that we only have so much time, and she waits us out. Finally, getting no response from her withered limbs, Peter and I load Carrie into the sling and lower her into the bubbling tank.

"Ah," she says, a blissful smile on her face, her body weightless. "That's better. That's a whole lot better." Floating, she flashes me a conspirator's grin. I reach to the edge of the tub, turn on the gentle bubbles she loves. "Guess what? I can fly, you know. I used to fly all the time. But for some reason, I forgot how. Now it's coming back to me. It's easy, really."

Oh fine, I think. You can fly and I can snap my fingers, get me and Alvin back the way we were.

"Don't tell Jimmy," she says. "But one time, when he was still a boy, I flew away on Mac. I had to. Do you remember Jimmy? Such a bonny lad, bigger than all the others. And me just a bit of a thing. It's a wonder, I always thought, a real wonder. Anyway, Mac was home that day. I think he was laid off then, just till the road bans were lifted. Mac lied to me you know. Back home, he'd talked on and on about his land in Canada. I was young then, and in love, too, or so I thought. How could I know that the only land he had was the gravel stuck to his boots at the end of a day on the grader?"

She sniffs, wipes her nose with the back of her hand. "And he never told me he didn't do a lick of work all winter long. But never mind about that, it's another story entirely."

Carrie's comment about winter starts me thinking. I wonder if Alvin has taken down the screens. Every year, he's done it religiously, the first of September, but this year, he doesn't seem to care. The leaves on the trees in our yard are already dry and brittle, turning yellow on the edges. It feels like early frost.

"On that awful day," Carrie says, "Mac was standing in the yard, watching Jimmy. Jimmy never had a nasty bone in his body, you know. A right little laddie, he was."

I smother a smile. Carrie's Scottish brogue is thicker than pea soup. When she tells her stories of long ago, her accent seems to grow proportionately with the length of her tales.

"That morning, the neighbour lads were over, playing in our sandbox. They got tired of it, I guess. Took Jimmy's pails and even his wee shovel and dragged everything across to their own yard. Jimmy stood there, watched them go. Mac strides to the middle of the yard, hollering. 'Come on, you goddamn lily-liver. Get over there and hang a lickin' on those thieving brats. Right now. I mean it.' Jimmy was shaking. 'They'll bring them back, Dad' he says. 'You don't have to worry. They always bring them back.'"

I swish the water around Carrie's bony shoulders, but she doesn't seem to notice.

"From my kitchen window, I can see Jimmy wiping tears from his eyes with the sleeve of his jacket. His nose is running, too. 'Come on,' Mac says, going to the sandbox, grabbing Jimmy by the arm and pushing him towards the neighbour's yard. 'Be a man.' I wanted to rush out there, to scream at him. He'd given Jimmy a couple of good shakes and Jimmy froze, looking up at his dad."

"Oh Carrie," I say.

"Then Mac drops his arm and slams his way across the porch and into my kitchen. 'A big boy like him,' he scowled. 'A big boy like that. He should be ashamed.'

"I don't look up, scrubbing hell out of the sink and Mac stalks over, sticks his unshaven face close to mine. 'Where did that kid come from, anyway?' he bellers. 'He's nothing like me.' Thank God, I'm thinking to myself. Thank God for small mercies. I hurry to Jimmy, out in the yard."

She's quiet for a moment, winces as I lift her arm. "Sorry," I say. "Just about done here. Carry on."

She glances at Peter, to make sure he's still listening, too.

"That was the day I flew away. Took Jimmy too, although I didn't know if I could fly and carry him as well. But after Mac's awful accusations, I couldn't leave Jimmy behind. Turned out I wasn't strong enough. By the time I got to the edge of town, I knew I couldn't fly with Jimmy, so I had to turn back. Oh, God forgive me, I had to turn back," she whispers, bitter tears shining in Highland green eyes. She shudders. I touch her shoulder, so she'll remember I'm here.

"I told Darrah. I told her I had to leave and she said, "Don't be silly. You can't leave Mac. He's a good man,

Carrie, you know he is. She never said 'Yeah I think you should go, you and Jimmy will be just fine.' She never said that, no she didn't, and that's a fact."

"Shh, shh, Carrie," I say, saturating the sponge and squeezing the warm water across her scrawny back. She's so thin I can count her ribs beneath her pearly skin. "Shh, shh, don't you cry, it's going to be just fine."

It's Carrie's birthday and Darrah brings her a new housecoat. It's pink chenille with a Velcro fastener at the nipped-in waist, fashionable as far as housecoats go. Darrah and Carrie sit on her bed, heads together, whispering like two schoolgirls.

When I bring around the five o'clock meds, Darrah is gone and I find Carrie's new housecoat draped across the garbage can.

"Really Carrie," I say, picking it up, smoothing the wrinkles and giving it a shake. "What were you thinking of? I'm sure you don't really want to get rid of this. It's beautiful. And you don't want to hurt Darrah's feelings. She loves bringing you gifts. I hope you at least said thank you." I hang the housecoat in Carrie's closet.

"Close that bloody door," she says. "I hate pink and Darrah knows it. She's hoping I'll have to wear it. She thinks the staff will insist, you know." A smile of sudden inspiration lights her eyes. "Why don't you take it home with you. Please, I want you to."

I explain that we can't accept gifts from the residents. "Sorry, Carrie, I'd love to have it. But those are the rules." I think of the pink housecoat wrapped around my shoulders after my bath. Alvin used to say that I was even prettier when I was wearing pink.

Carrie's eyes go dim. "Bloody hell, then," she says. "Give it to that Mary next door. Maybe it'll shut her up for a day or two."

"Go on. Do it," she says, motioning to the closet. "I don't need any reminders of Darrah hanging around here. I've got all the reminders I need, that's for bloody sure."

I'm looking a little blank, I guess, because she pulls me in with a curved finger, closer to her bed.

"Look at this," she says, pulling up the sleeve of her gown, showing me a round, multi-colored bruise on the inside of her elbow. I lift her bird-thin arm, feel the squish of blood beneath the surface of her translucent skin. The elderly often bruise easily, like over-ripe tomatoes, but Carrie's bruise is deeper than most that I've seen.

"Darrah," she says with satisfaction. "She pinches me, you know. Every time she comes. They won't believe me when I tell them. Don't be silly, they say. Your own sister? Ha! They don't know squat about Darrah. She's in cahoots with the devil, you know."

I sigh. "You've told me that, I think. And how your mother cried the day that she was born."

"But she can't fly," Carrie says, forgetting me again. "The bitch can't fly. At least I've got her on that."

I have a four-day stretch to rest and relax, but when the phone keeps ringing and there's no one on the other end, I wish I was at work. I wash Alvin's array of fine, new shirts, but before I scrub their collars, I hold them to my face and sniff. Mostly, I can't smell a thing. I am in the laundry room, sorting and sniffing, when the phone rings again, loud and shrill. "Okay," I'm going to say. "Let's get this over with.

You tell me what my husband's really been up to all this time. Then quit your damn calling and leave me alone."

"Hello?"

It's Marlene, calling from the Biscayne Lodge. "Twyla called in sick at the last minute again. I'm sorry. I know you're on a four day break but there's no one to cover. Could you possibly come in?"

"Give me fifteen minutes," I say. "I'll see you soon." I hang up the phone, relief weakening my knees. At least at work, there's people around.

Darrah walks past the nursing station and asks me how Carrie has been. I check Carrie's chart. "Not any more co-operative than usual in physio, but at least she's not crying as often. It's a step in the right direction."

"Thank goodness," Darrah says, blinking back tears.

I notice that her hair doesn't seem so red, its deep copper's fading and the roots are showing grey.

She sniffs. "I can hardly stand to see Carrie like this. She's always talking about when we were girls, about the awful things I did. She's imagining things again, I know she is."

I leave the protection of the high front desk, lead her to a chair.

"It seems like only yesterday that Carrie married Mac and followed him to Canada," Darrah says. "It happened so fast. Somehow, the war put everything into overdrive."

I pat Darrah's smooth hand, notice her fingernails, manicured and painted a soft shade of peach.

"I remember crying the day she left. When her letters came, I studied them, read them over and over until they fell apart along the creases where I'd folded them one too many times. Her life sounded so much better than mine."

"There, there," I say. It was what my own mother said. "There, there." I realize it doesn't mean a thing. Darrah sniffs again and I hand her a tissue.

"God, it's incredible when you think of it; all those war brides leaving home with stars in their eyes. They should have counted them when they were tallying up the casualties." She puts her hand on my arm, as if she's afraid I might bolt.

"Of course, when Jimmy was born, I had to come. I wasn't married, so it wasn't like I had a life of my own, or any commitments except a lousy secretarial job. Somehow, I thought Carrie and I would become close, like sisters are supposed to be, that our lives here would be grand." She shakes her head, as if waking from a dream. "Listen to me," she says. "That was years ago. Maybe I've been coming here too often. I'm carrying on as badly as she does."

She wipes her nose and gives her head a little shake. She stands, turns toward Carrie's room. "I suppose I'd better go in. She's probably been waiting for hours."

I notice her coat seems a bit short in the sleeves. It's royal blue: Carrie's favourite colour. Oh well, I think, it's not as if Carrie has any need for a coat right now, not like she'll be going anywhere soon.

I spend my whole shift on the floor, skipping coffee break, checking into Carrie's room a little more often. I softly open the door and see Darrah, her chair pulled close to Carrie's bed. She raises her finger to her lips. "Shh, the poor dear's finally sleeping. I'm going to sit with her for a bit. Of course, I have to get home, make supper for Mac, but there's lots of time yet. She really hates it when I leave without saying goodbye."

"Okay," I whisper. "If you need anything, come down to the desk."

"We'll be just fine," Darrah replies, edging her chair a bit closer and smoothing the wrinkles in Carrie's bedding. "And don't worry, if she needs you, I'll call."

I know when I've been dismissed; I leave, but I keep checking anyway, cracking the door every time I pass Carrie's room.

When Darrah finally leaves, I tiptoe into Carrie's room. She's lying in bed, so thin her body barely makes a ripple in the blankets. Her eyes are closed and tears pool in the papery creases at their corners. From the foot of her bed, I can see her bony chest rise and fall. Closer still, the pulse in the blue hollow at the base of her throat.

She opens her eyes, as if she barely has the energy for even that small gesture. "Oh, please," Carrie whispers, "Please, just leave me alone. It's that Darrah . . . it's always Darrah. She tells me I'm too old to fly."

I approach the side of Carrie's bed, gather her fragile body in my arms. The window is open, like the door to a dream. I wisp through the window, float high above the houses and the faint green shimmer of treetops far below.

At the edge of town, I hesitate, wonder, for a moment, if I should turn back. I gaze upon Carrie's lined and lovely face, her tired body weightless at last.

The Beauty Box

Rain has been falling steadily all day. My sister Connie and I are cleaning our bedroom driven by our mother's inflexible schedule. Monday is the washing; pancakes and bacon for supper. Tuesday is the ironing, the dusting, including the picture frames and the big old claw feet on the piano; pot roast for supper. And so on each day. Saturday is cleaning day, no excuses accepted, so we get to see the floor of our room once a week, although this is no big thrill. The carpet is brilliant tangerine, sculpted into swirls and whorls, but remaining relentlessly orange despite the distraction of its design.

Dad has gone to town to visit Grandma and he's taken the little ones, so it's just my sister and me. And Mom, of course. She likes to bake on rainy days. My dad took the kids so they wouldn't bother us by wanting to help. They've been gone since ten o'clock and it's now almost three-thirty. I check the window, impatient with this dreary day. There's no sign of my father on the dirt road from the farm across 'the flat' to the highway.

The flat is a strange piece of land spreading six miles south and east from our farm. It's like someone had taken a giant iron and carefully pressed the land until no creases remained, except the ditches. When Dad left this morning he was aiming to be home before teatime. "If this rain keeps up all day," he said, "the road across the flat will be a real mess."

My dad is always obsessing about the weather. Normally, he's cursing this dustbowl country for its lack of rain.

"The barley is already shriveling in the heads. Even the pasture's burning up. We'll have to move some cows if it doesn't rain soon. Might be able to turn them out on the south quarter, but that won't last. Christ, this country will drive me to drinking yet."

It seemed strange, then, to hear him so concerned about too much rain.

My mother, of course, will write about the rain. She keeps a diary, each day's entry recording the weather, what she accomplished that day, and not much else, nothing of what she's feeling, if her day was happy or sad. She let me use her diaries for a science report: weather patterns for the last ten years. When I read how many times she and Dad have been dried out, hailed out, froze out and stripped clean by grasshoppers, I thought it was close to a miracle they hadn't packed their bags and gone looking for an easier life.

On August 2nd, 1952, her firm and flowing script started off, of course, with the weather. *We've got a bumper crop coming*, she wrote, *the best we've seen in years. It never hails after the end of July, so now, thank God, we should be safe.*

There was a *PS* at the end of that entry. But the script, spidery at first, let a tiny hint of her soul peek through. She was describing hailstones piled in drifts against the house and how the crop was flattened so badly they couldn't even salvage it for feed. She added that the children had been excited, running out as soon as the storm was over to play in the piles of hail, how they'd gathered pails full of the stuff and had begged her to make home-made ice cream. *So*, she wrote, *all wasn't lost. I've never made ice cream smack in the middle of summer before. I have to admit I'm having a bit of trouble thanking Him for providing lots of ice.*

After that one interesting entry, it was pretty well back to dry and dusty and prayers for rain.

But this year, the rains have come. Good for the crops, but not for the roads. After months of sporadic traffic and no sign of the grader, the gravel migrates to the edges of the road, leaving hardpan grooves. The grooves are smooth and straight and driving the road in summer is like highway driving, as long as it's dry. After steady rain, however, it's another matter entirely. You have to keep your speed up so you plane on top of the mud, especially in the half-mile stretch from Frasers' farm to ours. If you slow down, the clinging muck can suck you in, and suddenly your car is bogged down solid. If you drive slowly, you better be driving something big and powerful, like a tank.

I turn away from the rain, back to our room, which seems smaller now, no longer a cozy refuge. The room is square, ten by ten feet with a large closet. The closet has a rounded corner, giving the bedroom an exotic, modern twist. The closet is merely decorative in our room. For some reason — unknown even to us — we usually throw our clothes on the floor. We don't pick them up in the morning either. No time. The school bus comes at seven-twenty and getting ready takes every second we can muster.

Connie is sitting in front of the beauty box, applying a third layer of navy blue to her lashes. They're thick with mascara; I can see the clumps from across the room. I'm about to mention it when she picks up the tiny comb and begins to separate the lashes carefully. Why is she bothering? Nobody will see her today.

My father designed and built the beauty box for my mother as a Christmas gift in 1960. She's a practical woman and I can't remember her ever using it, but she loved the idea, the thought of my dad drawing the plans and labouring over such an extravagant gift. When she tells the story, her eyes get lost, as if she's looking at something far away. "Imagine," she says. "A gift like that for a down-to-earth woman like me."

The beauty box looks like a large mahogany suitcase with a handle on top. It's hollow and has a three-way mirror mounted inside. When you open it up and position the mirrors at the correct angle, you can see the back of your head and make sure that the front and the back of your hairdo blend together.

The beauty box has drawers along the sides of the big mirror and drawers underneath as well, so all your combs and pins are close at hand. A little light is recessed at the top — you can work away for hours until your make-up is perfect. Flip the toggle switch on the side and the light illuminates all your beauty. Or all your flaws.

When we became teenagers, the beauty box was moved permanently into our bedroom. It sits on the little study desk that's angled into the corner of our room, but the only thing we study these days is ourselves. We look for any hint of a blemish, curl our stick-straight lashes, line our eyes with 'Blue Midnight' or 'Purple Passion'. An endless search for perfection.

There's always plenty of traffic around the beauty box. I don't know why our younger sisters — all three of them — feel free to come in here whenever they please. They could use the mirror in the bathroom, but hardly ever do. They forget their brushes or combs, the towel they've wrapped around their head, or any other piece of schoolgirl paraphernalia. And apparently, they never miss what they leave behind because it all ends up in a pile on the end of our dresser, right next to the beauty box. When the pile gets too high, we just give it a sweep of an arm and it lands on the floor, along with everything else. Our mother only comes into our room on Saturday afternoons — to make sure our cleaning has met her standards — and we are grateful for that.

Today, the cleaning has been much more thorough than our usual Saturday blitz. We picked up the debris from the carpet and shampooed the whole room. Unfortunately, the orange color hasn't faded despite the fact that we doubled the amount of shampoo recommended.

This morning, before the carpet cleaning, we repainted two walls. These jobs have been on our mother's 'to do' list for months. The walls are now soft beige, a big improvement over the unfortunate hospital green they were.

The blind is hanging at a cockeyed angle. I quit watching Connie comb her lashes and try to adjust it so everything will be perfect, if only for an hour or two.

I check the road again. Nothing. I'm craving black licorice, my father's favourite and mine as well. He usually picks up a fresh supply in town. He cuts the licorice in halves and stores the pieces in a tall glass sealer, lid screwed tight to preserve the freshness. I love the smell when he opens the jar. Sometimes, he slips me an extra piece or two. My mouth waters as I stare into the rain, dreaming of sweets.

Finally, Connie is satisfied with her work at the beauty box and she offers me the stool. "Want your hair fixed?"

I can't believe she's offered. Connie never wants to do anything with me. She's happy to work on any of her friend's hair whenever they ask, but she can't be bothered with mine. I haven't asked for ages. My hair is poker-straight and there's not much to be done. I usually just scoop it back into a ponytail.

"Okay," I say. "Go ahead if you want."

I sit down at the beauty box and watch as she carefully backcombs my hair, sprays it with super hold, and begins to backcomb again. She starts to arrange it, pulling wisps in front of my ears and fluffing the bangs, spraying as she goes. She's finally happy with the front; she starts on the back. When it comes to doing hair, you never know what Connie will try next. I don't want any surprises, so I fiddle with the mirror, trying to watch her, but I can't make it work.

"Will you sit still?" Connie yanks on my hair. She picks up her special backcomb and starts again.

"Ouch, you're pulling too hard." I turn my head so she has to reach. Then Connie notices the front of my hair, which, despite the super hold, has become hopelessly flat.

"I give up," she says, throwing the comb into the top drawer. "There's no hope with hair like yours."

I think she's probably right, but I don't often get a chance at the beauty box so I take up the comb, arranging my heavy bangs in a fringe across my forehead. They have no body and there's nothing I can do; I don't attempt to poof them. I decide to try the back. Maybe something can be done. Maybe I can give myself a whole new look, sleek and shiny. But I can't get the mirrors set; there's some kind of trick to it that I can't figure out. After three tries, I give up.

Now Connie is at the bedroom window, holding the curtain aside, scrubbing at the steam with the embroidered edge of the lace. She's peering into the steadily falling rain.

"Somebody's coming. Down on the flat. Can you see?" I stand beside her, straining to see past the steam and the drizzle falling from the eaves.

"Yeah, I think so. But it's not Dad."

She nudges me aside, trying to get closer, leaning into the sill. "Who'd be driving across the flat today if they didn't have to?"

We watch as the car creeps up the last mile from the crossroads to the lane. The car is going too slowly for the muddy conditions, slewing right, left, and sideways. I hold my breath watching its progress, feel the slow slide towards the ditch as the tires scrabble for traction on the sparse gravel. Just as my lungs are about to burst, the car slowly rights itself and continues its crablike crawl closer and closer.

"Hansons?" Connie asks.

"I think so," I answer, Connie now partially blocking my view. "Are they nuts?" The old Lincoln turns off the main road and heads up the lane to our farm.

"Hey Mom, we've got company," I holler as we head for the kitchen, tracking the car.

Our mother often bakes two or three batches of cookies at a time and gets herself into a jumble of baking pans and mixing bowls, the utensils all strewn across the counter for everyone to see. Today she has a dusting of flour across her nose and cheek, settling in the fine hairs near her jaw. The flour has added a soft sheen, like she's just powdered her nose for a party. She's looking around her kitchen in dismay. "Today?" she asks.

"Yeah, it's Hansons," I say, looking out the picture window from the dining room. The seal on the thermal-pane has been broken for years, so the view is foggy, with clear strips where the rivulets have broken free and run to the rotting wood at the bottom of the frame.

The car is closer now and Nancy and her mom are wavering through the steam on the window and the curtain of rain.

Nancy's mom and my mom have been friends from the moment they met. Anne was a war bride and always says how my mother's warm welcome kept her from getting right back on that train and heading home first chance she got. Although she's been living in this community for twenty years, her Cockney accent is still strong. I love to sit and listen to her.

Mom stacks gingersnaps and Aunt Amy's oatmeal cookies into an ice-cream pail and then wipes the counter clean. She doesn't like to be caught in a mess, not even if she's right in the middle of one. "I'll get the kettle on," she says. "You girls whisk around and get this kitchen tidied up a bit. Hurry up, they're on their way in."

We stash piles of *The Western Producer* and *Hockey News* out of sight in the broom closet and gather up the scattered dishes and baking pans, stacking them into the battered aluminum bread pan. We cover the pan with a dishcloth. Then we shove the whole mess under the sink. Later.

The inside door is open. My mother says the plinking sound of rain is music to her ears. I can see Anne through the screen, about to knock. She's wet as a result of her dash from the car to our porch, and she seems a bit shaken as well. She just got her license last year and doesn't drive often, especially not in weather like this.

Nancy is standing right behind her, shaking droplets of rain from her black hair, which has begun to curl into soft ringlets. She's standing close to her mother, not exactly hesitant, but as if she's waiting for some kind of signal.

"Come in if you can get in," Mom is apologizing, moving rubber boots and runners from the entryway and placing them neatly on the steps leading to the basement. Six pairs later, she's finally made enough room for Nancy and Anne to step inside, out of the damp air and into the warmth of our serviceable kitchen.

The smell of cinnamon permeates the air. There's a plateful of gingersnaps on the table and cinnamon rolls are cooling on racks along the counter, dripping their sweet, syrupy overflow onto the scarred butcher-block surface of the baker's nook. Mom has covered the rolls with a blue and white checked cloth and I lift the corner, scooping out a finger full of the cinnamon filling. Quickly, so she won't see.

"Lordy, that was a hair-raising drive. If there's one thing I could use right now, it's a cuppa."

I am already on tea detail, making sure the water has come to a rolling boil and carefully measuring three heaping teaspoons of loose tea into the bone china teapot. I pour the bubbling water carefully over the tea-leaves and replace the lid before carrying the teapot to the table. The pot rattles on the tray.

Connie spoons the thick, clotted cream from the pint jar in the fridge into the cream pitcher and places neatly folded napkins and the sugar bowl onto the smooth surface of the old oak table. In this house, there is no plunking the cream jar on the table, no dipping into the sugar canister to sweeten your tea.

My sister and I, however, have taken to drinking our tea from the everyday mugs and Connie starts to take them from the kitchen cupboard.

"That's quite the rain," Mom says to Anne. "You're dripping wet. If it weren't for your slicker, you'd be soaked clean through." Anne wears a yellow slicker when it rains, which of course, isn't very often. She is probably the only person in the entire countryside who does. She's about to hang her slicker on the back of a chair when she notices Connie and the mugs.

"If you don't mind," Anne says, "I'd rather have the bone."

Anne is a true tea drinker, like our mother. They don't mind telling you that drinking tea from a mug is close to a mortal sin. So Connie closes the door on the everyday dishes and goes to the china cabinet, taking out five Silver Birch teacups and saucers.

I don't love my mother's china. It's too busy for my taste. Full of trees and sky and lakes, all frozen in an anemic silver color. When she dies, I hope she doesn't leave it to me. As Connie begins to place the cups and saucers around the table, our mother interrupts. "Don't bother setting up for you girls. Anne and I'll just have a bit of a private."

There are six chairs around our kitchen table and one more against the wall. Mom's hand hovers, unable to choose. Our mother has rescued her precious chairs from auction sales and second hand stores, stripping and refinishing, oiling until she was finally satisfied with the smoothness of the wood. She's managed to get the colour closely matched, but each has a different pattern pressed into its back. Mom has been collecting antiques for years, loving old things when no one else did.

"That one," she'd say, pointing out a chair with a fleur-de-lis design, "I got at Wilson's sale. I had to go five dollars to bring it home. I was feeling so bad that day I could hardly bring myself to bid. But at least all of their stuff wasn't carted off by strangers. It makes me feel a little bit better, seeing it here."

"And this one," pointing to another, "I found at the nuisance grounds one day, when I was tossing out my chipped canning jars. Imagine, putting such a treasure in the dump. All it needed was a little elbow grease."

Mom used to tell the chair stories to anyone who seemed vaguely interested in her mismatched set, until one day, Connie asked her not to.

"It's bad enough we don't have a chrome set," she said. "But really, do you have to talk about those chairs every chance you get?"

I kind of liked her little histories, but I didn't have the nerve to say so. I just stood there, watching the tremor at the edge of my mother's mouth, the sudden flush on her face.

"You girls are getting mighty uppity," was all she said, but she doesn't talk about the chairs and where and how she found them anymore.

Mom settles on the ladder back with the turned spindles and reaches for the teapot, all the while studying Anne. "Why don't you girls show Nancy what you've done to your room?" she says. "Take your tea with you if you want."

We know when we've been dismissed. We take our teacups and leave. We really don't take offence. They never talk about anything interesting, at least not in front of us.

Our room is damp and steamy from the cleaning and the painting, and the rain. We have an electric heater turned on full blast to speed up the drying, but the only thing it seems to be accomplishing is a low-pitched hum.

Nancy sits on the little stool beside the beauty box. Connie digs around in one of the drawers, searching for God knows what missing beauty aid and I sit on the bed, leaning up against the wall.

"Can you get us some cookies?" Connie asks, not even bothering to turn around and look at me. "I forgot to grab some."

I know she's lying, trying to get rid of me for a while so she and Nancy can talk. She's forever dieting and if she's thinking about cookies at all, it's only to wonder how many calories she'll save by not eating a single one.

"Get your own," I answer, and immediately realize I sound far too rude. I have to be nice or they'll kick me out. "Well, okay if you really want me to," I say, "but what about your diet?"

Connie turns to Nancy and asks if she'd like a cookie or maybe a cinnamon roll. "There's lots of goop on them," she says.

Nancy answers no, she doesn't dare. She's got to be careful.

"Tell me about it," Connie interrupts, "All I have to do is look at a cookie and I gain a pound. Anyway, sweet stuff is hell on my complexion. Best to leave it alone."

They get sidetracked, wondering if it's sweets in general or chocolate in particular that attacks their skin, discussing the merits of covering zits with makeup or just ignoring them until they dry up and disappear.

They forget all about me, and the cookies, too. I love Aunt Amy's oatmeal cookies and almost decide to get two or three to hold me over until suppertime. I change my mind, crawl up on the bed and lean against the wall. I can feel the steady thrum of rain against the stucco. It lulls me and I listen.

"This weather is the shits. I don't know if Brian will even make it here tonight or if Dad will let me go if he does. Are you guys going?"

I didn't know about Connie's new boyfriend. Last I heard she was dating Duane.

I don't know why I should be surprised though. When it comes to boyfriends, my sister likes variety.

Nancy and Kurtis have been an item for so long you don't even have to ask if she's got a date. Of course she does, every single weekend and during the week, too, if her dad will let her go.

"I don't think I'll be going anywhere," Nancy says, "especially tonight."

Amazed, I turn my head to look at Nancy, but her long bangs curtain her eyes. I can hardly believe my ears. Kurtis and Nancy are always together, but there's a million girls out there just waiting for their chance. If I were Nancy, I'd do almost anything to make sure he didn't go dancing without me, or anything else without me, for that matter.

I fight down a little blip of hope. Once, Kurtis danced with me. He's so tall my arms got tired just from reaching up. He's got these amazing aqua-blue eyes and short blonde hair that looks ruffled, like someone's been running their fingers through it over and over again. Quarterback shoulders. On top of all that, he really knows how to dance.

I'm only two years younger than Connie and Nancy and their whole crowd, but it's like I was born a full century later, for all they have to do with me. Sometimes, if there's a dance or ballgame they have to miss, they'll say to me: "Keep an eye on so and so for me, will you?" Like I'm their official boyfriend guardian or something. Like I'm totally harmless. That's why I was so surprised when Kurtis asked me to dance. So surprised it made me dizzy.

I think Nancy was surprised, too. She and Kurtis were having a fight and she'd stomped right off the dance floor and into the ladies' room. By the time she came out, Kurtis was dancing with me.

"Do you mind?" Nancy asked, moving between us and putting her hand on Kurtis' arm. "My turn."

Actually I do. Catch you after this waltz. The words were there but I couldn't spit them out. My tongue was sticky, clinging to the roof of my mouth like mud to boots after a two-day rain.

Kurtis still had his hand on the small of my back. It was pretty obvious he had no idea what to do, so I backed away, over to the hard wooden benches lining the sides of the hall and sat down, wishing I could slide right through the floor. And that was it. But now, whenever he's around, I can't keep my eyes away from his.

"Do you think you can do something with my hair?" Nancy's got the beauty box open and she's looking at Connie. "Maybe cut the bangs a bit?"

Connie's a self-taught hair expert. She does dye jobs, touch-ups and haircuts. Since the beauty box, she even cuts her own hair. There's a trick with the mirrors. You have to do everything backwards. She gives herself excellent cuts.

"Sure. Can you hand me my scissors? In the drawer. Right there."

As she searches for the scissors, I notice Nancy's hands. Her nails are bitten to the quick, and she's chewed the polish off every nail on her left hand except for her thumb. It's not like Nancy. She's always perfect.

"Now, how much do you want off?" Connie asks.

"Just a bit," Nancy says. "And could you straighten my bangs?"

Connie bites her lip, frowning in concentration as wisps of ebony drift to the floor around the beauty box.

"There," she says, moving Nancy's head with her hand, tilting it so she can check the symmetry, making sure every hair is perfectly aligned. "That's better. Want me to backcomb it? It's kinda flat on top." She continues to work on Nancy's hair, arranging the soft curls to frame her elfin face, making her dark eyes enormous.

"I don't know why I'm worried about poofing your hair," Connie says. "Look at it out there. I think it's raining even harder now."

The rain is still falling, large splatting drops hitting our windows, the sound tinny, like pennies plunking into a pail. Soon, Anne calls. "Come on Nancy, I've had my cuppa. The roads won't be getting any better. We'll want to be home before your father, especially today."

Nancy stands in front of the beauty box. As she shakes the wisps of hair from her collar and begins to re-tuck her shirt, the button pops off her jeans. It falls, not right into my lap, but almost.

"Here, you lost your button."

"Thanks," she says, taking it from my outstretched hand and holding it in her palm. She's looking at it like she's never seen a button before. "Guess I might as well get used to this."

She runs her fingers through her hair one final time and checks her image in the beauty box as she turns to go.

I am staring out the bedroom window, mesmerized by the rain. I see them leave, the car swishing slowly down the lane, then onto the slick part through the flat, dancing with the ditches and finally making it to the crest of the hill. From there on, the gravel takes over, and they seem to be on solid ground.

There's no one at the beauty box, so I sit down, take up the brush and slowly begin to brush my hair. One hundred strokes, until it's sleek and smooth. I feel the weight of it, watch the amber gleams laced through the rich chestnut, everything highlighted by the soft glow of the beauty box's recessed light. The light seems golden, pooling across my shoulders like a soft warm shawl, holding back the sudden chill that shakes me as I listen to rain drum on the roof.

I take Connie's special backcombing tool and tease my hair until it's a solid mass. I begin to arrange it, watching myself in the mirror. When the front is perfect, one smooth wave from crown to jaw line, I turn, hands exploring the back of my hair. Moving as if under the weight of water, I stroke and smooth my silken hair. My vision shifts. This is uncharted territory, a place I've never been.

Talisman

Lianna is lost. Again. Directionally challenged, Douglas calls her. Sometimes he says she couldn't find her way if Jesus Christ himself was holding her hand.

She used to love the adventure of taking a wrong turn, but now, her stomach knots and she gasps at the strength of the sudden clench. Lianna's hands tremble as she tries to decipher the map. With her forefinger, she hesitantly traces a thick blue line down the left-hand side of the map and then stops when the blue intersects a smaller black line. "Shit," she mutters.

Lianna draws a deep breath and refolds the tangle of her map. Geese, drawn by shallow sapphire sloughs, circle and land. Hoarse honking fills the air. Lianna smoothes her khaki linen pants and fingers the top button of her white cotton shirt. When she shifts into low, the rumble of her Corvette startles the flock, ungainly cargo planes straining for flight.

She tops the rise, and sees a house like a mirage in the unseasonable heat of the early April day.

White paint flakes onto her palm as she pushes on the rickety gate. She picks her way across a sandstone path and carefully climbs the steps, rattles the door. "Anybody home?" A dog launches himself at the screen.

"Now, now, Chocolate," a rusty voice calls from somewhere inside. "No need to be so fierce in the middle of the day."

"Do you mind if I come in?" Lianna calls.

"What do you think?" the voice demands. "I been waiting for most of the day."

Lianna eases the door open, ignores Chocolate until the mutt, the creamy color of a Caramilk bar, comes close enough to brush against her leg. Then she reaches down, pats the silky head. "Nice puppy," she says, her hand lingering on the velvet behind the droopy ears.

"He scared off a prowler last night," Lianna hears. "Fierce, he was. He's still a bit skittery today. Can't trust people anymore. Always looking to steal something from an old lady. It's a good thing I've got Chocolate to guard my door."

Lianna is walking toward the voice, but she stops, disoriented by the tilt of kitchen tiles staggering toward the open door.

"You'll have to come to me," the voice tells her. "Easier that way."

At a dark walnut table, littered with papers and pictures, an old lady perches on a pressed-back chair. Lianna sees a walker positioned slightly to her right. Pictures plaster the walls.

"Trying to straighten out this mess a bit," the voice says, making a vain effort to pat down her wiry hair. "Good of Cherise to have you come. Surprises me though. Hate to say it of my own flesh and blood, but she's been pretty short of keeping promises, that one has."

She fixes Lianna with a sudden stare. "Don't stand there gawking," the old lady says, "or didn't she tell you? I'm sure you've seen a walker before."

"Sorry," Lianna replies. "I was looking at the photos." The largest photograph, framed in barn-board grey, is centred above the buffet. A lanky rider sits easy in the saddle, his lined face haloed by long silver hair. A small black collie stands by the horse, eyes riveted to his master's craggy face.

"Dawson," the old lady says, following Lianna's gaze.

"He's striking," Lianna says, her eyes on the photo but her mind on Douglas, his baby-butt cheeks, his hands unsullied by the smell of horse or dog.

"Yep," the old lady says, "and it wasn't just his name that made you take a second look. I used to call him *Dawson, my darling*. If I forgot and said it in front of the hands, he'd turn as red as the sky when the sun's about to set." Her lips are curved in a smile. "Dunno' to this day why he settled on me. Hazel," she says. "Even my name is plain." She is levering herself from the chair, but one hand slips and she plops down hard. Lianna turns to help.

"I'm fine," Hazel snaps, pulling her body erect. "But I could use some tea. Top left cupboard. In a red tin can."

All Lianna wants are clear directions back to the highway, but her query is killed by the high voltage of Hazel's sudden smile.

"Anyway, I'd rather chat than have you cleaning around me," she says. "I told Cherise I could manage, but she never was one to listen. At least not to me."

Lianna finds two china teacups and leaning on the backsplash, a painted tin tray. She steeps the tea, adds a luncheon plate and four shortbread cookies. The sugar is crusted in the bowl and she chips its surface with the edge of a spoon. She doesn't dare check the expiry date on the milk carton she finds at the back of the fridge.

She bears the tray to Hazel, who pushes her pictures aside and makes a small square of space for their tea. Hazel picks up a picture, a skinny boy of about fifteen with blonde hair, horn-rimmed glasses and a serious gaze. "Donnie," she says. "My boy."

Lianna pours two cups of tea. China rattles as Hazel's knotted fingers struggle with the delicate stem of the silver spoon. A fine dusting of sugar clouds the tabletop and she brushes it quickly to the floor with her leathered palm.

"Donnie stayed with me after Dawson passed," Hazel says. "Looking after me, I guess."

She holds the picture closer, peers into Donnie's face. "I told him often enough he'd better leave, find a life of his own. Look after your mother, Dawson said with his final breath, and make sure she doesn't sell the ranch. As if I ever would."

She rubs her thumb slowly across the boy's faded face. "Hell of a thing to ask," she says. "Not a bit like Dawson. But he was dying. Who's to judge?" She lays the picture aside.

"Donnie waited too long," she said. "Ended up with Gwen." Hazel gazes out the window, to the huddle of outbuildings dotting the yard. A cat jumps to the windowsill, winds its plumed ginger tail and settles against the dusted pane.

"You know," she says, picking up the picture again, curving it in her palm, "Gwen won't marry him. When I asked her why, she told me her first husband beat her. After I got to know her a little better, I thought to myself 'well, why wouldn't he'?" Her wicked grin fades at Lianna's sudden gasp.

"Touched a nerve?" The soft web of wrinkles around Hazel's eyes is stretched wide. "The point is," Hazel says, "Donnie has to sneak away when he wants to visit me." She touches Lianna's hand. "Sorry if I was out of line. Joking about serious things seems to be my way."

"Someone walked across my grave," Lianna says, attempting a smile. "It's nothing, really."

Hazel picks up another picture, a sinewy woman with the look of a runner, like the exercise fanatics Lianna avoids at the club. "Should pick a woman like you'd pick a turnip," Hazel says. "The small ones are usually bitter. Plump ones are milder, a little bit sweet."

Lianna feels the tug of linen, tight at the waist.

Douglas buys her elegant clothing tucked into crinkly tissues of boutique bags. His latest offering had been pencil straight slacks and a short, fitted jacket, butter-soft suede. The burnt caramel colour made her mouth water and she could smell candy apples cooling on sticks. She'd run her fingers over the detailing on the jacket, held the suede to her cheek. "It's beautiful," she'd said.

"Try it on," Douglas had replied. "It's perfect for you."

His sunlit eyes clouded over when she admitted she hadn't been a size eight for at least two years. "I'll exchange it tomorrow," she'd said. "There's lots of nice things in the larger sizes too."

"Keep it," he'd said, as he folded the purple bag carefully and put it on the top shelf of her closet. "Why not drop those ten extra pounds? There's nothing to it, if only you'd try."

Hazel passes Lianna another picture, a bespangled gypsy, eyes dark and full of secrets, hair hanging like a curtain across chiseled cheeks.

"Cherise," Hazel says. "I guess you'd know that."

"She's beautiful," Lianna says. "And her name is too." She can hear a dog barking somewhere outside. Chocolate lifts his head, listens for a moment. Lianna's intention to get some quick directions and make up the time she's lost meandering the back roads has dissipated, like smoke in the wind.

"I should have named her Annie," Hazel says. "Fancy name, fancy ideas. Got her off on the wrong foot and she just kept right on going, no matter what I said."

Lianna doesn't know how to reply, so she takes another slow sip of tea. "The bathroom?" she asks, and Hazel cocks her thumb. "Right there," she says. "Watch your step."

The bathroom floor doesn't quite come to the level of the narrow hall and Lianna would have stumbled if not for Hazel's warning. She steps over the sill, tries to ignore the underlying odor of urine as she checks the toilet seat for drips.

"How do you manage getting your walker over that ledge?" Lianna asks when she returns.

"I manage just fine," Hazel says, intent on her sorting, her cup of tea forgotten at her elbow. "Wouldn't mind though, if you started in there."

As she adds a final polish to the ancient taps, Lianna catches sight of herself in the mirror. Her face is flushed by the heat and hard work, and her lips curve in a smile. Me, she thinks, cleaning a stranger's toilet? I must be losing my mind.

"I can't find my danged guest book." Hazel is searching through the rubble on the table, moving pictures and papers, dust motes languid in the slanted rays of the sun.

Lianna finds a half bottle of lemon oil and a soft flannel cloth. With overlapping circles, she wipes dust from the buffet, polishes the walnut wood. She takes Dawson's picture from the wall, dusts it too. She examines the kindly light of his clear, blue eyes.

"Tuesday okay for next week?" Hazel asks. "Nice to have a body to talk to once in a while. Of course, cleaning's good too."

"I'll be here by ten," Lianna is surprised to hear herself say.

"About time this thing surfaced," Hazel says, offering an open book. "I knew it was in this rubble somewhere."

Lianna picks up a pen, watches script flow across the page. Lianna Delaney her signature reads, and she turns her palm, as if it the reason for writing her maiden name would somehow become clear.

Chocolate follows as she leaves. Lianna pats his shiny head. "Good boy," she says. "You look after Hazel now."

She slides into her Corvette, notes the coat of fine dust on the factory Baby Blue. I better run it through the carwash, she thinks, before Douglas sees.

As she smoothes Hazel's simple directions on her thigh, where she can check them as she drives, Lianna notices three white spots on her linen pants where she's splashed them with bleach.

Her husband's Gucci-soft shoes whisper on the front hall tiles, but Lianna remains at the island, where she's chopping green onions. When the salad is ready, she leans on the doorframe, waits for Douglas to look up. Five minutes pass and she finally clears her throat.

"Supper's ready," she says. "Mmm, sorry, dinner I mean."

"Be right there," Douglas says, glancing at his watch. "Busy day?"

She finds it surprisingly easy to tell him that she didn't do much of anything. Above the Business section, she can see only the curve of his neatly groomed brows and she doesn't have to meet his eyes.

Douglas walks into the dining room, stops behind her chair, and the fine hair rises on the nape of her neck. When he bends to kiss her, Lianna raises her hand to his cheek. She catches the faint scent of bleach and drops her hand.

Lianna thinks an entire week about calling Hazel, confessing she isn't really the cleaning lady Cherise had promised, only a directionally challenged woman who'd lost her way. But when Tuesday dawns she rises early, pulls on her jeans and an old tee shirt. She has to hunt to find those jeans, her closet now lined with linen and dry-clean-only clothes. When she pulls them on, they feel like a long-lost friend.

Hazel's top step creaks and Chocolate gives one short yip before he catches Lianna's scent. "Down boy," she says.

"Forgotten me already?" He gives her another perfunctory sniff before resuming his post on the small braided rug beside the kitchen door.

She peers into the dusky dining room. "Hazel?" Lianna asks.

"Here," she answers. Lianna thinks of Goldilocks when she spots Hazel deep in a blue easy chair, except that Hazel's hair is silver and smoke. She touches an unseen lever and the seat of the chair rises, nudges her upright.

"Damndest thing I ever saw," Hazel grins. "Don't use it much when I'm here alone. Scared it might buck me off. But Cherise says I have to have one. So I do."

Lianna turns to the sink. "How often does she come to visit?" Lianna asks, as she fills the battered aluminum kettle and sets it on the flame. She wonders how she will ever explain her presence here if Cherise shows up anytime soon.

Hazel looks out to the horizon. "A mother's job is to bring the young up to be self-sufficient. Done a bang-up job with Cherise, that I did. So I guess the answer to that would be I have no idea."

When the tea has steeped, Lianna pours.

"Did you ever see one of these?" Hazel has been sifting through trinkets in a red shoebox. A perfect Indian arrowhead, the black shot with glints of silver, nestles smooth and shiny in her palm. "Got a whole collection," she says. "It's against the law to have arrowheads these days, so I hid the rest. Somewhere safe."

She rubs the flat of the arrowhead against her cheek. "Smooth," she says. "Like finest silk. Legend says finding an arrowhead will bring you luck. And your one true love."

She hands the arrowhead to Lianna.

"You know," Hazel says, her eyes dreamy. "The day I found this arrowhead was the day I figured out Dawson was in love with me."

"How?" Lianna asks.

"We were rounding up horses from the gullies south of the ranch. Dawson was talking them in, soft and low. I was supposed to circle around, open the gate." Hazel's hand is rubbing slow circles on the table. "When I saw this perfect arrowhead, just laying in the dust, I had to pick it up. Dang things can disappear in the blink of an eye. Arrowheads are funny that way." She takes a small sip of tea.

"The big roan's hooves missed me by an inch, so Dawson said. He swore at me good, and when he was done cursing, he reached down and scooped me up with one arm. Held me right next to him on the saddle. Didn't let go for a damn long time."

Hazels' lips are curved, eyes filmed and far away. Lianna feels like a voyeur, the vinegar-dipped cloth limp in her hand.

"Until that day," Hazel says, "I was only his hired hand."

"A female hired hand?" she asks. "Back then?"

Hazel's head is bowed over the arrowhead and she buffs it with the corner of her shirt. "Yep," she says. "It's a whole other story. Maybe I'll tell you sometime."

I have a story, Lianna almost says, maybe I can tell it to you. But she turns back to Hazel's window, polishes hard.

Lianna has learned that secrets are bad. Twice she'd tried to tell Douglas how she'd found Hazel, gotten so involved in the old lady's life. The first time, he'd replied "uh-huh, mm-m." She'd stopped mid-sentence, and when he finally looked up from his paper, she realized he had no idea what she'd just said.

The second time, she'd sat on the arm of his leather chair, took his chin into her hand and said, "Douglas, can we talk?"

"Sure can, darling" he'd replied, "as soon as the call I'm waiting for comes through."

Lianna angle parks on main, intending to pick up some half-and-half, a treat for Hazel's tea. The post office is tucked at the back of the Lucky Dollar and Lianna asks the lady peering through the wicket if she can have Hazel's mail.

"Sure," the lady says. "I see your car at Hazel's all the time."

Lianna picks up two envelopes — Hazel's power bill, her gas bill and a Home Hardware flyer - and tucks them into the bag with the milk.

"Thought maybe you were one of Hazel's catch-colts," the lady says, "If you know what I mean." The woman stoops to put a parcel wrapped in brown kraft paper into someone's mailbox.

"What's a catch-colt?" Lianna asks.

The postmistress colours, dots of red flaming the apples of her cheeks. "I shouldn't have said that," she says. "An old woman's babbling. Just tell Hazel Alma says hello."

Traffic in the city snarls past Lianna. Horns honk and fingers are raised. When Lianna is almost sideswiped by a McGavin's truck, she steps on the gas. The long line of traffic behind her stays right on her tail.

"Wow," Lianna sighs as she pulls into her cul-de-sac. "I'm even starting to drive like a farmer. Dangerous business, at least around here."

The pale pink peonies along the front walk droop, their scent heavy and sweet. Sticky petals team with ants. Lianna makes a mental note to stake them tomorrow. The gardener isn't due for three more days.

When they'd bought the house, the front yard was bare. Lianna's head had been filled with plans for curved brick walks, for riots of flowerbeds and twisted fruit trees fragrant with bloom. Her fingers had ached for the feel of rich, warm soil. She'd dreamed of orange and yellow poppies, purple pansies and banks of fuchsia phlox, eager for May long weekend, when the almanac said it would be perfect to plant.

She'd looked for ways to kill time until the soil was warm and willing, waiting for her hand. When she'd booked her spring cut and colour, she'd told Douglas it might take most of the day. "Call me when you're ready," he'd said. "I'll pick you up."

She'd phoned him at five. Ten minutes later, a red Mustang rag-top pulled to the curb.

"Want a ride, good-looking?" Douglas had asked, his face flushed with the warmth and the wind. "This car was sold when the salesman said it's a magnet for chicks. Just seeing if it's true."

"Can we afford . . . ?" she'd started to ask, but he'd laid his finger across her lips.

"I've got a place or two I need to stop," he'd explained as he took a left instead of a right. At the liquor board store, he came out bearing two bottles of Chilean red. When he emerged from Dee-Dee's floral with a dozen yellow roses, she wondered what was going on.

He'd put the roses in her arms. "Come away with me," he'd said. "Everything is handled. I've even packed your bag."

As they sped along the highway, the wind wreaked havoc with the perfection of her hair, but she felt like Cinderella on her way to the ball.

"Two days of heaven," she'd whispered to Douglas on Sunday as they finished their breakfast in bed. "Thanks for the lovely surprise."

But the biggest surprise was a hundred miles ahead, at the end of their drive. While she and Douglas wined and dined, a crew had landscaped their yard. Poplar and elm edged the yard, straight and stiff, like soldiers on parade. The flowerbeds were orderly, pink and pale. Everything was on the square, perfectly straight.

"Whatever possessed you?" she'd said and Douglas had grinned.

"Making your life easy," was his quick reply. "I don't want my wife grubbing in the garden like some poor farmer's wife."

Lianna has always hated her orderly yard but when she mentioned cutting some curved edges to the flowerbeds, Douglas said no, it's perfect as it is. When she walks up her sidewalk, she always imagines it meandering a bit.

"Douglas?" she calls as she opens the mullioned door. The silence is complete. "Douglas?" she calls again. "Anybody home?"

He pokes his head around the corner and Lianna jumps. "Coming in the front?" he asks. "Again?"

"Don't worry Doug," she says. "My shoes are clean. See?" She lifts her right sandal for inspection and is almost pleased to see a bit of dog poop stuck in the deep groove of her new Birkenstocks.

When she first saw the garden spot beside the shed, Lianna asked Hazel if she could plant. "Sure," Hazel had replied. "But I didn't figure you for the gardening type. It hasn't been planted since my knees gave out." Hazel rubbed her knees with her palms, leaned from her chair toward the window Lianna had just cleaned. "I'll get Donnie to turn the soil."

Planting day was perfect, windless, so the feather-light seeds dropped straight into Lianna's careful rows. She patted the damp soil over them gently and firmly, like a mother patting a colicky baby's back. At the end of each new row, she pounded a yellow stake.

She was exhausted by the time Hazel edged around the southeast corner of the house, a Coke in one hand and a willow cane in the other.

"Don't stare like I was the Second Coming." Hazel gestured with her cane. "Dawson made a few. He gave most of them away, but I kept this one. Pretty, I thought. Look at the grain. I never dreamed I'd end up using the damn thing. Goes to show you, doesn't it?"

Lianna took the Coke, held its sweat-beaded coolness to the side of her neck. Hazel eased down onto the lawn swing, weathered and worn and in need of paint. Birds chirped in the caraganas and two monarch butterflies wafted across the yard.

"Wow," Lianna said. "This little garden has almost done me in." She pulled a clump of infringing grass and ran the damp soil through her ruined fingers.

"You've got it, you know," Hazel said.

"Got what?" Lianna asked.

"Hunger," Hazel said. "For the land. Once you get it, it never goes away."

Lianna's eyes swept the distant horizon as her fingers stroked the soil. The earth cupped her buttocks like a lover's hand.

"Come on," Lianna finally said. "Let's find some shade." She reached up and Hazel took her hand.

The maple tree outside Hazel's picture window has turned to shades of scarlet, pumpkin orange, yellows too. Lianna notices that some of the smaller leaves are beginning to crisp and curl.

"I'm almost ninety," Hazel says, shaking her head. "In two weeks time. When I pass a mirror, I almost say hello to the old woman I see. Gives me a start when I realize it's me."

"Ninety?" Lianna says. "Are you planning a big whoop-de-doo?" Lianna grins. The events she attends with Douglas at the club are definitely not whoop-de-doos and he'd cringe if he ever heard her use the word.

Hazel pats her steel-wool hair. "No party for me," she says. She holds a letter on thick, creamy paper. "Cherise wants to take me to a spa." She cocks her head. "Can you imagine? Wrapped in seaweed and massaged by some stranger?"

"You might like it," Lianna replies.

Hazel tosses the letter aside. "Not likely," she says. "Nobody's laid a hand on me since Dawson passed. I'll keep it that way. Told Cherise she could come out for the day instead."

"Cherise hasn't shown her mug around here for years," Alma tells Lianna when she stops for the mail. "Too fancy for the likes of us." She pushes her faded cardigan up her muscled arms. "Too bad Hazel's girl wasn't more like you. Faithful, if you know what I mean."

Lianna feels her cheeks go hot. Faithful, she thinks, isn't really the word for me.

She has looked up the word in Douglas' gilt-edged dictionary. *Infidelity: disloyalty or esp. unfaithfulness to a sexual partner.* Knowing that the literal definition doesn't apply to her hasn't really helped. Mentally, she ticks off the days, only four each month to start. But she's now spending almost half her time in a world that Douglas knows nothing about.

Lianna checks the tomato cages and picks two ripe, red beefsteaks for lunch.

"You and Donnie," Hazel says, when Lianna serves buns spread with mayonnaise and thick slices of tomato. "Working so hard on that little piece of land. But you've gotten it to bear fine fruit. Look at these tomatoes. Big as my plate."

Lianna doesn't answer, the sweet tangy tomato like sugar on her tongue. She has worked hard and she doesn't feel the lick of guilt when she bites into her bun, slathered with mayonnaise, and butter too.

Douglas has noticed her taut new shape. "Look at you," he'd said one night as she took off her robe. "I knew you could do it. Too bad you waited so long." His praise had seemed muffled to Lianna, like the beating of a far-away drum.

Lianna appreciates Donnie's helping hand in the garden and she wonders how much time he's been spending there.

She'd found his number scribbled on Hazel's John Deere calendar on the wall by the phone and she'd jotted it down, tucking the slip of yellow paper into her purse. She'd meant to call him, thank him for his help. But her days with Hazel slip by like a dream.

"You never come to the club anymore," Douglas says. "Arlene is always asking about you. She wants to know what you're up to these days."

Lianna takes a slow, deep breath, pinches a leaf from the geranium that is blooming on the wide windowsill. "It doesn't take much to keep me busy," she says, flashing him a smile.

"I'll make your excuses to Arlene," Douglas says, setting his briefcase on the island. He takes Lianna by the shoulders, turns her to face him and gives her a lover's kiss, soft and slow. The geranium leaf flutters to the floor.

"It might be nice if you'd make the effort to join us for lunch one of these days," he says. When Douglas smiles at her, Lianna notices muscles bunched at the edge of his jaw.

"Too bad," Hazel says. "You and Donnie would have made a good pair. Earth-bound, both of you." She turns to the window, watches a gold finch flutter to the chokecherry bush.

"He's a lot like his dad," Hazel says. "A spitting image, right down to his steel grey hair. Most importantly, he's got Dawson's good heart."

Lianna pours their tea. "I'd like to meet him," she says.

Hazel lowers her head, rubs her forehead with the tips of her fingers. "A power source," she says. "That's what you need, the both of you need, this old woman thinks."

Lianna is not sure what Hazel is talking about. Lately, her conversations wander more and more. "I've got them in a little tin," Hazels says. "I was going to give them to Donnie one of these days."

Lianna raises a brow. "I don't know. . ." she starts.

"My arrowheads," Hazel interrupts, with an impatient shake of her head. "If the government finds out, I'll end up in jail. Maybe you will too. After all, I've showed you one or two. Or Charlie will show up, steal the whole damn works."

"Charlie?" Lianna asks.

Hazel glares at Lianna. "That no-good," she says. "If a man will do such a thing to his dog, no telling what else he might do."

Lianna has never heard of Charlie before.

"Dawson and Charlie," Hazel says. "Like night and day. Thank God." She takes a ragged breath.

"Poor Goldie," she says. "Sometimes, I can still hear her howl." Hazel's lips are quivering, purple at the edges like raw liver on a plate.

"Hazel," Lianna says, touching her arm. "Don't. Whatever it was, it doesn't matter now."

"Oh yes, it does," Hazel says. "Great big boxer, sniffing around my little spaniel-cross bitch. I thought I caught him soon enough, but I didn't. Not by a long shot."

Hazel raises her eyes to Lianna.

"I wanted to shoot her," she says. "Put her out of her misery. Charlie forbade me. Let her labour until she split herself wide open. When he finally shot her, her spirit had been gone for hours." Hazel turns her face to the window, the furrows in her face diverting her tears.

"You can tell a lot about a man by the way he treats his dogs," she says. "I left Charlie right after Goldie died." She wipes her cheek with the sleeve of her green cardigan and straightens in her chair. "I'll never let him near Chocolate. If Charlie shows up here, I'll shoot him. Really, I will."

When she enters the house, Lianna smells cinnamon, hears B.B. King. She tippy-toes down the hall but Douglas has ears like a bat, tuned to the slightest hint of noise.

"Is that you Lianna?" he calls from the den. "I finally gave up, started cocktail hour alone."

She pivots, walks down the hundred-mile hall. The cinnamon scent wafts from candles flickering on the mantle and on the cold slate of the hearth. Shadows dance on the spent ashes. When she hesitates in the doorway, Douglas pulls her inside.

"I've missed you," he says and he kisses her cheek. From the pocket of his sports jacket, he pulls a small box, wrapped in red, tied with a pure white bow. "So I got you a little surprise."

She fumbles with the wrapping and hopes he doesn't notice her soft old jeans, the faded-out tee. "Oh my God, Douglas," she says, when she sees the oval amethyst, more purple than a bruise, nestled inside.

He lifts the ring from the box and she offers her hand. His thin, pale hand envelops hers.

"For Christ' sake Lianna," he says. "Look at your hands."

Lianna feels a sudden freeze of dry cold on her palm. "Like a migrant worker's or maybe even worse. How many times have I told you to leave the gardening to Bernie? That's what I pay the lazy bastard for."

Lianna bites her lip.

"Sorry about that," she says. "I'll book a manicure tomorrow. I'll call right now. It's not too late, I wouldn't think."

She reaches to kiss the planes of his shadowed cheek but Douglas moves away.

"Lianna," he says. "I work damn hard so you don't have to and what do you do? Spend all your time grubbing in the flowerbeds or whatever the hell else it is that's keeping you so busy this summer. Christ, I'll never understand."

He drops into his Lazy-boy, flips to some golf-game replay he's probably seen at least a dozen times.

"I love the ring," Lianna says, holding it in her palm. "I'm going to take a quick shower. Use lots of lotion, maybe it will help." She hates herself for groveling. She hears the commentator's whisper as she carefully closes the leaded-glass door.

The muted voices from the den are icy drops of water plunking slowly on her skull. She takes two Advil from her bedside table and washes them down with a glass of water. When Douglas finally glides into their room, she controls her breathing, soft and slow.

He sits beside her on the bed and tucks the quilt around her shoulders. Then he lifts her hand, curled on the pillow, and gently kisses her fingertips. When he stands and pulls the curtain across the French doors so the moonlight is blurred, Lianna fights the sudden rise of tears.

Lianna used to run. Her route was around the track and north along the highway, past the SPCA. One summer day, she took refuge there during a sudden storm. A brown and white puppy was lying listless in his cage by the waiting room door. Lianna made soft sounds until he lifted his head, and when she held out her hand, he sniffed her thoroughly before he finally licked her palm.

"Do you mind?" she'd asked the girl behind the desk.

"Go ahead," the girl said. "The poor mutts get precious little attention. We've got away too many puppies and not enough hands."

When Lianna left the office, the tiny, toffee cream mutt had a name. Muffin was nestled safe inside her sweatshirt, his soft curls ticking her chest. When she picked up her pace, she felt him snuggle closer, his cold nose like a welcome kiss.

Douglas was waiting. "Thank God you're back," he said. "I was getting worried. Some of that lightning is awful damn close, especially when my wife is out in it, running around."

He'd pulled her inside, enfolded her in his arms. When he felt the bump in her shirt, he'd pulled back. "What have you got there?" he'd asked. "Found time to stop by the mall and buy another pair of pretty shoes?"

When she'd told him how she'd rescued Muffin, Douglas shook his head.

"Lianna, how could you?" he asked. "You've got to learn to think things through." He took the puppy from her, headed for the garage. "That's all we need," he said. "A puppy pooping on the carpet and ripping up our yard. The landscaping cost me big bucks, in case you didn't know."

He found a cardboard box, put Muffin inside. "He'll be just fine here until morning," Douglas said. "Take him back right away, before you get attached."

She'd hesitated in the doorway and when Douglas turned off the light, she turned it back on. "So he won't be afraid," she'd explained when Douglas raised his eyes.

The pale sun held no warmth and Muffin and Lianna shivered in unison as she tucked him into her sweatshirt. Her legs seemed heavy, mired in mud, but too soon, she reached the SPCA. Lianna leaned against the door, a black blanket of dread heavy on her chest. The door gave beneath her weight.

"Back so soon?" the girl behind the counter asked.

Lianna reached inside her shirt, withdrew her puppy with a trembling hand. She kissed Muffin's cold nose and handed him back.

"Sorry," she said. "I'm allergic to dogs. Really, I didn't know."

She stumbled outside, sprinted until she thought her lungs would burst. Sometimes, she still dreams of Muffin's big, brown eyes.

Chocolate snuffs, groans in his sleep. "I better get going," Lianna says. "Too much yacking. Not enough work."

"You?" Hazel snorts. "I was the one running off at the mouth. Only excuse I have is that I'm getting really old." She smiles at Lianna, uses her forefinger to trace the map of veins across the top of her weathered hand.

"You know," she says, "I've had a happy life. There's not much I'd change." Hazel pushes back her steel wool hair with gnarled fingers.

"Can you do one more thing for me?" she asks. "Before you go? These old knees don't take directions very well anymore."

Hazel tells Lianna to go upstairs, first door on the left she says. "In the closet. There's a stack of boxes. Move them aside. Bottom shelf, right at the back. English mint tin with the hinged lid? Bring that down."

Hazel takes the red plaid tin from Lianna. "My jewels," she says. She opens the lid to reveal the arrowheads lined up on purple velvet like soldiers on parade. Their perfection takes Lianna's breath away.

"Here," Hazel says, shoving the box into Lianna's hands. "They're not safe here. I can feel it in the air. Take them home. Hide them for me."

Lianna closes the lid, tries to hand the box back to Hazel. "There's nothing in the air around here except dust and more dust," she says.

Hazel pushes the box back into her hands. "Give 'em to Donnie some day," she says. She clutches Lianna's arm. "Promise?" she says.

Lianna sets the box down and solemnly crosses her heart. "Okay," she says, "I promise. But I'll only keep them until you decide to give them to Donnie yourself. Now stop talking nonsense. You've making me shiver."

Lianna stands in her pristine bedroom, the tin of arrowheads heavy in her hands. Sunlight from the eyebrow window strikes a small alcove high on the wall. She grabs an oak barstool from the den. It wobbles as she reaches, tucks the tin back as far she can. She hops from the stool, dusts off her hands. She walks around the room, checking from every angle.

"There you go, Hazel," she finally says. "You can rest easy now."

She strips down to nothing, feels the soft wind feather her virgin-white skin. She hoes an entire row of ferny carrots and half of another. When she begins to tire, she stretches out between the rows. The earth supports her, warm on her back, and the tomato plants offer their mottled, bushy shade.

Arrowheads, carefully placed, outline her collarbone, trace the stem of a "y" between the rise of her breasts. A work-worn hand places the largest arrowhead in the hollow of her bellybutton. The arrowhead is large, golden brown, warm, like his hands. Rich, black soil crumbles from its edges. He circles her bellybutton with the tips of his fingers, works the soil until it is silk on her skin. She raises her arms to run her fingers through his thick, graying hair.

Her husband's smooth baldness against her palm startles her awake. She shivers, pulls the comforter across her shoulders, bare in the cool blue moonlight flooding their room.

Lianna stirs at the muted ring of a distant phone. "Some blubbering idiot," Douglas says, striding into their bedroom and throwing the French doors open wide. "Third time he's called. He keeps saying to tell you she's gone, that you won't have to do your cleaning anymore."

Douglas smoothes the satin ribbon quilt at the foot of their bed. "The guy's numerically challenged," he says, watching Lianna through hooded eyes. "I told him he's got the number wrong. Told him not to call here. Ever again."

Instinctively, Lianna rolls and curls. From the satin of her belly, an arrowhead falls, its jagged point piercing the shroud of her sleep.

Every Day She Kills Us and Always We Survive

"It's hotter than the hubs of hell up here. No wonder we had such a lousy sleep."

"You know, Carol," Sydney replies, yawning. "Mom'll flip if she hears you talking like that."

The heat is unrelenting and our bedroom has never really cooled off, so we wake up sluggish and out-of-sorts. When our mother calls, we drag ourselves out of bed and down the stairs, hoping the night breeze has at least cooled off the main floor.

In a hot spell, the faded red brick on the verandah gives off heat to the touch and you can feel it radiating to the bedrooms above, the breeze picking it up and blowing it through our open windows. Last night, when we couldn't sleep, we threw the covers off the bed, grateful for the gentle movement of air across our bodies.

We have oatmeal porridge for breakfast, although why our mother would cook anything in our already unbearably hot kitchen is beyond me. I try to disguise mine with brown sugar and lots of icy cold milk.

Sydney protests. "Mom, there's no way I can eat this. Can I have cornflakes?"

"No," our mother replies. "You eat what the rest of us eat. Get to it."

Sydney laces her porridge liberally with sugar and milk as I have, but she just pushes it around in the bowl and picks at the sugary portions. When Mom leaves the room, she quickly empties her bowl into the dog's dish by the door and Norm laps up the porridge, wagging his stump of a tail and looking at her with grateful eyes.

"Woof, woof, thank you very much Sydney. But I'd rather have cornflakes." Sydney's mouth is slightly open, her eyes scrunched in concentration as she tries to throw her voice.

She's studied the last section of her book for five nights in a row. Last night, I got tired of her bedside light shining in my eyes and made her stop. I should have let her read a little more.

Norm stops eating for a moment and watches Sydney, his eyes on the strange contortions of her face. Then he shakes himself and goes back to the porridge bowl.

"Magic still not working?" I ask.

"Do you think I wasted my money?"

"Probably not," I say, wanting to make her feel better, although I haven't seen a single indication that she'll ever be able to perform a magic trick, let alone the hundreds promised in the ads. In April, she'd mailed in her $14.95 for *Magic Made Easy in Fourteen Days*. She'd awaited the book's arrival like a pregnant woman two weeks overdue. As soon as she had the wrappers off, she'd shut herself away and worked at her magic for hours on end. Sydney's pretty focused for a kid who's only ten.

She tried the interlocking rings, which seemed welded together permanently; the silk scarves kept slithering from her hand; and blowing smoke rings was out of the question, at least around here. Her final try was the sleight-of-hand. When she lost track of the red ball, she gathered up the cups — red, blue, and yellow — and put them in the hall cupboard, right at the back.

Sydney dreams of being a great magician and I dream about Randy and me. I end my days by dreaming. Usually, I drift to a wonderful world where I'm the centre of attention and Randy's at my beck and call. But one night, our bedroom was too hot for sleep. When I felt Sydney tossing and turning too, I gave up. "Sydney," I said. "How about a little magic?"

She smiled at me then, a sad little smile. "I don't believe in magic anymore," she said. "When someone tells you how it works, the magic is gone."

She looked so miserable that I touched her arm. "Don't be silly," I said. "There's magic everywhere."

She was looking at me, eyebrows raised. I carried on. "What about the northern lights? Especially when they sing. It has to be magic, don't you think? Better yet, how about Uncle Charlie? He always finds a dime behind your ear."

"Yeah," she replied. "But you know darn well it's always really late when he stops by and usually, we're half asleep. Besides that, he's always got a half dozen other things going, like playing the piano a bit or joking with Dad. If we were really watching, we'd have caught that trick years ago. I've read about it in *Magic Made Easy* and it's no big deal."

"But *you* can't do it," I say. "Maybe it really is magic if
you've got the directions and you still can't make it work."
But my sister was twisting a strand of her hair tight to her
scalp, pulling harder and harder, so I left it alone.

Sydney's moved to the final section of her magic book
— *Ventriloquism for Beginners*. Every night before we turn
out the lights, she studies the mechanics of 'throwing your
voice.' Her mission is to make Norm the first linguistic dog
in Butte Valley. I think she's nuts.

Sydney twists her hair while Norm laps the porridge from
her bowl. When he finally looks up, she gives him a little
pat. "I think this time it's gonna work."

She takes a deep breath and her eyes go glassy. Her
eyelids droop, as if she's in a trance, halfway into another
world. Norm remains silent, not knowing he's supposed to
be a talking dog. He continues to lap the porridge. When
he's finished, he turns to Sydney and barks, a short little
woof that can't be considered anything except exactly what
it is.

"Very good," I say. "I think he just said thanks."

I laugh; Sydney doesn't.

I rinse my bowl at the kitchen sink. Mom is at the back
step, feeding the half-wild kittens that used to live in our
barn. Dad says if you make pets out of them, they'll never
be decent mousers. Our mother feeds them anyway. A
skinny cat will never have the patience to out-wait a mouse.

When the porch door slams, Sydney turns back to the
table, using her spoon to scrape the bottom of her bowl. She
licks it slowly and sighs, as if she'd just eaten one more bite
than she could possibly hold. Our mother isn't fooled and
starts towards Norm, maybe to let him out, or to check his

bowl for evidence. Sydney interrupts. "What's the plan for today?" she asks, golden ringlets corkscrewing over the collar of her shirt, the unrelenting heat encouraging her unruly curls.

"Peas," our mother replies. "And if I were you two, I'd skedaddle out there right now. Get picking before the heat of the day. We can take our chairs around to the east side later and shell them in the shade."

Our mother has been on the farm too long. She actually thinks that sitting in the shade shelling peas is a pleasant way to spend an afternoon. God, I can hardly wait to leave this place, its slow monotonous pace, every day the same. There's nothing to mark their passing except my mother's 'to do' lists, stuck on the refrigerator door. She checks her list daily, the jobs neatly stroked off as they're accomplished. At sundown, she takes the list, reads it over almost lovingly before she throws it in the trash and sits down to compose another list for the following day.

The garden, watered every other evening from the dugout behind the barn, is the only thing that flourishes in the heat. The irrigation water is green and slimy, thick with cow slobber. There are algae slicks floating everywhere, but still the garden grows. Somehow, using pipe he'd scavenged from the dump, a half-crippled water pump and his old standby — a bit of barbed wire — Dad had rigged the irrigation system. I was appalled to see how it pleased our mother. There's got to be more exciting things in life than watering the garden every other day.

And then there are the snakes. Drawn by the dank coolness under the pumphouse, they come by the dozens, hiding under the plywood platform supporting the pump, sometimes even coiling themselves around the base of the pump itself. There's a pulley-start on the pump and because Dad is usually still working come evening, it's my job, and Sydney's, to reef on the rope, pulling the choke and firing the pump. It doesn't start easily. We take turns of about five minutes each, grabbing the rope, pulling quickly and listening for the cough as the engine gasps to life. Sometimes it takes us a good half hour, because if we hold the choke open too long and flood the motor, we have to give it at least ten minutes before we can try again.

The first time Sydney saw the snakes she screamed bloody murder, running to the house like all of hell's demons were right on her tail. Mom said she was sure that one of us had finally been fatally wounded. "I thought you must have caught your hair in the twirling wheel of the pump shaft," she said. "I've told you a million times. When you're working down there, you're supposed to wear a ponytail. Or I thought maybe Sydney had fallen into the dugout. It makes me shudder just thinking about it."

Our mother is always imagining horrible deaths: how we will surely be maimed by the bailer, run over by Dad as he drives the haybine to the field, or perhaps squished beneath a truck when it falls from the jack. Every day she kills us, and always we survive.

The day that Sydney saw the snakes, our mother held her close, rocked her and patted her hair. "Shh, Baby, don't cry. Shh, shh, Momma's here. Don't worry, I promise, everything will be okay." Sydney was as white as the sheets hanging on the line in our yard; goose bumps rose on my arm and I had to turn away.

After the snakes, it became my job to start the pump, and no amount of bribery or bullying could induce Sydney to come anywhere near. Her terror has grown in tandem with the number of snakes in our yard. Her fear is instinctive and all the scientific information in the world can't convince her that the only snakes to fear on the prairie are rattlers and diamond backs, and that we don't have any such species around here.

At first I was mad, thinking it just another lame excuse to get out of doing her share. She's such a baby; it would be hard to guess I'm only three years older. She gets away with a lot more than I ever did. Mom seems to forget Sydney's old enough to iron and clean and gives her the fun jobs like burning the trash and feeding the chickens or Norm.

Sydney loves animals, and it doesn't take long to feed the chickens and gather the eggs. And in my opinion, feeding Norm doesn't qualify as work. Besides, it gives her more time to practise throwing her voice, although I don't think she's made any progress. I don't know where she's throwing it to, because so far, Norm hasn't said a single word. Sydney's used two whole Chapsticks this month. She has to keep her lips in shape so she can purse her mouth in the proper manner. She's getting real close she says; it's just a matter of projecting a little bit more.

Every second evening when I go down to the pump, I pull the rope a time or two — in case anyone's listening — and I do a little dreaming, sitting on the salt lick that Dad has set out for the cows.

In my dreams, Randy and I spend a day at the lake, go dancing at the hall by the beach, or sometimes go to the drive-in west of town. He buys me extra buttered popcorn, although I always say, "No thanks, I'm watching my weight." He says I look just fine to him and watches me as I eat.

When I'm finished, he licks the butter from my fingers, slowly, one by one, as his eyes hold mine.

Sometimes he buys me gifts, usually clothes or jewellery. I protest. After all, I say, it's not as if we're engaged. He's especially good about choosing rings. He likes the gold ones best, with large, chunky gemstones, but occasionally he buys me a cameo or pearl. He isn't much for silver and that's fine with me, because I prefer gold myself. It goes better with my dark hair. Silver is more for the blondes. My dream Randy isn't attracted to blondes.

"Carol, where are you?" Sydney says, calling me back.

"I'm here. Maybe if you'd come down and help with this stupid motor, it wouldn't take me so long."

"The snakes," she starts.

"Go back to the house, you baby. I don't need you anyway."

Then I try to start the pump and although it may be a long time before I coax it to life, all that extra reefing is worth it. I like having the world to myself for a while.

More and more, I crave time alone and decide to *use* Sydney's terror of snakes. I tell her all about them, how they coil their cold bodies around the sweaty pipes leading from the dugout, how their little heads waver in the breeze as they peer up from the hollow beneath the pump, watching me work. I tell her that they've already multiplied, coming first by the dozens and then by the hundreds, how they will soon be having their babies, and how, every year, they and their babies, and *their* babies, too, will return to the same spot. I tell her that when the weather turns cool in the fall they'll clump together, masses of snakes, writhing and watching, forming a great roiling snake ball and how they will remain entangled, cold and seemingly dead, but in reality, waiting for spring and the warmth of the sun. When the ground warms, they'll stretch and wriggle, the sun reviving them and giving them life.

Gosh, I say. I sure hope they don't find their way up to the garden. It's always so moist there. I sure hope they stay down by the dugout and under the pumphouse shack. Wouldn't it be awful if they started to migrate?

It's fun, teasing Sydney, until she develops a sudden allergy to the garden. I can see where it will lead: more work for me. I change my tune, promise Sydney that snakes pick only one place to set up their dens and that once they have chosen, they never leave. She doesn't think to ask me why they've moved here. We've never seen a snake around the place before. I would have told her they're just like colonies, and when they get overpopulated, one sector has to split off and start again. I've sharpened the hoe, I tell her, and if any snake dares travel that far from the dugout, I'll chop it in half. Snakes can feel these things. They know where there's danger and avoid it like hell.

She buys it. I'm free from taking on the garden alone. I worry that gardening will ruin my beautiful hands and when Randy buys a ring, he might take one look at my green and grubby hands and forget his preference for brunettes.

Funny how this family works. Sidney and I both hate the garden; the garden is our mother's life. Mom tells her friends that this year, despite the heat, her garden is producing almost double or close to it. I wish, not for the first time, that she'd talk about books or fashions, or else be entirely quiet, but she never does. I know she reads because she encourages me to do the same, but when Dad comes home, she tucks her book away and they talk about the weather or the awful price of binder twine.

"Sydney, quit doggin' it and get going. If you think I'm going to do your rows, you've got another think coming." I lift my basket, heavy with the harvest of precious pods. Sydney is squatting about half way down the row she's started on, gorging herself. She's not even trying to pretend she's working.

"Do you think I've eaten enough fresh peas to be immune to them yet?" she asks. "I sure hope so, 'cause man, they really give me gas." She is grinning, not even embarrassed that last night, besides the heat, I'd had to endure her endless rumbling and farting. My sister's on dead idle. Having her out here distinctly cuts down the pea package count at the end of the day.

That's another thing our mother does relentlessly: counts bags of produce she puts down each day, her freezer list a source of pride for her, and for us, another indication that she's been out of the world too long. Sydney and I have talked, and we're quite sure we'll never end up like our mother, counting packages of frozen peas. Our lives will surely amount to something more.

The phone rings. I run to the hall, grab the receiver. Randy? But it's only Tom Tisdale, trombone player extraordinaire and the leader of our high school band. Tom, my friend since we were six. Shit, I think, when I hear his voice.

"Hi Carol," he says. "Hot, eh?"

"Yep," I reply, impatient with his observation, the weather obsession that afflicts almost everyone. When I leave this place, I will never again talk about the weather.

"I got the car," he crows.

Tom almost never gets his old man's car. I can see why he's happy; I just don't see what it has to do with me.

"I'm heading for the lake at two," he says. "Can you come?"

Crystal Lake is really just a large spring-fed slough, but it's big enough for powerboats and the beach is white sand. A diving platform is anchored about forty yards out, close to the buoys; it's a good place to suntan.

"Hang on," I say. "Gotta ask Mom."

I find her upstairs, changing bedding in the stifling heat. What's the use, I wonder. They're just gonna get sweated up again tonight.

"Mom," I say, grabbing the bottom corner of a sheet and helping her tuck. "Tom's on the phone. Can I go to the lake with him today?"

"What about Sydney?"

"Mom, if I have to drag Sydney along everywhere I go, pretty soon no one's going to ask me anywhere. I'll be in seventh heaven if you let me go," I plead. "I'll make it up to her. I'll even play hide-and-seek with her next time she pesters me to play. You know I hate that stupid game."

There's another reason I don't want Sydney to go. In a moment of extreme boredom, I told her all about my crush on Randy, and she's such a blabbermouth, she can't be trusted. I must have been temporarily insane.

"I highly doubt you'll be in seventh heaven, at least I hope not," Mom replies, smiling now. "Seventh heaven is where the spirits of unborn babies reside while they're waiting for their chance to come back into the world. If you read a bit more and quit your constant daydreaming, you might find out an interesting fact or two. Really, it's good for the soul."

Mom and Sydney have this exchange going, each searching for useless bits of knowledge and trading their facts like they were signed baseball cards or a special cat's eye marble. I don't get it. My spare time is spent practising different hair-dos and trying out make-up, the ways of women new to me.

"Anyway," I say, as we unfold the top sheet. "Weren't we talking about *me* going to the lake? Tom's waiting, you know."

Mom pauses, flips the sheet onto the bed and smoothes it with her hand. "Okay, you can go," she says. "But don't forget your promise — play hide-and-seek the next time Sydney asks. I'll hold you to it."

I run down the stairs and grab the phone, tell Tom I can go.

"Make sure you're ready on time," he says. "If you're not, I ain't waiting." That's Tom for you. Obviously, he's never had to spend an hour doing his make-up only to find he's chosen the wrong shade of eye shadow. He has no idea how long the natural look can take.

Sydney and I shell peas steady until 1:30. "You finish," I say, standing, pulling the kinks from my tired back with a housecat stretch. "Tom's coming at two and I have to get ready. You've done less than your share so don't bother pulling any lip."

I take off my dust-laden sandals, leave them by the back door and pad up the stairs barefoot. The steps are smooth, cool on my soles. I shower quickly, work on my make-up and hair.

The clock in the downstairs hall is striking its second bong when Tom pulls up front with his dad's Beetle. He's got it loaded almost to the hilt, with Frank, Shelley and —

Oh my God! — Randy, jammed in the back. The front seat's saved for me.

I wonder if there's any polite way to get Shelley to move so I can get in the back, next to Randy. It's pretty squishy back there, and his shoulders are square and tremendously wide. Maybe he'd be more comfortable if he put his arm along the back of my seat. I might pretend I'm dozing, maybe let my head fall back. We'd be touching.

Cripes, I think, what am I doing? I pull myself back, flash Tom a sisterly grin. He's not looking at me. His eyes are on Sydney, standing on the step with her mesh beach bag in hand.

"Can I come, too?" she asks.

Dear God, no.

"Jeez," Tom says, "I wouldn't mind, but we don't have much room."

Shelley rolls down the window. "You can probably squeeze her in the front," she says. "I've got enough room back here to hold her bag."

I'm desperate for a clean getaway, but we've been idling too long. Mom appears on the verandah, a basket full of wet sheets balanced on her hip.

She smiles, waves to Tom. "If you don't mind taking her, it'd really be nice." She walks to the Beetle and peers inside. "It's so darn hot and she does love to swim. She won't be any trouble. Carol will keep an eye on her, won't you, Hon?"

It isn't a question. I bite the inside of my cheek. Damn!

I'll definitely ditch her as soon as we get to the lake. Maybe I can get her to head up to the mini-golf by the store or go play in the jungle gym. There's always lots of kids around there. Maybe it won't turn out so badly. Randy might be attracted to the fact that I'm so much fun my kid sister always wants to tag along.

We wedge Sydney into the front between Tom and me; I'm pushed right over to the door. I put my arm around her to steady myself, pull down the visor and adjust my hair. I watch Randy in the mirror.

The wind roars through the car as Tom speeds toward the lake, wreaking havoc with my hairdo. Should have used more spray, I guess. I can't believe Randy is sitting behind me, actually breathing the same air. Chuck Berry's new song comes on the radio. I reach across Sidney and turn it up. *"Riding along in my automobile, my old man's car and this is real,"* Tom sings, his bastard lyrics competing with Chuck's but his voice right on key. Music blasts from the extra speakers Tom installed beneath the dash.

Like magic, Sydney disappears completely and so does Tom. It's just Randy and me, cruising the backroads in his candy-apple red Mustang. I can't believe it. I'm the first person to ride in his new convertible. Moving a little closer, I kiss Randy's neck. I love the rush of the wind through my hair. I feel wild and free.

When Tom slows to pull the Beetle into the parking lot, I'm totally surprised, disoriented, thinking of Randy and his reaction to those butterfly kisses I'd been planting up and down his muscular neck. The lot's almost full and Tom has to drive through twice before he scores a spot in the shade of a big cottonwood. He opens the trunk and grabs both tire tubes. They're half deflated so he needs the pump. I hand it to Sydney.

"Here," I say. "Carry this. It's light enough."

Randy and Frank hoist the cooler and head down the path to the beach. Shelley and I follow, laden with blankets and bags.

Sydney's still standing behind the car. "What are you waiting for?" I ask. "The Second Coming?"

Halfway to the beach, I'm stopped by Sydney's scream. I see a baby bull snake, coiled across the path.

"Oh for God sake, Sydney. It's just a baby. And they're harmless, you know." But she's frozen, her eyes wide and staring. I know she's about to let loose again, and there are way too many people gawking already.

"Shut up," I say through gritted teeth, grabbing her arm roughly and pulling her around the baby bullsnake. "You're making a scene."

I finally steer Sydney down to the sand. It's hell-fire hot. The guys are already gone. They've got the tubes in the water and they're floating out toward the dock. Shelley strips off her T-shirt, revealing a tiny, black bikini, and heads for the water.

I shake the blanket, hand a corner to Sydney. "Here," I say. "Stop your damn snivelling and give me a hand." We spread our beach blanket: an old corduroy quilt.

"Remember what I told you about Randy and me?"

"Yeah," she says, wiping at the fine beads of sweat glistening above her upper lip. "How come he's out there at the dock? Isn't he just crazy for you?"

"I kind of made that up," I say. "Say one word to him and I'll kill you. I'm not kidding."

I've threatened to kill Sydney before, so she's not exactly terrified. She settles beside me, smoothing the sand at the edges of our blanket, making a little pillow of sand for her head.

"Don't get too comfy," I say. "When Shelley comes back, you take a hike."

Moments later, Shelley returns; Sydney doesn't move. "Here," I say, digging in my purse for some coin. "Go get yourself a Popsicle."

"I can't," she says. "What if there's another snake?"

Just then, we see a school friend of Sydney's. She waves, and Sydney waves back.

"Snakes never stay on the sand," I lie, "they'll shrivel up and die if they do. If you walk along the beach, you won't see another snake."

She shakes her head, doesn't believe a word I'm telling her.

"Cross my heart and hope to die," I say. "Now go see your friend."

"You mean Jody?" Sydney asks.

"Yeah," I say. I find a crumpled dollar. "Here," I say, "buy something for Jody too."

She hesitates, still doubtful, but I turn, ignoring her. The next time I look, Sydney's red suit is far in the distance, almost to the store. Jody is walking beside her, dragging a stick across the sand. They stop by the water's edge, squatting to inspect some wonderful piece of driftwood, I imagine.

Good. Now maybe I can figure out how to get Randy's attention.

I take the oil and rub my limbs, careful not to miss a single spot of skin. What I'm aiming for is the all-over golden tan. When I'm slick with oil, I lie down. Close my eyes. I'm sure when Randy comes back from the dock, I'll feel his presence. I don't need to see. Eventually, he'll get tired of Tom and Frank, tell them he doesn't want to give up his chance to spend time with me. I suck in my gut, wriggle my butt further into the soft sand, hoping I look really slim, although I know it's impossible for me.

A fly lands on my leg, takes a little walk. I flick him away, pull my bathing suit down a bit at the top of my legs. My skin is pretty darn white. I consider sitting up, maybe waving to Randy or walking down to the beach and riding with him on the tube for a while. The sun licks my eyelids and I slip on my shades. People are having a picnic on the grass, just above the edge of sand. Bit-by-bit, their voices fade. I can hear the wind sighing high in the poplars.

I have no idea know how long I've been asleep. I look down the beach.

"Anyone see Sydney?" I ask. Shelley, beside me on a striped towel, shakes her head.

Tom and Randy are still out on the floating dock, too far out to hear my question unless I stand on the shore and screech, like mothers do when searching for their children. I can't do that: I'm no frantic fishwife.

"Great." I get up, and head around the bend, expecting to find her digging in the sand, making castles with her friend.

But no one has seen her. They think she was sitting on the beach with another little girl — Jody — about half an hour ago, but they haven't seen her since. The clerk says Sydney was in the store earlier but she hasn't been back.

I first jog, then run along the beach, searching for her red Speedo suit. She's always loved to play hide-and-seek. Maybe she's playing it now.

"Please God," I bargain, as I scan the length of the beach once more. "I'll do anything. Just let her be okay."

I picked out the picture, the one they're using on the little folder that tells her name, and birth date and the date she died. I wrote her a poem about her and Norm, but my mother didn't think it was appropriate. She went with *The Lord is My Shepherd*. I don't think Sydney would have liked it much, would probably rather have had *Casey at the Bat* or maybe even *Crossing the Bar*, but Mom doesn't really have much interest in what I think just now, so I let it go.

Dad just stands around, silent, offering no opinion on any of the decisions Mom's made about Sydney's service, staring into space like he's lost.

People shouldn't die in summer, when the sweet peas are in bloom, the cornsilk is turning to gold and sunflowers turn their yellow faces to soak up the sun. People should only die in winter, when frost sparkles on the windows, there's three feet of snow, and the garden is sound asleep.

Today, our garden is drooping, and the grass in our front yard is turning brown. The irrigation system has broken down completely and needs some repairs, but Dad doesn't seem to care.

I stand on the brittle lawn, feel the heat from the nearby sidewalk and the rough yellow stucco of the chapel, but my shivering will not stop. "Please, Mom." I'm surprised to feel tears gathering in my eyes. How can there be any left? "Don't make me."

"You have to go," she says, dry-eyed, her face a mask, her hand squeezing my elbow. I am frozen, cannot take even one step. She pushes me toward the entrance of the chapel.

"You'll feel better if you see her one last time," Mom says. "It helps if you say good-bye."

Dad opens the door when he sees us and joins us as we step inside. He plants both hands on the back of the walnut pew, leans, and steadies himself. He's trembling, pant legs quivering as if they were alive. He sinks into the pew, watches with his hollow eyes.

Sydney lies slightly inclined, as if she's been waiting. I catch myself before I wave: a little, helpless, wave. She looks like a waxen princess, her smiling lips glistening with a hint of palest pink.

I didn't see her when they finally found her, tangled in the rope that anchored the dock. My parents had come by then and taken me home.

"Give her a kiss," my mother instructs, her hands firmly guiding me forward. "Today's the time for tears. Tomorrow, at the funeral, you have to be brave."

I kneel beside Sydney, bow my head. Weep. My mother's papery, blue-veined hands are almost gentle as she lifts me, supports me, nudging me closer. "Kiss her good-bye."

And so I do. I kiss those waxen lips and touch her hands, clasped so piously over our grandmother's prayer book. Sydney would snort if she could see. Or fart if she could squeeze one out. I want to grab those little hands, make one into a fist.

I whack my own, knotted fist on the side of her casket: solid, real. I feel the hollow thunk, the sound reverberating above the muted music. My mother starts, frowns. Laughter bubbles in my throat, and I want to slap Sydney awake. I want to grab her, sit her up, make her say anything and everything, cause the biggest ruckus anyone has ever seen in Butte Valley, Saskatchewan, population: one less.

Two days after Sydney's funeral, they send me to camp. I don't want to go but I don't really want to stay home. "It'll be the best medicine for her," I hear my mother tell my grandmother, when she calls to see how I'm coping. "The girls at camp are from Saskatoon, Regina: bigger places, and they probably won't know. She needs to be where something's going on. It's too quiet here."

I protest, but Mom insists. "Just try it," she says. "If you really can't take it, we'll come and pick you up."

I'm afraid of those girls I don't even know. What if they ask me about my family, where I come from, normal questions that anyone would ask? What if they ask me if I have a sister? I've spent a lot of time thinking about that. I don't know the answer.

The first time our camp counsellor takes us to the beach, my heart starts to hammer double time and I feel like I'm going to puke. I tell the counsellor I'm not feeling well, ask if I can lie in the back of the van for a while. She gives me some Gravol to calm my stomach, but it doesn't help.

After that, I avoid the beach, take my runners and back-pack and hike in the crispy, brown hills.

When I return home a week later, all of Sydney's things are gone: her battered old Pooh bear, her stuffed dog Wrinkles that she slept with every night, Raggedy Anne and Andy, all her toys and books. Her blue and yellow cuckoo clock will never crow again. Even her photographs have been taken down from the living room walls, their outlines on the ivy wallpaper growing fainter with each passing day.

Disappeared without a trace. Maybe it's easier for my parents this way but I miss her and wish I had something of hers, like a sweater or a jacket that I could hug at night, something that might still hold her scent so our bedroom wouldn't seem so lonely.

A whole month later, in the morning when I'm making our bed, I feel something move as I tug on the sheet. Sydney's book, *Magic Made Easy in Fourteen Days* is jammed under the mattress, close to my head. Now I sleep with it under my pillow. Sometimes, it helps.

Tom still comes over, though he doesn't stay long and we hardly talk. I spend a lot of time alone, mostly down by the salt lick. And when I'm down here, I don't dream about Randy anymore.

The ventriloquist positions his dummy. "Say hello to Sydney," he says. "Such a pretty name."

"Missing your friend?" he asks as he pulls a scruffy brown Wrinkles dog from the suitcase at his feet.

"Oh yes" Sydney says, hugging Wrinkles. "Remember when I used to be a girl? I lived on a farm with my sister and a dog named Norm. I can see them, sometimes."

"Interesting," the ventriloquist replies, "But it's time to sing. How about "Twinkle, Twinkle, Little Star.""

Sydney opens her mouth. Nothing. She tries again, then shyly buries her head in Wrinkles neck.

"I'm sorry," the ventriloquist says. "But my dummy's tired and we must say goodbye."

He kisses the dummy gently on her cheeks — right, left, centre — and touches her forehead with the inside of his thumb, like a priest baptising a baby. He folds the dummy, and smoothing her springy curls, sets her carefully in the case. He places Wrinkles in Sydney's arms and closes the lid.

    Somewhere in the audience, a child cries.

One evening, at the pumpshack, I hear a voice. "Hey Carol, you won't believe it. I'm not afraid of snakes anymore."

    I sink down onto the salt lick, squeeze my eyes shut.

    She keeps on talking. She must have finally learned to throw her voice. It is coming from everywhere.

Aurora Borealis in the Churchill Sky

Jack ambles to the dirt track edging the west side of Danny's spread, the babble of campfire voices receding, blessed silence a balm to his soul. Northern lights haunt the horizon, crystal blues, greens like Ponderosa pine, and pale, pineapple yellows, fading and faint. He can almost hear the lights whisper as they stir up the stars. The northern lights are women; that's what the natives up in Churchill say. If your whistle's sweet enough, you can whistle them down, get them dancing like crazy all across the sky.

He hadn't stayed up north long — six months tops — but the memories are as constant as the Aurora Borealis in the Churchill sky. Churchill, where the lights flaunt and flicker three hundred nights of a year. Jack's read about the lights, and has stood in awe watching their most vivid displays from November to March.

The intensity of the colours — violet blues or baby, clover greens or palest lime, the bleach of the whites — depends on the strength of the solar wind and gasses present in the upper atmosphere. Gosh, Jack thinks, as a jagged green javelin pierces the prairie sky, whatever makes them tick, they're as pretty as can be.

He loves to stand on his porch on crisp, fall nights now, looking for those lights, while far in the distance, a coyote howls.

The first good blizzard is a bonus to Jack. He looks forward to the downtime he feels he's really earned. When he hears his friend Dan bitching about the Saskatchewan weather, how it's 'cold enough to freeze the balls off a brass monkey' — too damn nasty to even be out bedding up the cows — Jack just smiles.

He'd never experienced the bite of true bitter cold until he'd been assaulted by the Churchill wind. Jack's job, driving a bus full of shift workers to and from the mine, had paid really well, so he'd sucked it up and ignored the cold as best he could. But the heater in the bus had barely put out and, sometimes, he can still feel that bone-chilling ride.

Money. That's what had sent him north. Even before he'd arrived at the pitiful scatter of metal buildings the company called a camp, he was counting his cash. There wasn't one goddamn thing to pass the time, except drinking, and gambling, and drinking some more. He needed five thousand dollars for a down payment on a spread of his own and he kept purple sage at sunset and his own fat cattle firmly in his mind. Gambling was out — it had never appealed to him — but when it came to drinking, he was right there, at the head of the pack. He'd hardly drawn a sober breath the whole damn time, even behind the wheel of the bus.

The lights dance on the horizon now. Sweet cedar smoke drifts in the stillness and Jack fills his lungs. It's a different world up there in Churchill, he thinks to himself. A whole different world.

Jack hears the soft strumming of an acoustic guitar, muted voices, the musical clink of silverware. Dan's branding had taken longer than they'd planned. Those black bastards got the whole herd in an uproar. It was uncanny; almost like they knew.

"Cowboy caviar, ready in five," someone hollers from the fire. Jack's mouth waters, anticipating the pop of the prairie oysters, fried golden on the outside, the insides satin smooth. He hears the crunch of gravel and Dan stumbles up with two frosty Pilsner in his hands.

"Beer?" He offers one to Jack.

"Thanks," Jack says, taking the sweaty bottle and swigging the icy beer. He turns his face to the stars, the cool slide of beer clearing his dust-clogged throat. Under the sky's vastness, he feels insignificant. "Took us long enough today," he says. "We're losing our touch."

The lights swoop down, twist and tease, wriggle away.

"You're sure as hell a big, wet blanket tonight," Danny says. "What's the matter? Take one in the nuts today?"

Jack shrugs, not bothering to reply. It had been a long day. He'd had enough of hot-dogging and cowboy bragging rights. Testosterone. He'd rather be in his special place tonight, the bluff in his north pasture, communing with the stars.

"Woman of yours raising shit again?"

"Yeah, a bit," Jack finally says. One night, after too many, he'd told Dan how he and Sarah had been trying to conceive for two long years and kept coming up skunked. How every spring, she got the baby blues. Every year, it affected her more. Birth and renewal. This year, she wouldn't even come to the pasture with him, watch the gamboling of his newborn calves. She used to love to see the brown and white babies, gangly-legged and awkward, bunting their mother's bags, looking for lunch.

This spring, when Jack's cows were all safely calved, he'd turned his attention to Sarah. She'd been remote, off somewhere he couldn't go. "Got us a date, all set up," Jack told her. "Get your fancy duds. We're goin to town." He'd made a reservation at The Keg. Maybe later they'd go to a movie at the Roxy downtown.

She was kneeling beside one of the free-form flowerbeds that meandered across their yard. "Jack," she'd said, touching the band that held back her long, blonde hair. "I can't. I'm a mess." Wind whipped around the corner and a dust devil danced across the drive.

"Too nasty to be digging today," Jack said. "Flowers can damn well wait."

Their drive to town was filled with the satisfying silence that comes at the end of a well-spent day. Sarah rested her arm along the back of the seat, toyed with the hair above his collar. Shivers ran up and down his spine.

He parked on Main, bathed by the scent of lilacs as he stepped from the truck. Somewhere in the trees, a mourning dove cooed. "Let's walk for a while," he said, and turned toward the park in the centre of town.

Jack has spent more time there than Sarah will ever know — every Saturday in June — when the farmer's market starts. An aboriginal woman sells watercolours there, mostly of children nestled in their mother's arms or little abstracts that look like sperm. Her table is beside a large maple tree and dark-haired toddlers tumble from her blanket when they waken from their naps. She gives them sips of water — a hug — and plops them back on their blanket in the shade of the tree. They watch her, patiently, like very old men. Jack's got more of her art than he can ever afford to frame, stashed in map rolls in the loft of his barn, but he keeps going back, drawn by the wonder in those wide, dark eyes.

Sarah stumbled on a tree root pushing through the pavement, and Jack took her hand. His eyes swept like laser light, returned again and again to the budding maple tree. "We've got about twenty minutes. Reservation's for seven."

Mothers and toddlers played in the park, pink setting sun painting roses on their cheeks. A blue baby carriage was parked beside a bench, a young mother cooing to the baby inside.

A woman, cumbersome with carrying her unborn child, bent to pick a tulip.

"Good evenin'," Jack nodded, touching the brim of his hat.

Sarah dropped his hand. "Can we go home?" she said. "I'm not hungry anymore."

"For God's sake," he said, stalled on the path. He lifted his cowboy hat, scratched his head. "Let's at least eat. I'm hankerin' for a three-inch sirloin, bleeding blue rare. I'm hungry enough to eat the arse-hole out of a skunk."

Sarah walked away, sat on a bench near the path. He had to move closer to hear what she said.

"Look around. Everyone seems to be pregnant but me. I'm so envious of those big, round bellies; it almost makes me physically ill."

She stood up, walked across the grass and slammed the truck door. Metal clanged, the sound bouncing like a ball between the brick buildings lining the street. Jack walked to the base of the maple tree, smoked a rollie he pulled from the pocket of his denim shirt. When he finally joined her, Sarah didn't say a word. He dropped his head to the wheel, sighed, and fired up the Ford.

After two years of trying, of taking temperatures, keeping charts, producing factory sex on demand, Sarah has somehow shifted the blame for their barren state onto him, as if he'd had only one chance for a son and he'd blown it years ago.

Sometimes he wished he hadn't said a word about his kid, to Sarah or to Dan. All he'd told Sarah was he'd been very young, and that somewhere in the world, he *might* have a son. He's tried his damnedest to blank out Churchill, to erase Charlene, her hair gleaming blue in the feeble light of his dingy little room.

The kid had never been an issue between them until Sarah realized they might not be having one of their own. Then, like a shadow, the boy slipped between them more and more.

The guitar is louder now, and someone is singing "Navaho Rug" by Ian Tyson. A simple song.

"Jack?" Dan says. "You and Sarah fighting? What's going on?"

"We're having our moments," Jack says. Out in the sage, a coyote howls. "The baby blues again. Getting a newborn can take years unless we want a mixed-race kid. I suggested it to Sarah but she turned me down flat. Said she wants a baby, not surefire trouble bundled in a blanket right off the reserve."

178

"Sarah be damned," Dan says, setting down his empty beer, the clink of glass on gravel interrupting the echo of the coyote's howl. "You can speed up the process. Buy yourself a surrogate. Be quicker. Shit load more fun."

Dan is like a mustang, Jack thinks, a wild look in his eye as if he were about to bolt and jump sideways over a ten-foot fence. Dan jumps the fence every chance he gets. Jack has always wondered how he pulls it off. After he's strayed, Danny shows up at home laden with gifts. His wife has more fur coats and diamonds than any woman around. Whatever their agreement, Jack thinks, it seems to work.

"I know someone who might help you out," Dan says, his face lit by a gap-toothed grin.

"Forget it," Jack says, grinding a clump of grass with the heel of his boot.

"Think about it," Dan says. "It'll cost a few bucks but it might be worth it. Sarah can be persuaded if she really wants a baby and wants one quick. Sweet talk her, like you used to."

Jack turns, searching the sky, but the northern lights have danced away. The sky is inky black and full of stars, but he's unable to locate even Orion, the most recognizable of constellations. His favourite. He pulls his jacket closer, shaken by an inexplicable chill. The fire winks, draws him closer and Danny tags along. He takes Jack's empty bottle, drops it in a box. Jack spreads his hands above the coals, rubs his leathered palms together, warming his bones. He hears the thud of kids kicking a ball out behind the house, their wild whoops echoing in the yard.

Danny's sister, here from the city, pulls a lawn chair up to the fire. Her son Tommy had seemed thrilled to be at the branding, getting in so close that Jack worried he might catch a good, solid kick. Lose some of his big, new teeth if someone didn't tell him to step back a foot or two. Jack was relieved when Dan finally did.

Tommy runs to his mother's side and she gives him a quick hug. He pulls away, blushing, and Jack pretends to be looking at the stars.

"Having fun?" she asks.

"Yeah," Tommy says. "Can we come to Danny's castration party next year, too?"

Jack snorts. Tommy's mother catches his eye across the fire. She lifts a palm and shrugs. Then she breaks out in giggles like musical notes, ringing in the chilly evening air.

Jack reaches into the frying pan, resting on the flat stones that ring the fire, and grabs a nut. He pops it into his mouth, savouring the taste.

"Jack," Sarah calls from behind a makeshift table near the house, where she's ladling beans. "Better fill your plate. I'm about to abandon my post."

As he fills his plate with potato salad and barbequed beef and beans, Jack notices deep, purple circles under Sarah's eyes. "Tired?" he asks.

"Yeah, eat up," she says. "I'm ready to go home."

When he's finished, Jack walks over, throws his paper plate on the fire and watches the edges smoke and curl before they burst into flame. Behind him, he hears Sarah sigh. He wipes his hands on the front of his jeans. "Be right back," he says.

Moments later, he returns, pulling his Ford up to the fire. He opens Sarah's door. Offers his hand.

"Thanks," she says, "but I'm not entirely useless, you know."

Jack is soothed by the satisfying rumble of his diesel. He turns south, starts the six-mile drive across washboard roads from Dan's spread to his. He reaches across the seat, pulls Sarah close, inhaling her faint cinnamon smell — the same scent that had attracted him years ago — the first time he'd asked her to dance.

"It's hot," she says, sliding back to the passenger side, leaning into the door, making herself small. She's staring into the night, her head turned away, neck muscles taut in the light of the moon.

"So what was the deal with you and Dan?" Sarah finally says, her voice like ice cubes clinking in a glass. "Is there some reason you two can't be bothered to join the rest?"

He clenches his teeth, concentrating on guiding his old beater over the Texas gate. Slowly, so he doesn't shake anything loose. The house windows blink, scatter broken beams of headlights all across his yard.

"Sarah, you know I love the sky. The lights are too bright by the house. I can't see the stars."

"Shoot," Sarah says, sniffing as her hands search her pockets for a Kleenex. He doesn't dare offer his hanky, although it's neatly folded and hasn't been used. She detests his polka-dotted hankies and he's not sure why. God knows, she never washes the damned things. She refuses to touch his jeans, says the stench of cattle in the denim makes her queasy. He's pretty sure he's the only rancher around who does his own laundry.

"It was nice of you to leave me alone all night," she says, sarcasm curling her lip. "I got stuck with Barb. She's treating me like some kind of freak. Like if I'd been born out here, I'd know how to get pregnant. I'm sorry I ever confided in her. And I'm sure she told Dan."

"Honey, she's probably just concerned. And me and Dan haven't even talked." He hates the lie, the way it rolls off his tongue. If she ever finds out how he's blabbed to Dan, Jack knows he'll be the next with his nuts in a pan.

Sarah sniffs, eyes red at the rim, lids puffy. She turns her head, and blonde hair falls across the delicate bones of her cheek. God, she's gorgeous, Jack thinks. Even tonight, when she's obviously the unhappiest woman for miles around.

You don't have the exclusives on that, he thinks and wonders what she would do if he told her the truth, how lately, he'd begun to dream of his son, imagine what he might be like. There's got to be a way to find out, if I really want to know. Dark hair? Brown eyes? Or a shadow of me?

Jack would be out riding — checking his fences — and he'd find himself in the middle of the pasture with no idea how he'd gotten there.

The boy's long, black hair gleams polished steel highlights in the noonday sun. Jack thinks it should be trimmed up a bit. But when the kid spurs his pony, Jack only sees how well he can ride. Took to the saddle like he'd been born in one.

Jack kills the motor, steps into the cool of the night and walks around to open Sarah's door. He hasn't forgotten how to treat a lady. At least they still have that.

The northern lights flash, their afterglow deepening the lines on his face.

"Two eggs or three?" Sarah asks as he slips behind her into the stream of sunshine, nuzzling her neck, inhaling her sweet morning scent. "I'm tired, Jack" she says, moving from his touch. Their lovemaking last night had been a disaster. Once, they'd been playful, like two colts finding their legs, but now everything had turned serious and there was no fun in it.

"Then don't bother," he says. "I'm not hungry anyway." He slams out the door and starts his truck, heading for the north pasture. He has fences to fix. By noon, fluffy white clouds are building in the sky and dust devils swirl at the edge of the road. Shit, Jack thinks, I'm gonna get wet. He bends to add a staple to the second wire of his three-wire fence, and feels someone's eyes, steady on his back. He picks up a handful of staples from the pile by the post, moves down the fence line, stapling as he goes. Still he feels the eyes. Then the wind picks up and the feeling blows away.

Six-thirty, Jack thinks, checking the horizon, searching for the sun. He feels battered and beaten and he's taken a chill. He walks into the silence of his house, straight to the shower, strips and turns on the taps. He stands there, pummeled by water as hot as he can bear, for as long as the forty-gallon hot water tank holds. He towels himself dry with a thirsty burgundy bath sheet, then wraps it round his waist. He searches for Sarah. He finds her tucked under a plaid cotton throw, curled up on the couch. His heart turns over when he sees her hands curled into her breast and a smile curving her lips. He reaches for her hand, changes his mind and for a moment, he strokes her hair.

He slumps to the kitchen — reads about the fragile environment of the Great Sandhills in the *National Geographic* — and eats the ham and cheese on rye that Sarah has left wrapped in waxed paper. A crust gets stuck crossways in his throat and he stands up, hunches over the table, coughing and fighting for air. Finally, he grabs his glass of milk and takes a big gulp. He lurches to the kitchen sink. He's weak in the knees, trembling, like the leaves on the weeping birch at the edge of the yard.

Sarah stumbles in, rubbing her eyes. "Jack," she says, "Are you okay?"

He's surprised to feel her body pressing against his back, her arms going around him as she blows sweet warm breath onto his back. He stands there forever, afraid he might spook her. Through the window, he studies the sky.

Keep your rope coiled tight, close to your side. Don't hesitate. Your calf will pick it up. Snake your rope. One smooth move. His son grabs the saddle horn, holds on tight.

A small noise startles him awake. "Sarah?" She's almost out the door, pressing her pillow tight against her belly, as if she's in pain. "What's wrong?" he mumbles.

"Nothing. I'm exhausted, and, in case you haven't noticed, you're talking in your sleep. Again." She holds her pillow closer, like a protective shield.

"Where are you going?" he asks, wide awake now, his heart beating a bongo against his ribs.

"The guestroom." She closes the door, the click of the latch echoing for an hour in his mind.

It is the start of an unsettling pattern. When she does sleep with him, she's rigid, keeping to her own side of the bed, faking sleep with deep and regular breaths so they don't have to speak, or do anything else. Most days, he works so hard and long, he doesn't really care.

Jack notices a tinge of scarlet on the leaves of the maple tree outside the kitchen window. Next to the maple, the leaves on the willow remain silver, undersides sparkling in the sun. He stands, glass in hand, thirsty, tired, lost in the leaves.

"We've got a home study appointment on Tuesday. Preliminary, of course, but they want it on file," Sarah says. "Our social worker's coming at ten."

He looks at her, and wonders if he can fool anyone besides Sarah when it comes to how he's starting to feel about adopting a kid. He knows they check out prospective parents with a fine-toothed comb. He's pretty sure they'll find a bug or two if they spend much time on him.

He'd planned on going to the Lawson Ranch production sale with Dan. Dan had been over to Lawson's twice last week, eyeing up the bulls. Beef on a bun before the sale and gallons of coffee and Coke. Free, of course. Fletcher Auctioneers ran a damn good sale. Dan had his sale catalogue folded and marked, ready to bid. As soon as the sale was over, Kenny Lawson and his boys would be setting up fold-out tables in the sawdust of the sale ring and hauling in boxes of booze, tubs full of ice. By the end of the night, cowboys — old and young, sober and drunk — would be wrestling on the floor, oblivious to the sawdust and the shit. The prize: a full year of bragging rights. Winner take all.

He and Dan never miss the Lawson sale, even when they have no intentions of buying a bull. Today, they're going over to the ranch to check out the sale bulls beforehand, maybe take some notes. It's easy to get carried away when you're bidding and Jack likes to have a good, solid plan. From his porch window, Jack sees a plume of dust. He likes to travel with Dan. When Dan says he'll be there by ten, Jack could set his watch.

He sits down, begins pulling on his boots, which he'd carefully cleaned and polished the night before. Sarah hadn't noticed, although she was quick to complain if he came into her kitchen with even a hint of shit on his boots. He sighs, cradling his remaining boot in his hand. "Sarah, can we talk?"

"There's nothing to talk about. We want a baby, right?" Sarah turns from the sink where she's washing fresh lettuce, the salad spinner whirring like a whisper.

"Yes, Darlin', we do. And we'll get one." He didn't know how he could make such a rash promise, didn't even know if he really wanted someone else's baby. Jack thinks of his cows, the ones with stillborn calves. Sometimes, you can fool them. They might take another's calf, suckle it, make it their own. But it doesn't always take, and when it doesn't, nothing can change the surrogate's mind. What if it happens with Sarah? With him? He'd be relieved if they could take their name right off the adoption waiting list.

October already. He and Sarah are raking leaves, piling them in the back. It's the first time they've done anything together for a very long time and its almost fun. Sarah drops in the middle of the leaves. "If we had kids," she says, "They'd be spreading these faster than we can pile them up. By the time we finally get a baby, we'll be too damn old to rake." Two spots of bright, rosy red blaze on the planes of her cheeks. Jack walks over, offers his hand. "C'mon, let's take a break. How about hot chocolate? It might warm us up."

He helps Sarah to her feet, admires her body as she brushes crunchy scarlet leaves from her long blonde hair. "Race you to the house," she says and takes off, running full bore.

"No fair," Jack hollers. "You're already half a mile ahead." She's laughing, pulling open the door to the screened-in porch. "Tough," she says. "It's the only way I can win against you."

They sit on the porch, chairs tipped and feet propped up on the sill, drinking their chocolate, which Sarah has spiced with a bit of Irish Whiskey and some real whipped cream. The cattle in the pasture across the road moo for their babies and the calves come running, straight to their mothers. A mystery to Jack.

Sarah reaches out and touches his shoulder. "Jack," she says. "I know I've been a pain in the ass lately. I'm really sorry. I guess this whole baby business is getting me down."

"Shh," he says, pointing outside. "Look. A goldfinch in the apple tree."

Friday afternoon. He's going to town. Jack finds Sarah out back, dirt clinging to the knees of her jeans. She's taken off her gloves. Sarah says gardening with gloves on is like sex with a dube. She prefers to feel the earth. She's mulching, a wheelbarrow of well-rotted manure parked nearby. Every fall, she put in dozens of bulbs, planting by the cycles of the moon. Sketches her perfect phantom garden in graph papers squares. She highlights successes, and strokes heavy black lines on the paper where plants fail to reach the standards set by pretty pictures in the Borden catalogue. "You've got dirt on your face," he says, brushing her cheek. "Anything you need from town?"

"Nope," she says, too busy grubbing in the dirt to look up for more than a moment. "But don't forget the mail. I ordered some bulbs. Hopefully, they'll be in today."

"I'll be happy to deliver your package, ma'am," he says, grabbing his crotch and giving her a wink. He's desperate to break the barrier between them, hoping even a lousy joke might be a start. She'd seemed almost happy the day they spent together raking leaves, but she's withdrawn again, back in her shell. Jack curses his own stupidity. He should have sat on the porch and talked things out. She'd given him an opening.

Sarah squints up at him, wrinkles her nose and keeps on digging.

"God," he thinks. "I sure feel old." He fights the foreign prickle of tears, jams his hat so it shadows his face. He hasn't cried in years.

As he drives across the Texas gate, an unfamiliar wave of relief washes over him. For a moment, he'd thought Sarah might decide to come along. That wouldn't do today.

The distinctive smell of hot grain drifts on the wind, bringing memories of sitting on his dad's knee as the combine munched its way through the fields. He remembers how one spring they'd carefully counted out twenty seeds and laid them on a plate covered with dampened towels. They'd wrapped the whole thing in plastic and set it on top of the fridge, his father explaining how the warmth would speed the germination time. Early the next morning, as he was about to climb a stool to have a look, his dad came in from doing chores. "Not yet, Johnny" he said. "Patience. Nothing grows overnight." He'd soon lost interest, not caring if the seeds were sprouting or not. From the time Jack was old enough to remember, horses and cattle were everything to him. He wonders, now, if his father, a farmer right down to his bones, had been disappointed, and if that disappointment could be measured, like rain in a rain gauge, like the depth of water down a brand new well.

He stops instinctively at the four-way stop. Jack shakes his head, thanking God he hadn't hit someone while driving unconscious, dreaming his dreams.

The post office closes at five. He fumbles with his key. Snatches the card from his mailbox and hurries to the wicket, the card wicking sweat from the palm of his hand. "Got yourself a big envelope," Juanita Morgan, the postmistress, says. "Must be important. Registered mail."

Jack signs, his signature wobbling from the pen, wavery and faint, like an old man's hand. The envelope — plain, legal size and bulky — has no return address. His heart picks up speed, the envelope heavy in his hand.

He hefts it, feels the weight of it. The detective he'd finally hired promised complete discretion and a written report. As he fingers the envelope, a gust of northwest wind sends icy, cold, fingers crawling up his spine. Churchill, he thinks, will that goddamn place ever let me go?

Frosted, frozen boredom had sent him into town. He didn't dare gamble, and besides the drinking, there wasn't much to do. His boots crunched the hard-packed snow, a sharp sound, like grinding the edges from chunks of broken glass. His path lit by the shimmer of the northern lights, he hurried to the Lyceum Theatre in the centre of town. He'd pulled his parka closer and snugged up the hood, blew on his fingers before he put them to his lips. His wolf-whistle ripped the silence of the Churchill night. Goddamn liars. The lights didn't dance; they shimmered far above him in the deep blue bowl of the pottery sky.

He was the token white guy in the ticket line and he wondered if, maybe, he should have stayed home. Two young boys, ahead of him in line, shoved and swore and laughed. One grabbed the other's cap. Serious shit. The hatless one threw a quick left jab and Jack stepped back, gave them some room.

When he looked down, he saw that he was standing square on the tip of a small red runner. "Excuse me," he said, raising his eyes. He saw right off how pretty she was. She wore a light denim jacket, half unzipped, and her thin white T-shirt obviously wasn't doing much to protect her from the cold.

"I'm sorry. Did I hurt you?" he asked. She blushed, a red tide rising on the copper of her skin. She'd dropped her eyes to the sidewalk and hadn't said a word.

Ten minutes later, the line-up hadn't moved. Behind him, Jack heard the chatter of her perfect pearly teeth. He turned. "Here," he offered. "Wear my parka till we get inside."

There weren't many places they could go in a town that size; they often ended up in his spare little room. She was sitting cross-legged on his bed, peeling an orange. The sharp tang of citrus tickled his nose. "I'm pregnant, Jack," she said, tearing the peels into tiny pieces she piled on his pillow.

"You're kidding." He'd been putting on his parka, about to leave for the mess, to pick up some fruit and chocolate bars, a carton of cigarettes that she could take home. The furnace cut in, the roar of the fan filling his head. A kid? His? Christ, he was still a kid himself.

"Have you made any plans?" He thought she'd hold him hostage for a few hundred bucks, but she never mentioned an abortion or money for one.

She looked up, thick black lashes like shades on her eyes. "Are you happy?"

He groaned, dropped his head into his hands. "I don't know," he said. "It doesn't seem real." He looked at her, sitting on his bed, stomach firm and flat. Only fifteen. Jesus, if he'd gotten into trouble like this down home, he'd probably end up doing time, but things were different up North.

After she left, he broke a small bone in his hand when he punched the fir frame of his bedroom door. The nurse at the first-aid hut wrapped it tight in tensor, asked him what he'd done.

"Slammed it in the bus door. Simple stupidity," he'd said.

He was so close. Two weeks away from having the cash, two weeks of overtime away from his dream. His own small ranch. He wasn't even sure she was pregnant, didn't know for certain if the kid was really his. And she wasn't wife material, that much he knew.

When his lay-off notice arrived, he'd nearly kissed the company logo at the top of the letter. A week earlier, he'd noticed lichens and miniature flowers blooming from patches of melting snow by the side of the trail. The bus laboured as he drove to the mine, softening tundra sucking at its wheels. When the frost truly went out, the entire road would sink out of sight.

His charter back to civilization was already booked. Take-off time Tuesday, eight AM. Not much time. Jack ran to his room, threw his few clothes into a battered duffel bag. Left out his toiletries. One more night.

He rifled through the gaping drawers. One final check. In the middle drawer of his desk he found a picture of Charlene. She was straddling his spindle-back chair, the harsh fluorescent light losing the battle with her hundred-watt smile. He held her, studied her face. In the end, he'd placed the picture on the scarred Formica surface of his desk, facing the door.

He tried to call her from the pay phone over at the mess. He listened as it rang, heard the fizzle of frost on the wire, buzzing on the line. "Hey, Char," he said, knowing that she wasn't there to hear. "Sorry, but it's time for me to go."

He sat, nose pressed flat against the window of the four-seater Cessna, as sub-Arctic forest — black spruce, white spruce, rocky outcrops dotted with pine — faded from his view. Churchill. He was never going back.

When his separation pay caught up with him, there was a letter, written on a piece of lined notebook, tucked inside. The note said a girl had brought it to the office and they'd decided to send it along.

Dear Jack, she wrote. *I'm sure sorry you didn't get a chance to say goodbye before you left. They told me at the mine that you'd been called home. I hope everything's okay.*

I have a real strong feeling the baby is a boy. I talk to him lots. I hope his hair is blonde, like yours, but the chances are slim. I'm going to name him John. It sure would be nice if you would write. Love Charlene.

Love? he thought. They'd never even said the word.

Jack settles into the truck, cranks the window down. The tobacco-stale cab closes around him as he picks at the flap of the envelope with his tobacco-stained thumb. Finally, he worries the envelope open, slides the bulky papers onto his knee. He folds the papers open across his rock-hard thighs and begins to read.

> *Report from Churchill: September 11th*
>
> *Subject located. Discretion assured, per your instructions. Private meetings on September 2nd and 5th. Information as follows: Charlene - married to a miner - living in town. Works the 7:00 AM to 3:00 PM shift at the Seven-Eleven every other day. One other child, seven years old. I've seen the boys when they come to the store. They are neat and clean, seem well cared-for. She has agreed to a paternity test for the older boy, Johnny, although she declines your offer of support if paternity is established. Please call the number on the letterhead and leave further instructions on the answering machine.*
>
> Randall Rutherford
> *Private Investigator*

Jack is shaking, holding the papers now with both of his hands. A picture falls onto the seat. He picks it up, stares at the boy. Shoulder length hair, black against the collar of his shirt. His eyes are wide, fringed with thick lashes. Definitely blue. Jack stuffs everything back into the envelope, slams his truck into gear and makes a quick U-turn.

He flees to his special place, the bluff overlooking his north pasture. When he'd first noticed the vague outlines of a circle almost obscured by prairie grass, he'd been intrigued, thinking it a random act of Mother Nature. He likes to think he knows her well.

When he'd seen a blip about teepee rings on *The Nature of Things*, he'd realized the treasure he had, out there in his pasture. He'd searched the library and found a book. He'd read and re-read the section on the significance of the rings, the sweet grass ceremonies held within, the way the circles called down distant dreams, visions from elders gone before. Christ, he thought. I knew there was something strange in the air out there. Now, he feels even more strongly the call of the spirits roaming the bluff and he's drawn there again and again by the mysticism that bathes the entire place.

He parks his truck in the sagebrush at the base of the hill, begins the steep climb to the crest. When he reaches the top, he stops to catch his breath. His hand strays again to his pocket, to the bulky envelope. Unconsciously, he strokes the leather of his tobacco pouch, closes his fingers around it instead, soothed by the soft silky feel. He withdraws his pouch and rolls a cigarette. Jack squats inside the circle, strikes his match on a nearby stone. He bends his head to the flame, inhales the sweet smoke to the bottom of his lungs.

"Sarah, I want you to meet my son."

It will never fly.

"It's just for the summer. I want to ride the pastures, take him along. Maybe teach him some roping, if he catches on quick." Nope.

Jack thinks of Dan, can almost hear him. "Yeah, you got yourself a little problem, damn straight you do. You been thinking about the kid all these years? And you never said a word. Jeez Jack, you are one deep son-of-a-bitch. Whoo-ee! Sarah will be wild."

Jack stares as the leaves on the sparse stand of poplars dance. Shadows move, solidify.

A man crouches by a slow-burning fire, the fringes of his buckskin skimming the dust. Tugging at its tether, a roan stallion rears. A woman hangs a pot on the tripod above the coals, her blue-black hair gleaming in the fading evening light. She touches the man's shoulder; a baby nestled in the cradleboard on her slender back bobs gently as she moves.

Instinctively, Jack's long fingers curve. He feels, for the first time, the wonderful weight of his child.

When the man drops a handful of prairie grass onto the fire, the smoke rises, thinly at first and then with increasing strength.

Heat licks his yellowed fingertips. Jack starts, surprised to see his cigarette burned down to its final twist. He stubs the ashes, drops the dead butt into the pocket of his vest. Deliberately, he rises, picks his way across the hallowed ground. Darkness drops, northern lights flirt with the edge of the sky.

Kenny

I snag my hair on a button and it takes forever to pull it
free. I'm in a hurry and my clothes aren't co-operating.
We're going to visit Kenny today.

My mom's excited and Dad is resigned. He knows she
won't be ready for at least half an hour, and we're already
twenty minutes late. When she gets in a dither like this, she
thinks of a dozen things to do. Like changing her dress. And
packing a box of oatmeal cookies — Kenny's favourite —
that she'd planned to take. It won't take a minute. Made
them special this morning. Then she remembers my school
picture. Kenny will want to see it, will want one of his own.
She'll just slip it into an envelope so it won't get creased.

And on it goes, until she's finally ready. I think she's
nervous. And before this day is over, I know she'll be sad.
Maybe that's why she doesn't really want to start, puts it off
as long as she can.

We said we'd be there by two. It won't matter to Kenny. He can't tell time anyway, but he knows we're coming, so he'll be waiting.

My dad is finally running out of patience. He's already outside, sitting in the car. He's starting to rev the motor just a bit. And it isn't even winter. It's a hot summer day. That's one reason we're going to see Kenny; so we can take him out.

"Kathleen, run out there and tell your dad to hang on," Mom says. "I'll be right out. I just have to find Kenny's sunglasses. I know I put them in this drawer somewhere. I'll be out in two shakes of a dead lamb's tail."

Whatever that means.

We finally leave. It's only a one-hour drive, east across the bridge, but it takes forever. I'm quiet. So are my parents. I've got the whole back seat to myself, and I'm yawning like crazy, but I fight the urge to sleep. I gaze at the horizon, straining to see. If I stare straight ahead long enough, maybe I can make the building appear in the distance.

I can feel the bumps on the highway. *Ka-thump, ka-thump.* The steady whump of the wheels and the sun on my shoulders through the window of our '64 Meteor makes me sleepy, but if I fall asleep, there's no place to lean, no shoulder to give my bobbing head support. No one to shove me back, over the lines, and into my own space. *Ka-thump, ka-thump.*

I think about my grade eight graduation. I'm the valedictorian and I'm not sure yet what I'll say. *Ka-thump.* I roll back the years, think about Kenny and me.

Kenny is six and I am five. It's my birthday. Dad brings home a new bike. He takes out his tools and looks at the training wheels. Reads the directions and tackles the job.

He paid them at the hardware store to put the bike together so he wouldn't have to. He's not too handy and doesn't mind admitting it. He's not happy about having to put the training wheels on himself.

"Well, this doesn't look too bad," Dad says, scanning the instruction leaflet. "Just a couple of bolts and spacers. Kenny, will you hand me the keyhole wrench?"

Kenny hands him the pliers and Dad sighs. Kenny looks at me; worry creases across his brow and a question builds in his eyes. He turns, searching the workbench and now he's got the pipe wrench. I find the keyhole wrench in the top drawer and hand it to Kenny.

Dad is waiting. He's holding the wheels in place and staring straight ahead. Like he's watching a home movie. One where the son grabs the right tool and squats down to help.

"Here, Dad, is this the keyhole wrench?" Kenny looks at my father expectantly, waiting for praise.

"Good boy, Kenny," Dad says. And he installs the wheels alone.

He takes the bike out to the sidewalk and I follow. I can hardly wait. I've wanted a bike forever, but my parents have always said no. Wouldn't be fair to Kenny. He doesn't ride one yet.

But Kenny's had a bike for a couple of years now. At first he tried. He tried so hard. Dad ran behind him, with his hand resting lightly on the seat. Guiding him, keeping him steady. But whenever he let go, Kenny would start to wobble and in no time at all, he'd fall right down. He did okay as long as Dad was there beside him but he just couldn't do it on his own. And one day, after he fell for the third time, he quit trying. Put his bike behind the garage and never tried again. No matter what Dad said. He was done.

Kenny finds something else he likes to do though. He's got an old iron wheel. I think it's the guts from a wheelbarrow because it's got axles on both sides of the hub, which Kenny uses for handles. He runs that wheel up and down the street for hours. His hand are calloused and sometimes blistered from the steel going around and around in his palm, but he keeps going. Keeps going until he's exhausted or 'till the sun sets, whichever comes first. It's like he's trying to make up for not learning to ride the bike.

"See me, Dad? This is hard, but I do it. I don't let go, even when I hit bumps. Sometimes, it hurts me Dad, but I just keep on going. Watch me Dad."

And our dad gives Kenny a pat on the back and tells him he's doing just fine. But he doesn't stay outside to watch Kenny. He walks to the porch and his paper, waiting by his chair.

Kenny stands for a minute, his eyes on our dad's retreating back. Then he turns back to his relentless wheeling. Up and down, up and down. Making grooves in the dirt with his wheel and grooves in his hands with the axle.

Now Kenny is standing beside my father, too. They're both waiting for me to try the bike. I've been waiting for years.

"Okay," Dad says, "Hop on and let's see you ride. You won't need me. You've got the training wheels. Just keep the front wheel straight and you'll be okay."

I'm afraid. I've waited for this day for so long. What if I can't do it either?

Then what will Dad do? And if I can, what will Kenny do?

Dad looks at Kenny and then at me.

"Okay, hang on. We'll get you going." And he runs beside me until he feels me take off under my own steam. And then he lets go and I am riding my bike. Alone.

I feel wonderful and I keep going. I'm not sure how to turn around, so I stop at the end of the sidewalk. Back by our gate, Dad is smiling. He's got his arm across Kenny's shoulder and Kenny is smiling, too. They wave and I wave back.

So it doesn't turn out to be a problem, really. Kenny and me ride together all the time. He just wheels alongside me and I pace myself to him. Riding in tandem, except my mode of transportation is a lot easier than his. I'm easy rider and he's the mule. Hunched over the wheel, running to beat hell, trying to keep up.

One day, Kenny hits a dirt lump. Sometimes he gets watching the wheel — round and round and round and round — and he forgets to check the road.

He has a huge wreck. He bashes his mouth on the iron wheel and cracks his front tooth. He has to have it fixed and Kenny is scared to death of anyone in white. Or any place that smells like antiseptic. Mom says it because he spent a lot of time in the hospital when he was little. It's different now — he's healthy and strong — but Kenny doesn't forget. Even our barber has to take off his long white smock before he can get anywhere near Kenny.

Right after the wreck, Kenny parked his wheel behind the garage with his bike. He never looked at it again.

My training wheels are long gone and now I have to ride alone. I miss him, miss having my pacer. I'm not sure how fast to go by myself. I keep at it until I learn how fast I can take the bumps, when to start braking, how to stand up and jerk the wheel, jumping over obstacles that are in my path. I learn about speed, and freedom.

Kenny comes up with something new to keep himself occupied. He's got a million dinky toys, which he keeps in a box. Now he's got himself another box and a little board about four inches wide. He puts all his toys in one box and sits with the box on his right side. Then he puts the empty box on his left and balances the board on his knees. He slides the little cars and trucks down the board, which he calls his slide'l down. From his right side to his left side, never stopping until the box is empty. Then he switches the boxes around and starts again. He won't stop in the middle. Can't, I guess. If we have plans, if we're going out, we have to wait. We can't go without Kenny and there's no way we can leave him here alone.

Mom tries to schedule his slide'l down days, but she can't, not always. Sometimes he just needs to do it and so he does. No matter what.

Kenny is ready to start school. He has his own knapsack and books and he's so proud. Mom walks him to school every day for a week before school starts so he can practise, and he loves it. He can hardly wait to go.

One morning, Kenny comes downstairs, his slide'l down board cradled in his arms. His knapsack is lumpy and it clinks when he moves. "I'm ready to practise," he says. Mom shakes her head.

"Kenny," she says. "When you go to school, you won't be able to take your slide'l down board."

He holds his board closer to his chest and runs his fingers down the smoothness of the oak. Mom puts her fingers under Kenny's chin, lifts his head so she's looking in his eyes.

"And your knapsack isn't for dinky toys," she says. "It's to carry your books." She tousles his thick, blonde hair. "Your teacher will have all kinds of new things for you to try," she says. "You won't have time for your slide'l down board. Now, run upstairs and put it away."

When Kenny finally turns and trudges up the stairs, I hear the slide'l down board thump on every step.

The first real day of school, we stand on the porch and watch him set off alone. Our mother waves and I stand beside her, watching Kenny go.

She is crying. Her dress has a large blue collar, and the teardrops plopping down darken the blue to mottled purple, like tiny bruises biting the softness of her skin. She wipes her eyes, notices me. Sniffs and tries to smile. "Come on, let's go inside and have tea. You can have honey in yours today if you want."

I wonder what I've done to deserve this bonus, but I don't ask. I just follow her into the kitchen and stir big teaspoonfuls of honey into my teacup. She doesn't even notice, she doesn't tell me tell me that my teeth will all fall out and that any self-respecting Englishman doesn't need honey in a cup of tea. I make the most of it, drinking three cups of tea, stirring in enough honey to make it thick and syrupy. I love this day, Mom and I sitting quietly, drinking our tea in the kitchen.

It turns out Kenny loves school and can't wait to go there. He learns to write his name. K-e-n-n-y. There are big spaces between the letters and his name heads downhill

— right to left — every time. But he's proud and so are Mom and Dad.

He prints his name everywhere. In his books, on his bedroom walls, on the white clapboard porch. Even around the bottom of the town water tower, which is across from our house and a little to the north. He uses yellow chalk. Dad rubs at the chalk, but he can't really get it off. Kenny has gone a bit too far, printing on the water tower. People complain. So Dad has to paint every week, and Kenny has a mission.

"Kenny, you sure can print your name. But you have to be careful," Dad says gently. "You can't just put your name anywhere you want. Just at home okay? You'll have to leave the water tower alone."

But next time we look, Kenny's name is once again scrawled across the base of the water tower. Dad paints over it and Kenny just goes and prints his name there again. I think he likes it there because he can make it so big. He can see it from our front yard.

Finally, I'm ready to start school, too. Mom buys me new books and new clothes and I get a red knapsack. I have a twenty-four set of crayons and ten new pencils. How will I ever use up ten pencils? But I guess if I write my name as often as Kenny does, the ten pencils will be gone soon enough.

Mom stands on the porch and watches me leave for school with Kenny. I keep looking back, but she's not crying. Not that I can see.

I like school. I like my teacher and she helps me discover a love for numbers. Two plus two makes four. It's logic. If you do this, that will happen. If you count by twos, you can get to ten faster. It's so predictable and I love it.

There's a blight on my days at school. Some of the kids tease Kenny and it drives me wild. There's a guy named Jeff, big for his age, who's already failed grade three and he torments Kenny every chance he gets. The rest just follow along like stupid little sheep.

Kenny, Kenny. No he can't. Kenny, Kenny try.

Kenny, Kenny, no he can't. And Kenny don't know why.

I run at Jeff, try to kick him, get him to shut up and leave Kenny alone. I hate it that the others just stand there. Even when they don't join in, they never tell Jeff to stop.

Kenny just smiles at them, looks down, and writes his name in the dust with a stick.

I end up in the principal's office with Mom.

"Yes, I understand she can't just go kicking and scratching people on the playground, but have you listened to her side of the story? It's not fair to her or to Kenny if what she says is true. And I believe her. She's not in the habit of lying to me. I think you'd better look into this further before you discipline her. There's more to this than meets the eye."

But no one will own up, least of all Jeff. Kenny doesn't realize what those kids are doing. He thinks they're his friends. So I end up with detention. Lots of detention. And Kenny keeps going to school and writing his name. Over and over.

Pretty soon, I'm past Kenny in school. I move on to the next grade, and the next. Kenny moves too, but not very far and not very fast. How can you leave your big brother behind? I can't, so I keep watch over him and they leave him alone, at least when I'm around.

One day, Mom and Dad have a big conference with the teachers and the principal. I sit on the hard yellow bench outside the principal's door and strain to hear. Kenny's gone as far as he can, they tell my parents, and he can't go to school here anymore. He's getting too big to be in grade two again and that's about as far as he's ever going to get in regular school. They suggest a residential school, where Kenny can learn other things, like woodworking or cooking.

"No," I hear my dad say, his voice echoing through the empty halls. "You're wrong about Kenny. He's making progress. Believe me, I know. Sending him away to school would break his heart. Can't you see all he needs is a little extra help? He's my son. God help me, I believe I should know what's best."

They talk for a long time and my Dad's voice gets softer until finally, I can't hear anymore. When they leave the office, their shoulders are stooped, their eyes sad. Dad seems surprised to see me sitting there.

"Let's go home," he says. "We've got some talking to do." He rubs his forehead as if trying to smooth the creases that have multiplied across his brow. "I don't know how Kenny will take it."

When they tell him, Kenny heads straight for his room and the slide'l down board. He spends the next six hours sliding his cars up and down, up and down, until finally he falls asleep slumped over the full box on his left-hand side. Dad goes in and gently carries him to his bed. I notice he has trouble lifting Kenny, that he staggers slightly as he carries him. Mom has pulled the covers back and when Dad lays him down, I tuck Kenny in. He doesn't even wake up. Just snuggles down and smiles in his sleep at some dream that's making him happy. .

I've never tucked Kenny in before. Somehow, it makes me feel older, snugging those blankets around his shoulders, making sure he's warm. I've grown up and Kenny's stayed the same. I used to be the little sister but now I'm not. I'm in grade eight. I wish for the past.

Kenny loves babies, like most people do. He loves to hold them and rock them. He's got a special touch with a fussy baby. When Mom's friend Marlene comes over for tea, her baby usually fusses a lot. Kenny takes over, holding the baby and rocking, rocking, rocking. Marlene's been Mom's friend for years, so she understands about Kenny, how proud he is to be helping, but when we go downtown, and Kenny tries to peer into a carriage or goes over to goo-goo at someone's baby, people stare and get scared. I want to smack them, tell them Kenny likes to make babies smile. What's so odd about that? He might look a little different, but he's just like anyone else when it comes to babies. But mothers hurry out of the store and don't look back.

Some are almost rude. "Excuse me, but I don't allow strangers near my baby." As if anyone in this town is a stranger. But that's what they say to Kenny. And he smiles and goes away, just like he's been told.

I buy him an ice cream cone and take him home. I give him a cloth to wipe his face when he's done, then I go to my room and cry. And Kenny goes to his room and plays with the slide'l down board for hours and hours. Sliding his little fleet of cars and trucks up and down, up and down. Sometimes, I wish I had a slide'l down board, too.

Dad still tries with Kenny. He takes him out to the garage and shows him the tools and tells him their names and what they're for. "Okay, Kenny. Do you remember this one?" He's holding the keyhole wrench in the palm of his hand.

"It's a small wrench for small jobs. Do you remember what we use this one for?"

And Kenny reaches for Dad's hand and takes the wrench. Picks it up and feels it and looks at it, first one side and then the other. He's concentrating hard, his brow creased with thought.

"It's for opening the paint can, right?" He looks at my father and waits.

Dad sighs and takes the wrench from Kenny. "Yeah, you're right," he says. "I guess you could use it for that." And he turns away.

Kenny wants to help. "Next time you have to paint, Dad, I can help you open the can. I know you like to paint, Dad, because you're always painting the water tower, right Dad?"

Kenny has not forgotten how to spell his name. He still likes to write it, over and over again. And my father keeps on painting, over and over again.

I have a ninety average. I have to. I have to be the best at everything. Mom and Dad tell all their friends about my marks, how I excel at science and math. They talk about my sports teams, how I'm the representative from grade eight on the student council. It's like I have to be twice as good, to make up for Kenny. So they won't feel like it's their fault, like there's some genetic flaw they inadvertently bestowed on poor Kenny.

One and one is two; or two and zero is two. Mathematics: my strong suit.

Sometimes, Dad gets his back up about Kenny. I've never ignored or been embarrassed by my brother. He's just Kenny. Always has been. The only time I questioned his purpose in life was when I had to take on half the damn schoolyard in his defence. Pretty hard to fight a mob all by yourself. But I used to try.

That's why I felt kind of guilty when Kenny had to quit going to school. I did miss helping him with his shoes and his coat in the morning, tying his scarf and pulling his mittens, missed walking to school beside him, but I never missed the taunting, the teasing, the stares. When he had to stop going to school, the torture stopped for me. So Kenny's misfortune made my school days easier. I enjoyed my life more and as time went by, I missed Kenny less.

Anytime he drinks, which, luckily, is not very often, Dad gets a chip on his shoulder about Kenny. He's not usually the argumentative type. He just shrugs away his troubles and looks forward to tomorrow. But whiskey changes all that. He starts worrying about the future, about what will happen to our family, to Kenny when he grows up. He asks me all kinds of questions.

"When you go away to school and make new friends, will you tell them about Kenny? What about when you get older and get a boyfriend? Will you bring him home? Or will you just forget to mention Kenny?"

"What are you talking about? Of course I'll bring friends home. Why wouldn't people want to meet Kenny?" Sometimes, I don't understand my Dad. He doesn't even listen when I try to answer his questions, just keeps hammering away with new ones so

I pretend to be studying and, thank God, he has enough sense to leave it alone. I have enough to worry about — keeping my marks up, practising piano, scoring the winning run for my ball team — without starting to worry about the future. I live for today. Just like Kenny.

Two months from now, I'm going to graduate. Grade eight graduations might not be any big deal, but it'll be the only graduation some of these kids will ever have. Seeding and summerfallow come first, pre-empting school, like storm warnings cutting into the final scene of Bonanza. Sometimes, after the farm work is done, too many school days have slipped by and there's no chance of catching up. School is over, the real work begun.

Kenny is graduating, too. But not from school.

He starts to spell his name wrong and then he quits printing entirely. No more "Kenny" anywhere. Dad puts his paintbrushes away and the town water tower is safe.

Kenny starts to stay in his room most of the day, playing with his slide'l down board. He stops coming to the kitchen to help. He doesn't even go to the garage to pass Dad the wrong tools anymore. When Dad comes in and asks for help, Kenny ignores him, as if he didn't even hear. Sliding his cars up and down, up and down. Day after day. Without end.

Psychologists and learning specialists come to our house with charts and graphs and questionnaires. Puzzles and shapes and songs. Kenny just ignores them and concentrates on his slide'l down.

Finally, they pack up their stacks of notebooks and cartons of gizmos and games. They stand on the porch and tell my parents that Kenny is regressing. That if he keeps it up, he'll be like a baby. A large, unmanageable baby. "If you continue to keep him at home, he'll never progress. He's putting a huge strain on your family and your marriage and the environment in your home is not helping Kenny. He needs guidance, a firm hand. An atmosphere conducive to learning. He can learn basic skills such as cooking and cleaning, maybe even some assembly line sewing or riveting. He needs stimulation, a chance to grow. We have brochures from several excellent schools. We suggest you study them, and keep in mind what's best for your son."

After they leave, our parents stand on the porch, unmoving, as if zapped by a stun gun. Dad lifts his hand to his collar, drops it without bothering to straighten his tie. Mom opens her mouth. Nothing happens. Finally, she finds her voice but it's rusty and low. "I thought we were doing the best for Kenny. Loving him and accepting him. He's part of our family." She rubs her hands along her arms, stops at her shoulders, holds herself to stop the shaking. "How can we possibly send him away? How could we explain it to him? He'd never understand."

Dad reaches for Mom, unwraps her arms and takes her hand. He strokes it over and over, but doesn't say a word.

They procrastinate. They talk to Kenny more. They try to get him to join us, to be part of us again. If they insist, he'll leave his room and usually come when we go for a drive. But when he comes downstairs, he doesn't sit around for long and when no one is looking, he disappears. Back to the world where he's happy. Back to his room and the slide'l downs.

Finally, reluctantly, they choose a school. They go there to meet the administrators and see the facilities. Talk to Kenny about it, and talk to me. At night, I hear the murmur of their voices, looking for a way out.

Kenny graduates before I do. He leaves home with his favourite knapsack — the koala bear that clings to his back — and one suitcase with wheels. At Kenny's new school, the students wear uniforms. His room is smaller than his room at home and he has only one dresser for his personal items; he has to leave a lot of his precious things behind. No toys or books from home. They have a whole new program for him to follow and they want to break the ties to his old life. To *make him over*, so he can be a *productive member of society*.

He doesn't even have a stuffed animal to take with him. I give him my favourite, a hippopotamus named Charlie, with a fat belly and big brown eyes. He's worn and smooth, but he comforts me. Kenny might like something to hug, I think.

I'm not sure Kenny understands why we leave him there, on that first day. I hope he doesn't wait for us, knowing we've always been there for him, that we would never leave him. Waiting alone as the sun goes down, watching. Like he used to. Sitting on the front porch, waiting for Dad's car to pull around the corner. I can still see him running out to the gate, hollering. "Dad, Dad, it's me Kenny. Hey Dad, I'm right here, waiting for you."

We don't return for a whole month. They say it's best if we don't. Kenny needs time to *acclimatize*, to get used to his new way of life, *his new home*. He doesn't need to be reminded of how things used to be. "Don't worry, if any problems arise, you'll be the first to know. We pride ourselves on how well our residents adjust. Kenny will love it here. Just give him some time to settle in."

So today is our first visit. I can see the cords taut on the side of my father's neck, and the silence is thick in the front seat. Mom and Dad don't know what to say to each other, or to me. Nothing can make this easier. The balance of this day belongs to Kenny. He's holding the scales, has the power to set their minds at ease or make the rest of their days intolerable. I close my eyes and pray.

Kenny is on the porch when we arrive. He's been waiting since breakfast time by the looks of it. A piece of toast curls on his breakfast tray, the jam dried on its surface and he hasn't even touched his orange juice. I think he's been sitting there, rocking back and forth, back and forth, waiting for his father.

His face lights up as we mount the steps. He gives Mom a kiss. Me, too. But he is shy with Dad, offering his hand. A handshake from Kenny. Is this progress? I'm not sure and I don't think Dad is, either. He wants to hug Kenny, actually starts to reach for him and then notices the outstretched hand. He takes Kenny's hand in his and shakes it, over and over.

"Well, Son, you look fine today. Are you okay?"

"Hey, Dad, wanna see what I made? I made it all by myself, Dad. And I held the drill. Come on, I'll show you, Dad." And he leads us on, saying "Dad" every third word, as if to reassure himself.

After Kenny shows us around, the administrators want to meet with my parents. They have kept a half-hour block of time open for a conference. My parents want to spend every second with Kenny, but how can they say no?

So they go, but only after telling me a dozen times, "Make sure to stay with Kenny. He's been looking forward to this for a long time. We don't want to disappoint him."

Kenny wants to show me his room. We walk through a labyrinth of hallways. Kenny leads and I follow.

Signs are posted everywhere. VISITING HOURS BETWEEN TWO AND EIGHT, NO SOLICITING, KEEP

VALUABLES IN SAFE AT ALL TIMES, ALL VISITORS
REPORT AT FRONT OFFICE.

Kenny heads for his room. I wonder if it's become his sanctuary, just like his room at home. He closes the door and jams a chair under the doorknob. He digs under his bed, between the mattresses and pulls out seven dinky toys. He takes the pillows off the bed. He squats on the floor behind the bed, feels around under the springs and pulls out a ruler he must have hidden there. Then he starts to play slide'l down. Only the ruler is so pathetically small, his cars keep sliding off sideways and he retrieves them and tries again and again.

I watch him and I feel a squeezing somewhere. It's really hard to breathe. He finally gets all seven of his little toys to slide from the pillow on the right to the pillow on the left. He smiles — a huge, sun-drenched smile — and puts his stash away. I guess he's doing something that is not allowed.

Kenny: my big brother, my little brother. He smiles at me, co-conspirators, and I smile, too.

We go back to the common room where the other visitors are waiting and we look out the windows at the beautiful day.

Our parents return. We go outside and have lunch on the deck, which overlooks a creek. Kenny notices three ducks bobbing by and points them out to me. Some of the others, eating their meals outside, don't even look up from their plates, seemingly unaware of the beauty surrounding this place. The food isn't bad, although the salad's a bit warm and the soup is cool. Kenny's table manners have always been the best, and he's quick to thank the aide who brings him his tea. Our mother smiles.

When we go back in, Kenny shows us the workshops and the exercise room. Then he takes us to see his room and the day is gone.

It's time to go. Mom and Dad kiss Kenny and hug him long and hard. He hugs them back, but he doesn't cry. Mom does.

I look at Kenny, silently making him a promise. I know what he needs. The next time I come — and it'll be real soon — I'll be bringing it. His slide'l down board. It won't be quite as long — I'll have to take it out to the shop and adjust the size so he can slide it between his mattress and the box spring — but it'll be enough.

The Merc and Me

I'm looking for Katy. Last time I saw her, she was guzzling
beer like there was no tomorrow, biting the caps off the
bottles to impress her friends. So far, she hasn't got so much
as a chipped tooth, but it makes me shiver to watch her,
biting with a quick twist and handing the open beer over
with a smile. When she's drinking beer, she's almost always
smiling. At least there's that.

Right now, she's smiling at Murray, offering him a sip.
It's surprising, because Katy doesn't share her beer. It
makes me wonder if they've got something going. Hard to
tell, with Katy, but it would be really weird. Last night
Murray tried to kiss me.

Somehow, Katy got the car so we could come to Maxine's
cabin at Clearwater Lake. I think she only asks me along in
case she gets too drunk. I'm the kid sister, so how I ended
up being her keeper is beyond me.

We were supposed to be water skiing today, but that
never happened. At Clearwater Lake, there's no water

skiing on Sundays, so we've already missed our chance. I feel like crying, because that's why I came.

What happened was the whole damn group ran out of beer — a real emergency — so Katy took our car and got some more.

Our family's only got one car and Katy doesn't get it often. I don't suppose our dad has any idea that Maxine's parents are gone and won't be back 'til Tuesday. If he did, this day at the lake would have been out for sure.

Now it's time to go home. I'm ready, but Katy isn't.

"Come on Katy. We promised we wouldn't be late and it's almost suppertime. We gotta go. Now."

It's an hour drive from the lake to our farm, but Katy isn't concerned. She looks up at me from her perch on a full box of beer. "Chill out, kid. I'm gonna call Dad. Will you relax if I call and get the official go-ahead?"

So I promise, although I doubt that even Katy can appease Dad while we still have possession of his precious car. Mostly, she gets her own way if she talks long enough, but sometimes, even she strikes out.

There's a telephone booth across the road and down a bit from Maxine's. Katy is searching her pockets for a coin. She comes up empty, of course. "Got change?" she asks, and Maxine flips her a dime from a jelly jar full of change on the windowsill. Katy ambles down the lane, taking her own sweet time. I follow, because, really, you can't trust her very far.

"Hi, Dad? Yeah, it's me, Katy. Uh huh, I know we're late." She's got the receiver tucked under her chin and she's gesturing with her hands, as if Dad could see. "Of course not. Well, maybe just a couple." She holds up two fingers, waves them at me. "Oh no, I'm sure I can still drive . . . Oh, no, don't worry, it'll be fine with them . . . Okay, okay, I won't. Yup, I promise. And don't worry. We will."

She bangs the receiver down, gives me the thumbs up. She's gotten us a reprieve, promised Dad we'd be home by 10:00 AM. Sunday, no later, so we'll still have time to make it to church.

After that call, it's all systems go. The cops show up at about 3:00 AM, and their flashing lights jerk me right out of a nice, sound sleep. It takes me a long time to drift back down but at least Katy and Maxine and the crew damp down the noise for a while.

This morning the lake is dead calm. So is everything else around the cabin. It's a far cry from last night when the cops showed up and everyone scattered, in a big rush to hide their booze, tripping and pushing and cursing holy hell.

The sun is rising over the hills, spilling light across the lake towards the beach and public campground. On our side, the shade still holds, so it'll be cool for another hour or two.

Those lucky enough to be solidly laid out from last night's beer might get another couple hours of dreamless sleep, but not me. I'm looking for Katy. I've already checked all the rooms, including the can, just in case she is in there horking. God, I have no idea how many beers she downed last night. Her capacity amazes me. Scares me.

I pick my way across the verandah littered with empty bottles and partiers.

Their bodies are curled up for warmth, most of them sleeping where they dropped. Maxine's sprawled on a sleeping bag and there's a guy right next to her, but I can't tell who. He's got his leg thrown over her hip and his head is tucked into her shoulder. I'm not sure if he's breathing, he's lying so still.

Katy, I see, has at least had the sense to drop on the lounger on the south side of the verandah. Someone even threw an old sweater over her. I wonder who's been taking care of her.

"Come on Katy, it's already eight. You promised Dad we'd be home in time for church. We've gotta stop for gas and by the time we get home, we'll be just under the wire. Now haul ass. You're the one who made the promise."

She snuggles beneath the sweater and starts to gently snore. I poke her. No response. I poke her again. "Get up. Right now."

"Jesus, will you at least make yourself useful? I need water."

"Shit. Who was your servant last year?" I grit my teeth, look out to the lake. A seagull dips and dives, flashes silver. He flips a perch, gulps and is gone. Katy groans. "Okay, Your Highness," I say. "I'll get your water, but you better be up when I get back." Inside the dark and quiet kitchen, I find a clean glass. I take her the water.

She's dead to the world so I shake her, hard. She groans, rolls over and comes up swinging. If there's one thing Katy hates, it's someone waking her up before she's ready.

I throw the water into her face. She splutters and curses, throws a few left hooks and a solid right.

I'm already running toward the car. I jump in, fumble with the keys, and start the engine.

"You better turn that damn car off. We've hardly got enough gas to make it to the service station as it is." She bashes her fist on the hood and glares at me through the windshield.

I shut the car off and wait.

She's checking her jeans, searching in every pocket. I guess she forgot about the beer run. She spent every cent we had. Luckily, I managed to snag a fin and put it in my own pocket. Thank God.

She glares at me. "You've got some coin I hope."

"Five bucks," I say.

"I'm driving." She opens the door and waits for me to get out. She's quite the sight this morning. Her eyes squint against the sun, mascara streaked across her cheeks, accenting the paleness of her skin. Her hair is wild and she reeks of smoke.

"Okay," she says. "Fork over the cash."

I do it without thinking, pulling the bill from my pocket, holding it in my open palm. She snatches it. In the blink of an eye, the five is gone. She's eaten the goddamn thing. She takes about three chews and swallows it. Opens her mouth and shows me.

"Are you nuts? I screech at her. "Or still drunk?"

She stretches, a big housecat stretch. Looks at me and grins. "Ha!" she says.

"Gonna have a hell of a time driving home without gas. Maybe we can borrow some money later. No use waking anyone now. They'll just be pissed off. Might as well sleep a little longer."

She heads back to the verandah, anticipating sleep. She's laughing, digesting the cash and enjoying it at my expense.

I dig in my pockets, find a dime to call home. To say the least, Dad is not pleased when I tell him we've got a nail in our tire and the tire guys won't be at work until noon. He doesn't believe a word I'm saying.

I feel like crying and I'm too damn mad to sleep, so I go into the gloom of the summer kitchen and boil the kettle. I fill the old tin dishpan and wash the dishes. Then I clear the remains of last night's festivities. I dump the ashtrays, put empties back into cases and wipe the table, sticky with booze. When I'm done, I grab a magazine and sit, tapping my foot on the cool linoleum, wishing it was Katy's head.

I should never have come with her to this stupid party in the first place. I might have known I'd end up babysitting. You'd never know Katy's two years older than me. She just doesn't give a shit about anything. She goes full out, parties till she pukes. Then she passes out, and lets things work themselves out. Which they usually do, when I'm around.

I'm feeling guilty about missing church, about making Dad and the others miss it, too. One thing about our Dad, when he makes a promise, he follows through even though taking six kids to church every Sunday can't be fun. Before our parents could even get married, Mom says she had to give up ownership of her ovaries to the Catholic Church. She and Dad promised to raise their yet unborn babies in the Catholic way. Mom bore the babies, but making proper Catholics out of us was entirely up to Dad.

Us girls know how to act in church, but our stupid brothers haven't a clue. The two of them sit there and try their damnedest to fart or burp and almost every other Sunday, my brother John pulls a faint. He'll do anything to escape before Communion starts.

The kids will be relieved if we don't show up with the wheels on time. I can't say the same for Dad. He's not going to breathe easy until we pull up the drive.

In the coolness of Maxine's kitchen, I shiver, whether from the cold or dread, I'm not sure. I head for the verandah, looking for a place to rest. No use doing anything more around here. Nobody will even notice and when they finally wake up, they'll no doubt just mess the place up again.

Why should I worry anyway? It's not my parents' place. We could never afford a place at the lake. Maybe if Dad would sell machinery, instead of going to auctions and buying blades and harrows and old harnesses every time he's got a nickle to spare, we could buy a cabin before we're all too old and feeble to hang onto a ski rope.

His equipment takes a lot of repairing and all he does is fiddle and fix and scratch around all day in his little piece of God's green earth, as he calls our farm. In a family like ours, even owning a car is a luxury.

I find an old patchwork quilt thrown in the corner, grab it and head for the big wicker rocker. I pull my feet up and tuck them under my butt, wrap the quilt around my shoulders and stare out at the lake. Light glances off the ripples in the water and breaks into glints of purple and amber and green. By afternoon, the boats will have it all churned up, but right now, the ribbons of colour are bobbing beneath the water, touching the sand. You can feel the silence.

The sun is piercing my eyelids and a sweat bead breaks free, trickles down my upper lip, tickling me awake. I look around, find the place deserted. Where is everyone? I see our car is out back, so at least Katy hasn't buggered off to some other party without me.

I gather up our towels and bathing suits and walk out to the car. Maybe if I get everything ready, Katy will have enough sense to head for home. If and when she finally decides to show, most likely Katy won't be ready to go home. Dad can work up an awful head of steam if you give him the chance, and we're walking a pretty thin line as it is.

The plastic seat covers protecting the red velour upholstery are sticky in the heat, so I roll down all the windows. Someone has set a beer on the Merc's hood and it's tipped over, Bohemian washing down the front of the car and drying on the grill. I grab the bottle and set in on the porch steps.

I find a sodden T-shirt on a kitchen chair and take it out to the car, begin rubbing the hood, trying to erase the beer stains while checking the hood for scratches. Hopefully, the idiot who left his bottle at least made sure it wasn't sandy before he set it on my father's car.

The beer is dried in foamy streaks and I can smell the hops in the sun. If I can smell it, I know my dad will too, so I sneak through the bushes to the cabin next door and grab a red plastic pail from the kid's sandbox.

I walk toward the lake, moving along the side of their cabin with care, not making a sound. I imagine these were the folks who called the cops last night, so I don't suppose they'd look kindly on me stealing their kid's toys.

It takes me three trips to the shore and back before I'm satisfied. The car looks better than it did when we left the farm. Beer works really good for removing bugs. It also seems to work well for removing brains, cause now it's one-thirty PM and still no sign of Katy.

On the verandah, I go through every pair of tossed jeans I can find, looking for a dime to make another dreaded call, when Katy and Maxine, with Murray and two other guys I've never seen, pull up in someone's rusted out Chevy.

They pile out like rabbits from a hat, and I wonder how they managed to get everyone in to start with. They open the trunk and begin unloading vast quantities of beer.

"Katy, where have you been? Sometimes I think you don't have a brain in your head. Dad will be furious, and we still haven't got any gas."

She flashes me a confident grin and as the last beer case is unloaded, I spot a red jerry can at the back of the trunk.

"Here" she says "I've been out getting the gas while you sleep like you don't have a worry in the world. Better not say I never help out."

And she waves toward the gas can as she heads to the verandah and grabs herself a cool one.

The can is heavy and I have trouble heaving it over the lip of the trunk. I'm in a hurry, want to get on the road before Katy has time to drink more beer. One is okay and two is still fine, but getting her to come home anytime after number three will be damn near impossible.

I'm not sure I'll be able to accomplish my task within the two-beer time limit when I feel someone's hand on the heavy can, almost covering mine. I look up from my determined dragging, and there's Murray, looking at me and smiling his big lazy smile.

"Here, let me give you a hand. This can's way too heavy for a little girl like you." He lifts it like it's bone-dry and walks to the car.

I'm so grateful I feel like crying. No one else has even noticed; they're all so intent on getting their first beer while it's still frosty. Not that Murray doesn't like his beer, too. Last night, when he tried to kiss me, he was so drunk he missed my mouth and ended up kissing my left cheekbone. I'm sure he doesn't even remember, but I do, and I feel my face start to flush.

He empties the can into the gas tank and looks at me, smiling. "There, that should get the old girl back on the road." He gives the fender a pat, finishes screwing on the gas cap and throws the jerry can into the back yard.

I notice the muscles bulging against the shoulder of his ripped T-shirt.

I feel the flush creep up my neck again. Damn this blushing! If I could just control it. But of course, I can't, not any better than I can control Katy.

"Okay, Kiddo, just toss me the keys and we'll see if we can get her fired up.

She was almost sucking air so it might take a pump or two. Gotta watch you don't flood her."

I hesitate, looking for Katy. She's sitting on a lawn chair down by the beach, using her lovely white teeth to twist the cap off yet another bottle of beer.

Murray's waiting. "Toss me those keys and let's see what happens."

I look at him, sitting impatiently in the driver's seat, but I don't toss the keys. I walk around to the passenger side and get in. He flashes me a grin and brushes my palm lightly as he lifts the keys from my hand.

The old Merc starts first crack. That's one of the reasons my dad bought it.

It might not be a great beauty, but it's big, and reliable, too. Dad's so damn proud of his car it's almost sad.

"Thanks a lot," I say, as I open the passenger door, gingerly arranging my sunburned legs so they don't stick to the hot plastic seat covers. "Can you tell Katy we're ready to roll?" But Murray has no intentions of leaving. He reaches across my body and pulls the door closed again while throwing the car in gear.

"Not so fast," he says as he guns the motor. "We might as well take her for a spin." He flips a u-ball out of the yard and onto the narrow gravel road, fishtailing like crazy. He's started out too fast, and, for one heart-stopping moment, I think we're going to slide off the gravel and into an approach. Thankfully, he eases off the gas and at the last possible moment, he straightens out.

"Want to do some ditch dipping?" he yells, over the sound of the wind whipping through the windows. He doesn't wait for an answer and now we're in and out of the shallow ditches, still at breakneck speed.

"No, please, you've gotta stop!" My tears dry instantly in the hot wind. "My dad will kill me. No one but Katy is supposed to drive this car. We promised. For God's sake . . . "

He's holding the wheel lightly with one hand. The ditches whirl around us, up and down. My stomach lurches every time the old Merc does and I hang onto the dashboard for dear life. The waves of wheat lining the roadside fly by in a blur as we top the rise onto the gravel road, heading west toward the highway.

"Great, eh?' Murray says, grinning.

"For God's sake, slow down!" I holler above the roar of the wind.

"Okay," he says, "I will, if you slide over a little closer," and he pats the seat beside him.

I'll do anything just to get him to stop. As I slide over, he slows the car to normal and I begin to breathe again, my body sagging against his in relief.

Suddenly, he drops his arm, which he'd been resting on the top of the seat behind me and his hand grazes my breast. I lean forward, fiddle with the radio and ignore him. His hand slips away. Maybe it was a mistake. After a few minutes I relax.

Next time he makes his move, there's no mistake as his oil-stained fingers slide down my breast. I jerk from his touch, grab the wheel and give him a good solid elbow at the same time.

He reacts by flooring the old Merc, wrestling the wheel from me as he holds down the gas. We slew wildly down the gravel leading to the intersection.

The approach to the highway is too steep, and as Murray tries to straighten the wheel, our tires lose contact with the ground.

Murray is still steering, but it's having no effect. When we hit the dirt with the wheel twisted sharply left, the old Merc just can't right herself. She begins a slow cartwheel, ungainly and awkward, like a two-ton ballerina.

Everything has slowed down, even my screaming. It seems endless in the hot afternoon. The car finally comes to a rest on its roof, having done a whole flip and half of another. My heart has stopped, and it doesn't start until the pain in my shoulder gives it a jolt. I reach up, feel a shard of glass, and with shaking hands, I pull it free. Somewhere close by, a meadowlark sings.

I check. My limbs still move. I start to cough, a gut-wrenching hack, full of dust and dread. I wipe a gob of spit on the hem of my shirt before I crawl toward the blown-out back window. The shattered glass crunches beneath my butt and I'm careful where I put my hands.

The rim around the back window is jagged, teeth of glass glittering in the sun. Metal groans and I hear a hissing sound. I shinny across the glass moonscape. With my forearms, I pull myself through the dirt until I'm clear of the wreck. I feel like I've been on the working end of a jackhammer for a whole day.

Murray. I can't see him anywhere. I go back, crouch by the car, but he's not inside. I wobble to the front of the car, my long, muscular legs suddenly failing me. Maybe he's crushed beneath the hood. Then I hear him moan and find him in the long grass, lying on his back.

"Jesus," he says, shading his eyes and looking up at me, seemingly unhurt except for a light scratch across his cheek and a shirt that's ripped from armhole to hem. "Didn't know your old boat had the guts for a ride like that. Wanna help me up?"

I reach down to give him a hand, but stop halfway and smack him, hard, leaving the rosy imprint of my hand on his cheek. I kneel on him, pushing my full body weight into his belly.

"Take it easy, Babe," he says, tatters of the clouds above us reflecting in his wide blue eyes. "You don't hafta flip."

"You idiot," I holler, pushing harder against his ribcage. "You just wrecked my dad's car and you don't give a shit. Anything to cop a feel, right?"

His eyes are wide and I can feel his muscles knotting, his entire body tense.

"Okay, asshole," I say, "You're so interested, take a damn good look."

And I strip off my T-shirt, throwing it into the wind where it sails for a glorious moment before it hits the dust in the summerfallow behind me. I undo the clasp of my bra and drop the straps.

Suddenly, Murray is deathly still beneath my body. I stare down at him and he turns his head away, closing his eyes.

"Chickenshit," I say, as I stand, spitting in the dust beside him.

I walk away, scanning the horizon, looking for Katy.

My Brother's Best Dress

Gordon steps from the summer porch, the snap of the screen door echoing in the silence of the yard. He lifts his head, like a bloodhound searching for a scent. Smoke in the air? He curses his neighbour, Michael Mahoney, and his damned diversification plan. The man would sell off his children if he could get a decent buck. Mahoney had converted part of his orchard to an RV camp three years back. Now the apricot section is dotted with campers and tents and — if the campers don't bother picking them — the sun-sweet apricots rot on the trees. But it's the fires in the campsites that worry Gordon every night. One stray cinder and his cherries could be cherries jubilee. The grass fires he's seen sweep across the prairies roar in his mind as he walks among his cherry trees, searching for a spark.

Fire. It's always been fire. Gordon's entire family is peopled with pyromaniacs.

Light the two silver tapers that traditionally flank the Christmas buffet, and a room full of chattering relatives will fall strangely silent. Light the large crimson pillar at the centre of the feast and one by one, the whole crowd begins to stare.

He walks back to the lane, thinking of family reunions. He's watched in the evenings when the guitars come out and the campfire is lit. Without fail, cousins make lighted figure eights and circles with sticks they've held in the flames, embers smoking and glowing as the fire sticks swoop through the night. They don't seem to notice campfire singing; they rarely stop their fire-play to join with the rest. Gordon worries a spark flying off one of those sticks will start the whole prairie on fire. Late at night, when all that is left of the campfire is glowing embers, all his cousins will be staring — silent and transfixed — into the coals.

Gordon shudders to think of the next family reunion, scheduled for his orchard in two years time. The prairie branch of his family has multiplied faster than he can keep track. He can't even remember the little ones' names. His own family has shrivelled and dropped from the tree; now there's only him and Cy. When the prairie folk show up, there will be no fires burning long into the night, no glowing figure eights among his beloved cherry trees. Gordon has already decided to put a ban on bonfires for the entire event.

He pauses, hand on the smooth silk bark of his oldest cherry tree. When he'd moved to this B.C. valley, thirty years back, he'd had no knowledge of orchards. He had to learn by reading and watching. Now he's an expert at pruning and grafting, and he's proud of the way the branches weep toward the ground, huddling over their precious fruit, making his cherry picking easier than most other harvests at his end of the lake. Still, harvest is a worry.

Rain at the wrong time can cause cherries to split and he worries about the picking itself: will he get enough men to come, and at the right time? Cherries must be picked at their peak, not too soon and not so ripe that they fall to the ground with a careless touch. Cherries without stems are graded much lower, and those with scars or splits, lower still.

Gordon often chastises his workers, cautions them to be gentle with their large, rough, hands. He'd rather pay for an extra hour or two of labour than have his cherries damaged before they're off the tree. He can't control the weather, of course, but he can oversee the picking.

He wants top-notch workers, but whom can he hire? He's thought of bringing in the migrant workers like some of the orchards further south, but he's wary. Look what's already happened. After the internment camps, the very people who were relocated and forced to do the manual labour somehow ended up owners of the land. Their kind has now taken over most of the orchards in his valley. He doesn't want that, not for his beloved land.

At the end of the lane, he hears a faint meow. It's that wandering calico cat. Gordon never leaves Precious outside for the night. When he'd found her shivering at the end of their drive fifteen years back, she was a tiny ball of fluff, eyes not yet fully open. Gordon would like to have found the bastards who dropped her there. He'd checked with Silent Sam, who lives across the road with his wife, Arlene. Sam's anything but silent; he likes nothing better than telling the world whatever he knows. Insomnia haunts him. He paces on his porch, watching in the night, while normal folk sleep. But on the night Precious appeared, Sam had been reading, and hadn't seen a thing.

His and Cy's mother had taken the shivering bit of fluff from Gordon's hands, draped it across her flowered bosom like a tattered shawl. "Oh, isn't she precious," she had crooned, the old wicker rocker creaking beneath her weight. She raised her eyes to Gordon's. "I believe I've just named the cat."

"But, but I . . . " Gordon began. After all, he'd been the one to find the kitten and Calico seemed like the logical name. Then his eyes were drawn from the verandah to the rocky ridge above the valley where his father lay beneath a black, granite stone.

"Honour thy Mother," he'd whispered, "I know, I know." He'd reached out to pet the kitten, who'd begun to purr like a diesel on a cold winter morning. "Precious is a perfect name," he'd said.

Now that Precious has grown old and slow, Gordon keeps track of her comings and goings, always worried that she won't be quick enough to avoid the white-walled tires of tourist cars whizzing along the newly paved road.

He sees a flicker of light under his largest Golden Delicious tree and hurries over to investigate. It's not Precious, reflecting the light of passing cars in her cat-green eyes and it's not an errant ember from Mahoney's damned campground. He slowly stomps his way around the base of the tree one more time before he's satisfied the spark he'd seen must have been a firefly.

Gordon finds it difficult to call "Here, Precious, Precious, Precious," with his new set of large, white teeth so he settles on "Here Kitty, Kitty, Kitty," and hopes that she comes.

He sees the glow of Cy's cigarette on the summer porch. Damn him, Gordon thinks; he's not supposed to be smoking out there. When it's just a porch, Cy can smoke there all he wants, but in the summer, it's become a bedroom too, and Gordon is not partial to anyone smoking in his room. With the heat lying heavy in the valley, the old house gets too hot to bear. All the windows upstairs except one have been painted shut; there's no way to get a cross breeze going. Every first of June, Gordon gets the rollaway cots from the basement and moves them onto the summer porch, where he camps until fall. He's begun to look forward to his summers on the porch. At the end of a long day in the orchard, he doesn't have to climb the stairs to his bed.

Occasionally, Cy sleeps in the summer porch, too. Gordon finds it comforting, the two of them camping out like they had when they were boys. Sometimes at night, he hears his mother's voice. *"Be quiet, you two, and get to sleep. Tomorrow, there's work to be done."*

"Gordon," Cy calls from the porch, raising his voice despite the stillness of the night. "If you're looking for Precious, I just let her in."

Gordon washes up in the kitchen and hangs his overalls on a hook by the door. He pours some half-and-half for Precious before he makes a sandwich for himself: two thick white slices and some farmer's market jam. The kitchen light is dim, obscured by the crispy bodies of flies trapped inside its globe. As Gordon seats himself, he makes a mental note to remove the frosted glass and clean it as soon as he gets the time. He eats slowly, savouring the jam's jolt of sweetness. As he rises from his chair, using his hands for leverage, he's surprised to hear himself groan.

He finds Cy sprawled on his cot, mouth hanging open, buzzing like a saw. A paperback — *Wild Heart Wilderness* — is open on his chest. Gordon glances at the picture on the back cover, a red-haired woman, breasts spilling from her corset. He shakes his head and drops the paperback in the wicker rocker beside Cy's cot.

From the summer porch, Gordon can see across the lake to the lights of the town. When they'd moved to the valley years ago, he missed the afterglow of prairie sunsets and found the mountains dark and foreboding, the black of night descending in one instant. The sudden darkness had made him uneasy. Now lights have spread from the town all along the hillside, pinpoints hanging above the lake like patio lanterns. Huge houses have taken up a lot of the arable land. The new summer people irritate him, like the mosquitoes used to back home.

Summers used to be different for Gordon and Cy when their mother and Aunt Emily were alive. The sisters never got over being separated, one uprooted to the B.C. orchard, the other remaining on the flat homestead land, the mountains rising between them like a solid wall. They wrote incessant letters, but both lamented it wasn't the same.

"She's coming soon," their mother would say, crossing off one more square on the calendar with a thick, black stroke. "Ten more days."

Aunt Emily always arrived the last week in June to visit their mother for a week or two. By the time she actually left, early frost would be thick on the branches of the trees.

Every year, she took ages to unpack her extensive wardrobe. She studied *Chatelaine*, kept up with the latest trends. She was two inches taller than her sister Mary, and of a much slimmer build. "That is what they are wearing in the big cities this season," she would say, pulling another elegant dress from the pile she'd made on their mother's bed. Gordon noticed that his mother watched Emily's fashions, her manners and her hair-do. Before the first week had passed, she'd copied every one.

It was Emily who'd brought the cornucopia of candles to their house.

"What in the world have you packed this time, Aunt Emily?" Gordon had asked as he struggled up the stairs, the suitcase leaden in his grip. Maybe she'd begun to transport her house from the prairies brick by brick. If she could reassemble it next to her sister's, the two might finally be content.

"Nothing special," Aunt Emily had replied. "Just a little treat for your mother and me."

Later, when he and Cy had smelled the acrid air and found their mother and Aunt Emily kneeling by the bed, all of Emily's smuggled candles in glorious flame, they'd gently taken the old girls downstairs after blowing out the candles one by one.

"Come Momma," Cy had said. "It's teatime and Aunt Emily must be tired after her flight." While Gordon made and served the tea, Cy returned to the guest room, clearing out the smouldering papers and taking custody of the candles so the aging pyromaniacs wouldn't set the house on fire.

The candles and the burning slips of paper were instruments for attracting the full attention of God. Their mother and Aunt Emily knew if you took the twisted little slips and held them right in the fire, watching as they burned, the messages would go straight to heaven in the flames.

Cy tried to broach the subject of the fires. "Momma," he'd said, "I know why you and Aunt Emily are making little altars in your room. Best to leave that business to the priests. The dear ones can hear you without the flames. If you wait for Mass, you can light all the candles you want. I'll give you the dimes."

Their mother lit votives at church every Sunday: one for her sister Jessie, who had died from kidney failure at the age of ten; another for her husband — emphysema had taken him — one each for her father and her mother, and on and on. Was she drawn by the Shepherd, or was it the jewel-coloured votives, burning in profusion, the flickering flames that inexplicably called to her?

Gordon heard a story once, standing outside a family funeral, the ease of the telling a give-away as to how many times the story had been told.

Aunt Emily had been babysitting for her sister, Mary, when they both still lived on the prairies. Emily and Mary were overprotective mothers, sure their children were in mortal danger at every turn. Emily had been watching the baby every moment herself, but a bit of insurance must have seemed perfectly logical to her. She'd intended to go straight to God to ensure He too, was keeping watch over the child. On that day, Emily had placed Mary's son in the crib with candles circling him on the floor. But she'd twisted too many papers and when she held them in the flames, the papers first smouldered, then exploded. Emily's husband had come running when he'd smelled the smoke, and had put out the fire before it got out of control.

He'd run outside with the baby, given him mouth-to-mouth in the fresh prairie air and the little fellow's colour quickly returned.

They never explained to Emily's children why they'd taken her away. Back then, treatment for mental illness was harsh. Maybe they thought it better the children not know.

"Can you imagine it?" one of the uncles had laughed. "Counselling for Emily? You could counsel her till the cows came home and you'd never talk her out of lighting candles."

They'd passed the bottle then, one to the next, each adam's apple bobbing at least three times before the bottle moved along. The talk turned to the weather and how many bushels the crops would go if they could get another inch of rain. It was a lovely day for a funeral, but the story had given Gordon a chill.

The temperature on the front porch is quite pleasant, the breeze blowing the scent of ripening cherries through the screen. Gordon is awakened by the sound of running water. When he rolls over carefully on his cot, first taking hold of the edge so he doesn't fall out, and sees Cy still asleep, a small wave of concern crests in his chest. He walks to Cy's cot, close enough to hear his smooth breathing. Relieved, he walks to the darkened hall. He finds the antique buffet standing in water, its claw feet immersed, and the ceiling above sweating and sagged.

"Cy," he calls, wading across the hall, afraid to touch a light switch. "Wake up. I think there's a disaster in the works."

Gordon was relieved to learn their insurance would cover the cost of repairs. The old house was solidly built, sufficient for their needs, but they hadn't done a single renovation since they'd moved here from the prairies. They'd only kept up the paint on the siding and touched up the trim every year. On the surface, the place looked fine.

The kitchen was dated, but who was to care? They had actually grown used to the old oak cupboard with its flour and sugar bins and its battered cutting-board top. The tiny counter space around the sink had room for a draining rack and Gordon thought it was all they could possibly need.

When the flood forced the renovations, Gordon was baffled by the change that overcame Cy. "Do you like this one?" he asked Gordon one night as they sat drinking their bed-time cup of tea — Cy adding a good portion of Amaretto to his when Gordon's back was turned — and he fanned out the folders from the plumbing shop downtown. "I'm kind of partial to the purple." His finger stopped on the grandest brochure of the bunch. The plumbing fixtures came in shades of pink and purple, pale blue and an awful, gizzard green. Gordon preferred the white claw-footed tub that came with the house, but didn't say a word.

"I think we can slip in a couple extras, without the insurance boys noticing," Cy said. "Might as well replace the vanity, and all the tiles. What about a colour for the walls? The decorator from the paint shop has offered to give us a hand."

Gordon was perplexed. What was wrong with beige?

He had been thinking of how to approach the topic of money to Cy. Gordon was quite sure they couldn't add such an extensive renovation to the insurance bill without being found out and he wasn't about to kick in half of the cost.

Their supper of broiled steak and lemon potatoes with a fresh spinach salad — it being Cy's turn to cook — is superb.

"Good grub," Gordon says, wiping his chin with a large red and white-dotted hankie. "I hope you got the steaks on sale. I'm tapped out just now."

Cy leans back in his chair and opens his wallet. It's bulging with cash.

"If you're worrying about the cost of the renovations, and I'm sure you are," he says, "don't. We can put a fair amount of it onto the insurance without anyone the wiser and I'll pay the balance."

Gordon's eyes pop. "Where in hell?"

"Won it," Cy says. "Down at the bar." For years, he's chipped in on a single lottery ticket with Scotty and Dave. Haggling over what numbers to play has been a good excuse to meet every Wednesday. Social gambling, Cy called it, when Gordon asked if he could afford the price of a weekly ticket and his turn at buying a round.

"This isn't all of it," Cy says, squeezing his wallet closed. "I just want to see how it feels, carrying around a large sum of cash."

"Goodness," Gordon says. "I didn't think you'd ever realize a cent from your gambling. But good for you Cy, good for you."

As far back as Gordon can remember Cy has been content with his work managing the bar. But now the hotel has been discovered by the summer folk and he's had to hire extra staff. Cy often comes home nursing a headache and heads straight for the bottle of Aspirin they keep in the cupboard above the sink.

"Training young folk these days so they take some pride in their Caesar's or the coldness of the glasses when serving a beer is like butting your head against a solid brick wall," Cy says.

He'd been horrified to see his newest barmaid mix a Caesar and not take the time to salt the rim or garnish the drink with celery, let alone add the pickled asparagus that Cy stocks for his regulars. She'd looked at him, completely mystified, when he'd pulled her aside. "What's the big deal?" she'd asked. "It's only one drink, and he'll be ordering another soon enough."

Gordon knows first-hand how difficult it is to get dependable help. A faithful worker is a gift and the owners of the bar have never properly appreciated having a man like Cy. Poor Cy's been working for little more than peanuts most of his life. Now, with his winnings, things have changed for him.

Gordon has tended his money as carefully as his orchard and he thinks it's truly amazing how his initial investments have multiplied. He thinks its lovely the way money can grow. He's often wished Cy had learned a little about the proper way to handle cash.

Business decisions had always been handled by their father until one soft, spring night when he'd pushed his ample belly back from the table, belched the loudest belch Gordon had ever heard and toppled off his wooden chair, instantly dead.

For the first time Gordon could remember, their mother seemed at a loss. She spent the next few weeks wafting like a ghost from room to room, carrying his father's frayed old cardigan and humming a tuneless song. During their mother's temporary lapse, Gordon and Cy made their only joint decision. When she recovered, their mother insisted on casting the deciding vote.

Gordon often felt guilty about the way he and Cy had divided up the household bills. He hadn't foreseen the advantage to himself. The gas bill, they decided, should be an even split. Cy had taken the power bill, Gordon, the phone. But the price of power had spiked quickly, the bill rising as sharply as the Rocky Mountains did.

Gordon has religiously policed the use of the phone and he allows long distance calls only after six PM, so his bill has remained almost the same. Gordon has been thinking of renegotiating their deal, but since Cy won the lottery, he's put *that* idea to rest.

Gordon is rearranging the rubble in the basement and as he clears the top shelf of the fruit cupboard, he finds his little stash of Christmas cards from Anna Louise. She's sent them faithfully every holiday season for twenty-six years. He undoes the red ribbon, holds the bundle to his chest, and reads. Anna Louise. A nice, quiet, girl and beautiful to boot — blonde like Doris Day — but his mother had scared her off like thunder scares a dog. Gordon carefully puts the cards back in their proper order, with the most recent year on top, re-ties the package and places it on the shelf. He begins to throw the jars of mouldy, discoloured peaches and cherries — the fruits of his mother's long ago labour — into the tin garbage pail he'd found beneath the stairs.

Cy's never had a girl. Gordon wonders if they'll come calling now. It doesn't hurt if you can flash a big roll of cash He has heard too many stories of old men making fools of themselves over women half their ages, just because they can. He's hoping Cy has the sense to keep his cash to himself.

Gordon is taking a break with a nice jam sandwich and a fresh cup of tea. He drops two tea bags into the pot and pours the boiling water, tucks the pink plaid cozy around the base of the pot. He rubs at a scratch on the surface of the new chrome suite. God, he sure hopes that Cy doesn't see. He feels some nostalgia for the round oak table now relegated to the basement. When he was a boy, he'd carved his initials into the wood. Running his fingers across the scarred surface has been comforting to him. Funny, he thinks, how people are.

The old chairs had been a lot sturdier too, not apt to scoot across the new linoleum leaving him flat on his arse as the wheeled chrome units have on more than one occasion. It's a danger, really, for a man his age, and he wonders how Cy manages to corral the damn things when he comes home late and bleary from the bar and has a bite to eat.

Precious is missing again.

"Have you seen anything of Precious?" Gordon is standing at the end of the lane, shoulders heavy with the weight of the air as he gauges the threat of rain. Silent Sam has just finished trimming the lilac bushes that grow along the edge of his yard.

"She hasn't been out at all today," Sam says. "Not that I could see. Probably hiding in the house."

The house has been over-run with plumbers, and men with hammers ripping things apart. Gordon's thoroughly tired of the mess, just as Precious seems to be. Precious hasn't had much luck lately, hiding in the house. Gordon thinks it likely she's somewhere in the orchard, curled up in the grass beside a cherry tree.

Yesterday, their decorator stopped in. "Have you thought of updating the paint?" she asked with a wave of her hand in the downstairs hall. "I hope you don't mind. I couldn't resist taking a peek in your living room. It's got really good bones and you'd be amazed what you can do with faux-finish paint."

Gordon had no idea what faux-finish paint was and he didn't care to ask. "I believe we painted the living room six years back," he said. "I'm partial to beige."

She'd given him her card — pushed it, really — into his hand. "If you change your mind," she said, "Just give me a call. I'd be happy to help."

Gordon blesses the day the renovations are finally complete. As the last painter packs his brushes and ladders, Gordon holds the screen door. "Just send the bill to Cy," he says as the contractor loads his truck. Gordon pours himself a good stiff brandy before he starts up the stairs, drinks it down in one big gulp.

The bathroom is a masterpiece, its lavender jet tub tucked into the corner and a three-way mirror above the new sink. The flooring — which looks like oak but is actually a laminate — is guaranteed to last. At least Cy had the sense to pick something that is low maintenance and comes with a lifetime guarantee. Gordon is relieved to think that the money hasn't gone entirely to his head.

When Gordon walks into his mother's room, he gasps for air like a fish washed up on shore. The bay window is wide, flooding the room with light, doubled and doubled again in the mirrored doors of the closet. The crown moulding is a pale shade of pink, contrasting the mauve on the walls and softened by a glaze of light cream. He's sure the painters will no doubt charge a pretty penny for every fancy stroke.

In the evening, when they've finished their macaroni and cheese — it being Gordon's turn to cook — Cy clears his throat.

"I've been thinking," he says. "I like the way Mother's room looks now the renovations are done. I might as well move in there. If you'll give me a hand, I can probably get most of my stuff settled tonight."

Gordon is suddenly dizzy, forced to grab the edge of the new chrome table. He stands there, slowly shaking his head, as if trying to clear the clinging remnants of a dreadful dream.

"It's just as well," Cy says. "I've got so many clothes they won't fit in my closet anymore. And you know what a time I have sleeping when I've worked the late shift. It's a lot cooler and darker in Mother's room, being it faces north."

What could Gordon possibly say? That he was uncomfortable with the idea of Cy sleeping surrounded by their mother's precious things? Although much in their mother's room had changed, her silver brush and comb set remained side by side on the dresser as if awaiting the touch of her hand. Her compact, faced with mother of pearl, lay perfectly parallel to the dresser set, the powder not even caked, the colour still rosy and clear. The iron bedstead remained, now painted pink, and at the foot of the bed, her ornate cedar chest sat covered with a mantle of yellowed lace, the family Bible squarely in the middle. Gordon could feel his mother's presence as strongly as ever when he walked into the room.

"What about your own room?"

"Two years from now, the cousins are coming from Saskatchewan; the family reunion's being held right in our yard. Surely, it hasn't slipped your mind?" Cy says. "I've offered my bed to the oldest of the oldsters, any time they want."

Gordon thinks moving out of his room right away in case someone wants to use it for a weekend in two years time doesn't make a lot of sense. "I can't help you tonight," he says. "Not at all. When I was draining the macaroni, my back went out."

Gordon doesn't mention his reservations, how he's always taken great comfort in the thought of his mother's room left undisturbed. Maybe he should have protested when Cy began to use the space beneath their mother's bed to store his cases of vodka and rye. Perhaps that was the start of it.

When Precious goes missing yet again, Gordon trudges up the stairs, to his mother's — *Cy's* room — to look for her. She isn't curled up in her customary spot in the middle of the bed and although he calls all through the house, she refuses to appear. Finally, at noon, she stalks haughtily up the lane, ignoring Gordon as he opens the kitchen door and lets her in for her long-delayed treat. She's put out about something, he suspects, and seems to be taking it out on him.

She goes so far as to shit in the upstairs hall, something she has never done before. "Precious," Gordon scolds her, eyes watering and stomach heaving, as he cleans up the mess, "I know you're upset, but you mustn't do this, not ever again. Just be a nice kitty-kitty and everything will be fine."

Cy begins to change. Gordon notices subtle differences, intensified with every night he sleeps in their mother's room. Cy has always enjoyed a ribald joke, and sometimes, Gordon is almost embarrassed by the language he uses. Now the off-colour jokes and bad language have entirely stopped.

Cy has always been a man who clings to the last remnants of sleep, hitting his snooze button again and again until he has burned up every available moment between waking and leaving for work. Now he's up very early, lingering in the bathroom as he prepares for the day. He's even developed an aversion to any talk of bodily functions, something he and Gordon have always discussed. Ever since they were boys, they've both taken great joy in huge, noisy farts.

Cy has been inclined to let his hair get rather shaggy when he's busy down at the bar, but he's begun to have his hair trimmed every two weeks. Gordon is concerned, thinking of the price of haircuts, wondering if Cy can afford — lottery winnings or no — to be trimmed up every other week.

When Gordon catches the familiar and foreboding smell of candles and scorched paper in the air, he is drawn like steel to a magnet. God no, he thinks. His leaden feet lead him up the stairs. When he finds Cy kneeling by their mother's bed, the candles flickering and smoke curling, Gordon blanches.

"Don't get yourself all worked up," Cy reassures him, rising from his knees. "I was just digging through mother's cedar chest. I thought maybe it was time we got rid of her things."

Gordon's pallor increases.

"And I found the candles. The wicks are all bent over and stuck so I straightened them. I was just checking to see if the wax is still good. I didn't mean to light them all. I just got a little carried away."

Gordon can't bring himself to ask about the twisted bits of paper. He backs out of the room and closes the door.

He'd goes to feed Precious, hoping to find her curled up on one of the kitchen chairs, but she is nowhere in sight. He pours the half and half slowly, watching it curl into the bowl. Since Cy's move, Precious has begun sleeping at the foot of Gordon's cot on the summer porch. He takes comfort listening to the rasp of her purr.

Cy, on his way out the next morning, gives Gordon a two-fingered salute.

"My God, Cy," Gordon says, "Are you going to the races? You're not dressing for comfort, you're dressing for speed."

Cy looks at Gordon, in his red-tab overalls, patched at the knee. "Maybe you should check the fashion magazines," he says. "Coveralls are out."

Gordon brushes his hands across the faded bib of his soft coveralls. They aren't so fancy he can't use them for a wipe.

"Pick me up a pair of nice Levi's if you don't like these," Gordon calls to Cy's receding back. "You know my size." But Cy is already gone.

Probably off to town to shop, Gordon thinks. Again. No more lounging in sweatshirts and jeans for Cy. Almost every other day, he'd been bringing home bags of Dockers and open-throated shirts. The closet in their mother's bedroom is stuffed. Now he's graduated to dress pants and buttoned-down shirts, his belts colour-coded to his pants. His selection of elaborate ties slithers from the over-loaded rack and cascades to the floor, a pool of rainbow silk. Certainly, Gordon thinks, it is strange behaviour for a man who's always been content with clip-ons when he wore a tie at all.

"Holy smokes, Cy," he says one morning as Cy lingers by the mirror in the hall. "I didn't know you'd learned to tie a double Windsor."

Gordon catches Cy's eyes in the mirror, notices the hint of a blush. Cy has never been able to master the double before, always ends up cursing and swearing as he yanks on his tie. Gordon would wait until Cy's face was almost purple with frustration before he offered his help. Cy would stand still as a statue while Gordon tied his tie in a meticulous double Windsor knot.

"There's a thing or two you don't know about me," Cy says, snugging up the knot and reaching for his keys.

Gordon doesn't see much of Cy for a week or two — he is working the late shift and Gordon is spraying his cherry orchard early in the morning when the air is still and cool — somehow, their paths never cross.

One evening, when the spraying is finally done, Gordon waits up, reading and dozing, listening for Cy. He'd felt suddenly lonely, tending to his orchard in the stillness of the afternoon, and he's been longing for some talk.

Cy struts in, wearing burgundy tuck-pleat pants, a pale pink shirt and a tie of pastel rainbow hues. "Jesus, Cy," Gordon blurts. "You look like a goddamned peacock. What's going on?"

"Don't worry," Cy says, smoothing the pleats across his round little belly as he walks past. "I can afford it."

Cripes, Gordon thinks, it's got nothing to do with the cash.

Gordon needs his mother. He longs to hear the murmur of her voice. At sixty-two, the desire to feel the touch of her hand surprises him. He ventures upstairs, heading for her room. The new door, much lighter than the old wood-panelled one, warped from years of wear, swings open softly at his touch. Mid-step, he halts.

The bedstead is draped with pantyhose of every colour — blue, black, taupe, tan and even nursely whites — all neatly washed and hung to dry. Gordon blinks. He stumbles backward through the thick purple pile of the carpet and softly closes the door. He pushes his forehead into the coolness of the old plaster wall in the hallway, steadies himself until his legs stop shaking and he is able to walk down the stairs.

As if he were partially paralysed, he uses his muscular arms to ease himself down to his bed on the summer porch. Unable to settle, he tosses and turns, the pantyhose drifting in his dreams, their colours bright in the harsh light of day. The wind picks up a purple pair, sucks them toward the sun, where they hang for a moment before floating down to the cherry trees below. Gordon grabs at his neck, strangled by the long silky legs. His own rough hands around his neck pull him fully awake. Gordon sighs and climbs from his cot to wait up for Cy.

When the lights of the Buick pull into the lane, Gordon pours two cups of hot chocolate, with a side of Schnapps for Cy. He hesitates for a moment, and then pours a double into his own chipped mug.

Gordon intends to bring up the subject of the pantyhose, but as he searches for a tactful way to start, he realizes there isn't one. "What do you think about the price of the super-sheers?" is all he can come up with, and he realises it just won't do. At any rate, there is no way he can bring it up without confessing he's been in Cy's room.

Yawning, and slurping the last of his schnapps, Cy rubs his eyes. Gordon draws a deep breath when he sees a dark smudge, like mascara, on the circles under Cy's tired eyes. *My God*, he thinks, *Oh my God*.

"I appreciate the company," Cy says, rising from the table, "Really, I do, but I think I'll turn in. It's getting awfully late, even for me."

Gordon rinses the cups, puts them in the sink. Perhaps we can talk in the morning, he thinks. Things always seem brighter in the light of day.

As Cy leaves the kitchen, the light from the new halogen fixture accentuates the dark shade of chestnut and glints of golden highlights in his hair. Gordon doesn't pay much attention to anyone's hair, hasn't since his own had thinned and lost its pigment. But the last time he'd noticed, his own sparse hair and Cy's thick thatch were the same shade of grey.

"Well, cheers," Cy says. "Sleep well."

Gordon lies in the summer porch, unable to settle. Finally, he gets up, dresses in the pale watery light, and slips outside. He stands beneath the spreading arms of his cherry trees and watches licks of candlelight waltzing on the rosy shades of Cy's new room.

Gordon is ambushed at the mailbox by Silent Sam, who always has something to say. "No letters today," Sam says, not even embarrassed about being caught red-handed rifling through their mail. Again. "Thought a letter from your kin in Saskatchewan would be just about due." He pauses, scratches his chin. "Has something happened to Cy?"

"No, don't think so," Gordon says. He clears his throat and begins to fan the mail. Bills and more bills.

"I watched him yesterday, looking for Precious before he fired up his car. You know he's always worried about running over that damn cat. He was mincing along like a hooker in six-inch heels. Thought he must have turned an ankle or maybe got himself a bad case of gout. In his line of work, it's a hazard of the job."

Sam's comment niggles. Gordon has indeed noticed the change in Cy's walk; how it has become slightly swishy in the last few months. At first he'd attributed the change to Cy's array of fine new shoes, imported from Italy, of the softest leather and in every shade. Cy even owns a pair of sandals, fastened with silky-looking rope. Cy'd never worn Jesus-boots before. Gordon has seen the price of Italian shoes in Borden's downtown. He shudders to think how much money Cy has spent on his footwear. But the shoes would surely be well broken-in by now, and Cy's wriggle-walk remains.

"He probably had a hard night down at the bar," Gordon says. "Too much time on his feet. He's not getting any younger. None of us are." With that, he took his flyers and bills and turned up the lane.

It isn't anyone's business how Cy chooses to walk and Gordon makes a vow to avoid his little chats with Sam. The man has a way of ferreting information. Gordon is determined to keep his lips sealed, especially when it comes to Cy.

The harvest is in. The cherries he takes to market bring a record price. Gordon is toting up his columns at the roll-top desk. He shivers, squints in the amber light of the autumn afternoon. He glances at the fireplace: today might be the day to light the first fire of fall in the smoke-darkened hearth. He reaches for the matchbooks, stored in a Blue Ribbon baking powder tin at the corner of his desk. The tin isn't there.

"Cy," he calls. "Have you seen the Blue Ribbon tin?"

No reply.

He walks around the crowded living room, moving magazines and trinkets as he searches for the tin. He checks the marble mantle but finds only a layer of thick, grey dust. A hint of smoke reaches his nostrils and he bends, hands outstretched.

The ashes are cold.

"Cy?" he calls. The scent of smoke grows stronger. He stops, hand on the newel post at the bottom of the stair, and fights a wave of dizziness that almost knocks him down. He waits until it passes, then starts up the stairs.

Gordon is assailed by the smell of burning paper, of candle-wax wafting in the upstairs hall. He touches the door of his mother's room with the palm of his hand. The door swings wide on well-oiled hinges, as if awaiting his touch.

Cy is there, kneeling before a candle centred on their mother's cedar chest, his hands clasped in front of his breast. There are candles on the windowsill and in circles all around the bed. Soft purple shadows pirouette across the walls. The sleeves of Cy's silky blue housecoat flutter, inches from the flame.

Gordon sinks to the floor, his hand falling on their mother's Bible as he eases himself down. No words pass between them. They are beyond words, as brothers, or lovers, or lifelong friends, often come to be. A wisp of smoke tendrils to the ceiling. Cy unwraps a large white candle, balances it on the open Bible, and Gordon lights the match. A breeze flutters the wispy curtains, pulls the smoke out toward the orchard, over the cherry trees and up; a message, at last, that might reach God.

BONNIE DUNLOP is a Swift Current writer who has developed a strong and growing readership in Saskatchewan and beyond. Her stories have appeared in many literary journals, and have been read on CBC radio. This is her first book.